# EVERY
# WORD
# A
# LIE

Published in the UK by Scholastic, 2023
1 London Bridge, London, SE1 9BG
Scholastic Ireland, 89E Lagan Road, Dublin Industrial Estate, Glasnevin,
Dublin, D11 HP5F

Text © Sue Wallman, 2023

The right of Sue Wallman to be identified as the author of this work has been
asserted by them under the Copyright, Designs and Patents Act 1988.

ISBN 978 0702 32406 2

A CIP catalogue record for this book is available from the British Library.

Typeset in Minion by M Rules
Printed and bound in Great Britain by Clays Ltd, Elcograf S.p.A
Paper made from wood grown in sustainable forests
and other controlled sources.

3 5 7 9 10 8 6 4 2

www.scholastic.co.uk

# EVERY WORD A LIE

## SUE WALLMAN

SCHOLASTIC

To James, Tom and Niamh

# CHAPTER 1

"Seriously, how much of this is going to be actual event planning?" asked Aden. He stretched his arms so his rowing club T-shirt rose up to display a few centimetres of his muscular stomach, and yawned. "I can stay awake if gossip's on the table."

Hollie put her feet on the coffee table in front of us. Her trainers were new, and I could just make out the tops of her socks, yellow with pink moustaches. We loved not having to wear school shoes and school uniform now we were in the sixth form, although Hollie had been playing fast and loose with the uniform rules for years. "The fact is, we do have to plan the next event." She moved her feet so she could admire the trainers from a different angle. "Come on, one event down, four more to go. Then we can slap 'charity committee' on our CVs and personal statements and we're good."

The five of us were occupying the prime spot in the café: the two sagging sofas next to the large window which overlooked the school gates, so we could see who was coming and going. We were a gang – me, Stan, Aden and Hollie – and we did everything together. It was as a unit that we had put ourselves forward for the charity committee because it would look good for uni applications. And Jada had wriggled in too, of course.

Our enthusiasm for running charity events was waning after the initial excitement of our first event, an orange-themed day where sixth formers had to pay to come in orange clothing, enter a Terry's Chocolate Orange raffle (featuring all available varieties, including the weird white chocolate one), guess the number of shreds in a jar of marmalade and buy muffins with orange icing, made by my brother, Harry, who thought he was the next Paul Hollywood.

"As long as I don't have to count marmalade shreds again," said Stan. He looked flimsy compared to Aden. He had brown shiny hair nearly to his shoulders and a face which didn't give much away unless you knew him as well as I did. He wore his customary black jeans and his favourite black hoodie. Footwear by Nike with pale grey socks; he had a few colourful pairs but he saved those for big days, and today was as ordinary as they came.

"We need to decide the next event by the end of today,"

said Jada, tucking a strand of her black hair behind her yellow bandana. She sounded decisive and sure of herself, and I marvelled again at how she'd managed to inveigle her way into our little group which had been so tight since Year Seven. Stan and me, and Hollie and Aden. Two best friends from primary school who'd met another couple of best friends at secondary school and decided we could all be best mates together. And now, one outsider.

Jada had only joined the sixth form in September. Her mum had wanted to move to the area to be closer to her family and had persuaded Jada she'd get better A-levels at Markham High than her former school. She was in the same English literature class as Hollie. Hollie was the charismatic one, the one everyone gravitated towards because of her energy and sense of fun – and Jada Simmonds had been no exception. The two of them had hit it off. When Hollie had signed us up for the charity committee, she had put Jada's name down too.

"Why her?" I had asked.

"She's keen," Hollie had said. "Jada's super-ambitious, wants all the right stuff on her personal statement. Also, she's really nice. It'll be fun having her."

I hadn't been so sure. Aden and Stan hadn't seemed bothered so I'd kept quiet.

"Whose idea was it to do this committee anyway?" moaned Aden. He squished his cheek up to his eye and went deliberately cross-eyed, one of his signature looks. He let go and it bounced back to his standard-handsome face.

"It's very time consuming. We spent weeks planning that ridiculous orange event. Is it worth all this effort just so we've got something to put on our personal statements? I'm not even sure I want to go to uni." He looked at his hands, then held them up. "Did I show you my blisters from this morning's training? Man, they hurt."

Hollie raised an eyebrow at him. The other thing about Hollie was she was gorgeous. Her hair was so blonde it was almost white, and her eyes were green-blue. "Would you have rather been on the environment committee?" she asked sweetly. "With all the hassle from that new try-hard geography teacher? At least nobody gets too involved with us. We're free to come up with our own fresh, innovative ideas." She looked eagerly at the rest of us, as though hoping we'd come up with a fresh, innovative idea – but the truth was we'd peaked early with orange-themed day.

I opened a bag of crisps and offered them round. Prawn cocktail. Stan was the only person who took one, which I could have predicted. We shared a love for prawn cocktail crisps, even though neither of us was remotely interested in eating an actual prawn. "Bake sale it is, then," I said. "Harry will make a load of cakes, and Stan's mum can pick us up some doughnuts on the way home from work, can't she?"

Stan, who was glugging on a bottle of water, gave a thumbs up.

"It'll be zero effort and pure profit for us," I said.

"If not for our parents," said Stan, indicating to me he'd like another crisp.

"I'll make bags of popcorn," said Jada. It was nice of her to offer but we didn't really need anything extra.

"Amazing!" said Hollie.

"What d'you think's most popular – sweet or salty?" Jada asked.

"Marmite flavour. Go on – do it!" said Hollie, laughing. "Wait. No. We want to make money, don't we?"

"I'll do some of each," said Jada, but Hollie was already on her feet, yelling across the café for everyone in the room to vote on whether they preferred salt or sweet popcorn, counting hands energetically. Jada watched her, grinning. They were similar in some ways, Hollie and Jada – wanting to be involved in things, leaping in with both feet, but Hollie did it with a lighter touch. Jada always struck me as just plain irritating, thinking she knew best.

"Classic Hollie," said Aden admiringly.

"Anyone want to play *Gartic*?" asked Stan hopefully, waving his phone at the rest of us.

"We're not done with the meeting," said Jada firmly and Stan lowered his arm extra slowly.

"Not sure we've got anything left to discuss about the bake sale, though?" said Aden mildly. He liked Jada all right, I reckoned, but he was always going to be more loyal to Stan. "I need to fit in a quick nap before class. Last night's rowing training's taken it out of me."

"Let's wait for Hollie," said Jada, folding her arms. "There might be other things to discuss."

I rolled my eyes at Stan and made a point of asking him

about our fortress in *Colony Survival.* "Had a chance to check out the alien damage from last night?"

"Nope. Let's check after school," he said.

I nodded. Stan and I were into gaming, Aden was into sport, specifically rowing these days, and Hollie was into being popular and fun. Still, it worked.

Hollie headed back, flushed and smiling, with her tally of popcorn votes. "FYI, more people prefer sweet popcorn but we could always" – she paused and checked we were all listening, especially Aden who was peeling a banana – "make it a popcorn lucky dip. You might get salty, you might get sweet, you might get *Marmite.* Up the stakes? What d'you reckon?"

"Hilarious," said Aden. "Let's do it."

"Nah," said Jada. "You can't prank people when it comes to food."

"Hmm," said Hollie. "Maybe you're right."

Jada knew how to handle Hollie, I'd give her that.

Aden pulled a face. "Yeah, Hollie, remember that time you took the white filling out of Stan's Oreo cookie and replaced it with toothpaste?"

Jada let her jaw drop. "Get out!"

"It was funny," said Aden. "Very Hollie."

"But Stan hasn't eaten an Oreo since," said Hollie, turning to him. "Sorry about that." Stan rolled his eyes in response, and she leaned back.

"Didn't you convince Hollie that a raisin in her porridge was a mouse dropping after that, Stan?" reminded Aden.

"Oh, yes!" said Hollie good-naturedly. "I totally fell for that – for maybe twenty seconds."

"Earth to Stanley?" I said as Stan was looking out of the window vacantly. "The mouse dropping in the porridge incident?"

Stan blinked and was back in the room. "You completely dissected that raisin, Hol," he said.

"So, moving on," said Hollie. "We're agreed on the bake sale for the next event? I'll go to the sixth form office and get it put on the event calendar. Hmm. Bit of a walk actually. I'll email."

She got her phone out, and Jada laughed. "Why walk when you can email?"

Hollie smiled at Jada, and I felt the quick hot flicker of something in my chest that wasn't indigestion. It was jealousy.

I let the conversation move on without me, thinking about the online fortress Stan and I had made and how we needed to make more food to feed our guards.

Jada was talking about a girl she fancied, someone in her previous school, which was miles away. It was – clearly – never going to happen. Then Hollie began talking about Liam Henderson, whom she'd been fixated on for months. I exchanged a bored look with Stan. Liam was a predictable crush for Hollie – too predictable. Boring. The most unobtainable boy in Markham. He didn't go to our school, he went to Markham's private school, Ivy Green, which made him that bit more mysterious, and he was the year above us. He also was the closest thing Markham had to a celebrity, because he played tennis at a near-professional level – he had a world ranking – and was unquestionably fit in both senses of the word: tall and broad shouldered, with wavy brown hair he held back with a band when he was on court.

Hollie had recently seen him interviewed on a sports channel saying he was single and didn't have time for a girlfriend, but "if the right person came along" he might make room in his life for them. Hollie had forced me to watch the interview several times. I'd thought his slight American accent sounded fake, but Hollie said it was legit, a result of several tennis camps in the States.

Hollie turned to me now. "Amy, can't you persuade your boyfriend to big me up to Liam?" she said. "Introduce us?"

This was new. "What? How?" I frowned. "I'm not sure Dom even knows Liam. He never mentions him."

"They go to the same school, for god's sake," said Hollie, stretching. "All I need is an introduction and I'll take it from there. We'd get on so well."

"Dom's in our year," I said. "He doesn't hang out with the Year Thirteens."

"Some friend you are! And, Aden, you see him at the Canbury Club all the time and you've done nothing about it," said Hollie. "You've repeatedly failed me."

Aden laughed loudly. His family were wealthy enough that they could easily have sent him and his older brother to Ivy Green, but they'd failed the entrance exams, a fact neither was remotely fazed by. He was happy enough to hang out at the exclusive Canbury Club, though, with its excellent sports facilities. "Nice try, Hollie. I'm not going to fanboy over Liam Henderson, even for you. Anyway, I play football and golf there, never tennis. I hardly ever see him."

"Fine." Hollie pointed to Stan. "What about you? Why haven't *you* helped facilitate this? Liam lives on your frigging road, Stan!"

"Up the other end," said Stan, as if "the other end" was a different part of town, which it kind of was – the houses were much fancier further along his road. "Anyway, you don't even like tennis, Hollie. Name the last time you watched it. You and Liam Henderson wouldn't have anything in common."

Hollie was affronted. "I don't *watch* tennis, but I like the *concept* of it."

"What's the *concept* of tennis?" asked Jada, with her wry smile.

"Glad you asked," said Hollie, her eyes sparkling. "Tennis is a wholesome sport and it's associated with strawberries. There's lots to like about it. Liam is a particularly good example of a tennis player. Tall, strong, good teeth."

"Right," said Jada, laughing now.

"Have you never seen his Instagram?" said Hollie. "You are missing a treat."

The bell went and I got to my feet. Jada had done an image search of Liam Henderson online. She tilted her head, considering him in his tennis whites. "I wouldn't have thought he was your type."

Hollie, who was swamped in the enormous sofa, held out her hand to me and I heaved her up with a practised manoeuvre. "He's very much my type," she said. "Look at that one from the summer…" And she and Jada went off to their Eng lit class, Hollie pointing out her favourite photo of Liam. I knew which one it was – Liam with both feet off the court, doing a slam dunk, or whatever the tennis term was for bringing his racquet down on the ball with maximum force.

"Look at the guy in the front row!" I called. Hollie had showed it to me on the first day of sixth form and we'd cracked up at the man's expression of horrified surprise as the sandwich he was about to take a bite out of fell apart.

Neither of them heard me.


Stan and I had psychology together next period. It started with a discussion of the reading we'd been set for homework, and when that was over and some worksheets were being handed round the room, a kid from way down the school came into the classroom with a note.

"Stan and Amy," called our teacher after reading it. "Mr Ferris says you're to go to reception. Make sure you catch up on work missed, please."

I looked at Stan in confusion.

"Who's Mr Ferris?" muttered Stan.

"The new try-hard geography teacher who's running the environment committee," I said, not that that explained anything. Neither of us did geography or knew anything about the committee. The small student was waiting for us to go downstairs, smiling now that we were on our feet, as if we were a gift he was going to present to Mr Ferris.

"What's this about?" asked Stan when we'd left the classroom, walking to the staircase that would take us directly down to the reception area.

"The Big Tidy Up," said the student, as if it was obvious. "It's this afternoon."

"The what?" said Stan.

The student repeated, "The Big Tidy Up campaign." He ran ahead down the stairs and said, "Here they are, sir," and we saw a group of maybe ten or twelve students from different year groups, each wearing a yellow hi-vis vest over their uniforms. There were no other sixth formers.

"Hello, you two," said Mr Ferris, who was in pink hi-vis. "Nice to see some older students are keen to participate. Leave your bags in that trolley and grab a hi-vis."

"Why?" asked Stan.

"Litter picking round the school grounds. Did you forget?" said Mr Ferris. He was young and eager, with wavy, bushy hair. "Thanks for signing up." He flashed a clipboard at us, and I saw our names on it.

Ah. "Hollie's handwriting." I rolled my eyes at Stan and we shook our heads and laughed.

11

"Someone put our names down for a joke, sir," Stan explained.

"Oh," said Mr Ferris. He looked crushed. Then he brightened. "Still, now you're here, grab a jacket!" Stan and I looked at each other and Mr Ferris continued. "It'll be fun! You'll have a blast!"

Stan shook his head in amused resignation. "Oh, well, at least it's not raining. Come on, Amy."

We left our bags in the trolley, put on hi-vis jackets and trooped outside as a group, then Mr Ferris directed us to different areas in pairs. Stan and I took our black rubbish sack and made our way to the food shack. Stan grabbed a banana skin first and pretended to almost drop it on my head before dumping it in the bag. Two empty drinks cans and a Crunchie bar wrapper later, we heard a banging noise. I looked round and saw Hollie and Jada at the window of an English classroom, waving with huge grins on their faces. I wondered if Hollie hadn't come up with this prank on her own – had Jada helped her? Or had it been Jada's idea?

I lifted my grabber up and jabbed it in Hollie's direction, as menacingly as I could. Then Stan and I had a mock fight, duelling with our grabbers, until Mr Ferris shouted, "You two! Give that a rest. You're supposed to be role models."

The other yellow-jacketed people were racing to pick up litter. There was probably some reward for the pair who returned with the most rubbish. Like a singular merit.

More people were looking out of windows, smirking at us. Hollie had obviously gathered a crowd.

"How about you move on to the PE kit, guys," called Mr Ferris. He gestured at a tree near the food shack where a black Adidas drawstring bag had been chucked over a branch. A bird dropping glistened next to the logo.

"I'm not sure I can take any more of this fun," I said.

Stan was looking at the PE kit. "How are we going to get that down?" He leaped up, swinging the grabber, and was rewarded with a shower of leaves. I could see people at the windows laughing.

"Let me have a go," I said. I jumped, hoping to dislodge the bag with my grabber, only I accidentally let go and sent it flying further into the tree.

Stan suddenly broke into giggles, then proper laughter. He had to lean forward he was laughing so much. It actually made me really happy – he'd been a little distracted over the last couple of weeks, as if something was bothering him, although he swore nothing was.

"Glad this amuses you," I said.

"Amy," called Mr Ferris, "go to the premises office and ask for a stepladder."

"A ladder." I tutted. "He could have mentioned that earlier."

"We're going to get that PE kit, whatever it takes," said Stan in a movie voiceover growl.

The only stepladder available was heavy and we were sweating by the time we'd carried it to the tree. When Stan finally got his hands on the PE kit and my grabber, me holding the stepladder steady underneath, we could hear sarcastic cheers from various classrooms.

"I'm going to kill Hollie," I said through gritted teeth.

"Don't worry, Ames," said Stan. "We'll find a good way to get her back. Something she'll never see coming."

# CHAPTER 2

Stan and I went back to mine after school. I slammed the front door hard behind us, my back hurting from holding the stepladder steady on the bumpy tarmac. After that we'd had to fish leaves and something so gross I didn't want to imagine what it was out of a drain.

"I need a tea and a sit down," I said, sounding like my granddad.

"Your face when Mr Ferris said we should join the *next* Big Tidy Up was unforgettable," said Stan. "Like an angry zombie." He stood in my hallway and dropped his jaw and made his eyes go starey.

"Accurate," I said. "At least I didn't tell him I'd be there, like you did. You wuss."

The kitchen door opened and my brother Harry appeared, wearing his navy baking apron. "Welcome home, litter pickers," he said with a grin. He was in the year above Stan and me, and usually managed to get home first because he took the bus rather than walked.

Harry didn't look much like me. He was bigger, rounder, with lighter hair and Mum's blue eyes. He often had red cheeks – from sunburn, steam from cooking or running for the bus.

"How do you know about that?" I demanded.

"Coops," said Harry. He delved into his apron pocket and brought out his phone and showed me a photo his irritating friend Cooper had sent him from a ground floor window of me jumping in the air with my litter grabber. Cooper had circled me in neon-green, and slapped a crying-with-laughter emoji next to it. "There's some even better ones," said Harry. He went to swipe his phone but I pushed him away.

"You're good, thanks, Hazza-Chops," I said, as I went into the kitchen with Stan behind me. On the table there was a Tupperware of cupcakes waiting to be iced. "Hollie set us up," I said. "Another one of her pranks."

"What I want to know is why you had to wear fluorescent yellow to litter pick," said Harry. "Was Mr Ferris worried about losing you?" He batted my hand away from the cakes. "You can't eat any of these," he said. "They're for Brenda over the road's nephew's thirtieth."

He always made extra when he had a job in case any

16

didn't turn out right. Harry wanted to be a baker when he was older and took his commissions very seriously.

"OK, OK, don't be so controlling. How many did she order?" I question, peering at them. They looked perfectly uniform.

"Hands up and back away," said Harry in the manner of a US police chief, then in a more normal voice, "Wait until I've iced them then you two might be able to have *one*."

I flicked on the kettle. "Tea?" I asked Stan. "While we think of a way to get Hollie back. This time, I swear, it's revenge."

"Yeah, tea. Cheers. I'd rather play *Mario Kart* than plot revenge, though," he said. He looked tired, I thought. There were dark circles under his eyes and his face was drawn.

"Are you sleeping enough these days, Stanley Maloney?" I asked.

"Yeah, I just stayed up late doing that assignment for psychology," he said.

I nodded. "Fair." Stan could be a bit disorganized and forgetful when it came to school and it usually fell to me to keep him on track. I'd forgotten to remind him about the assignment, probably because my head had been full of Dom recently.

"Amy always beats you at *Mario Kart*, mate," said Harry, reaching for the icing sugar.

"Not always," said Stan, with an edge even though he knew Harry was winding him up.

We went into the living room with our mugs of tea and played our default characters – Yoshi for me, Donkey Kong for Stan – and started with Mushroom Gorge. A while later, Harry came in with two cupcakes which were two-parts cake to one-part thick swirl of chocolate icing. Each had edible glitter and shavings of white chocolate on top. He put them on the coffee table and went back to the kitchen.

"You're welcome!" he called.

"Thanks!" I shouted after him. We took a break from *Mario Kart* to eat them and Stan looked at my phone.

"Hollie's video-calling," he said.

I grabbed my phone and, when the call connected, I held the cupcake up to the screen. "I need this, Hollie, after what you put us through," I said.

Hollie was on her sofa at home, white-blonde hair piled on top of her head, fluffy cushions around her. She had a serious, contrite face on her. "I'm sorry, guys." She couldn't hold her face any longer and collapsed with laughter for a moment, then pulled herself together. "But you did look lovely with your yellow jackets and those litter picker things. Not at all like you were doing community service."

"It was fun in parts," said Stan, leaning his skinny frame back against the sofa.

"It so wasn't, Stan," I said. "And now we've got to catch up with what we missed in psychology."

"I didn't think you'd actually *do* it!" said Hollie. "Why didn't you tell Mr Ferris it was a prank?"

"We did, but he was so desperate for people," I said. "He

even persuaded us to pose for a photo at the end, for the newsletter." I shuddered dramatically.

"You're going to be in the newsletter too? Oh, my!" Hollie grinned. She propped her phone up on a side table to redo her hair and the gold chain bracelet I gave her for her last birthday – her sixteenth – slipped down her arm. I loved that she always wore it. "Payback time for me walking into the clingfilm you put across Stan's kitchen door." She slapped her hand over her mouth with amused embarrassment. "Remember how I bounced backwards? I still can't believe I didn't see it."

"Walking into clingfilm took a moment out of your day," I said, "but that litter picking went on for hours."

Hollie cringed then smiled again. "Sorry, but it was funny!" She held up her hand. "Don't worry, I'll rein in the pranks now we're in the sixth form."

*Yeah, right*, I thought.

We moved on to our plans for the weekend. Stan was doing a uni taster day in computer science which he was sweetly buzzed about, and I had a last-minute cat-feeding job for my main client, Mr Peaty. Mr Peaty lived in a flat a fifteen-minute walk from us and travelled a lot for work, so he paid me to play with his neurotic black cat Hector, as well as feed him. This time it was just for four days, but every little bit of cash helped.

And I was going to see Dom. Obviously. My still fairly new boyfriend. My stomach swooped at the thought of his gorgeous face. After Harry had first met him, he'd told me he thought Dom was "too cocky, a bit full of himself, a typical Ivy Green boy". I disagreed; Harry could be overprotective. Dom was confident, naturally at ease with himself. Nearly three months later, Harry was finally warming to him. A bit. Mum and Dad certainly loved him and no wonder. Dom was pretty much the ideal boyfriend to introduce to parents – great grades, sporty and polite. He swam for Ivy Green School, and was always reading articles about things like proportional representation.

It didn't hurt that he was incredibly fit as well.

"Ooh, yes," said Hollie. "You're going out to dinner with Dom and his parents, aren't you? Good luck!"

Dom's parents were both lawyers in the same firm and completely intimidating. They liked to talk politics and current affairs and it was honestly like a formal interview every time I met them. Dom insisted that they liked me, but I got the impression they didn't think I was good enough for their son. I'd hinted as much to Dom after the first time I met them.

"They said you're funny and lovely. And go-getting," Dom had told me. "And they like that you don't get upset when the dog dribbles on you."

"Don't forget good at arm-wrestling," I'd said, and we'd ended up in a happy play-fight, after which I'd asked him what he meant by *go-getting*. It turned out his parents admired how I had built a network of animal-feeding jobs via friends of friends, and organized them with an Excel spreadsheet. For some reason the detail about me using an Excel spreadsheet had made Dom and me fall about laughing.

"I'll need all the luck," I said to Hollie now. "I'll be OK if I can get the conversation on to Dom's family dog. His mum loves their Labrador more than she loves Dom, I reckon. What about you, any plans?"

"We're going to that new Korean barbecue restaurant for my dad's birthday," she said. "Can't wait. Jada's coming too."

"Oh," I said.

"I know, I know," said Hollie. "*You're* my traditional plus one! But you'll be with Dom and his parents."

I nodded. The Lintons were always very generous with their invites. I was spending more time with Dom these days and Hollie wanted someone to go with her to her dad's dinner. It was fine. I couldn't have it all my own way.

But I wished it didn't have to be Jada.

# CHAPTER 3

I'd pretty much forgotten the litter picking by Monday morning. The dinner with Dom's parents had gone better than expected. We'd spent ages talking about dog shows, and I'd made Dom's mum laugh by telling her about Granddad's dog learning to wave.

I'd also had the best dessert I'd ever tasted – a dacquoise: layers of nutty meringue and cream. I'd photographed it for Harry, which led to Dom's dad looking up Harry's baking blog and saying it was impressive. Maybe now he thought my whole family were go-getting.

Dom had walked me home and we'd stood outside my front door kissing for the longest time, before I'd pulled away to find my keys, kissing him once more and feeling the sort of happy that comes from knowing you've been your best self.

On Monday I got up early to go to Mr Peaty's to feed Hector and lay on his sofa with the large cat on my lap for five minutes purring like some kind of machine.

It would have been quicker to walk straight to school from there, but I doubled back to Stan's so I could walk in with him. Like always.

"How was your uni taster thing?" I asked as he pulled his front door closed behind him.

Stan beamed. His animated description of the tasks and the people he'd met lasted until we reached our form room. We made our way to the back of the room where our group sat, having laid claim to three tables.

Aden waved. "I can't believe you guys are a meme now!"

I groaned and dropped into my seat. "Please tell me you're joking."

Aden showed us the group photo of the litter pickers from Friday which had the word *Rubbish Students* above it. Mr Ferris had done a hideous job of the group photo. Several of us were pulling random faces, including me.

"Oh, god," I said. "Gruesome."

Stan looked over my shoulder. "Is that honestly the best photo Mr Ferris could take?"

"At least you look almost normal," I said.

"It's been doing the rounds, getting some interesting comments," said Jada. She looked pleased with herself, and I wondered how the dinner had gone with Hollie's family. Did they like her more than me? I pushed the petty thought away. Hollie and I went way back, since being put in the same group for dance in Year Seven, and screaming our way down the zip wire on the team-building day shortly afterwards, where I landed on top of her at the bottom when she failed to get out of the way in time. Jada couldn't compete with that history.

"I don't want to know," I said.

"Wise decision," said Jada, visibly disappointed. "Best to take it on the chin and move on."

"We are," I said cheerfully.

Hollie said, "I still feel guilty."

"Don't," said Aden. "It was just a joke."

I coughed loudly. "Er, I think it's up to me and Stan to forgive her. And we don't. *Yet.*"

"Oooh," said Hollie.

Stan and I winked at each other knowingly. We hadn't actually come up with a plan to get revenge, but it was good to keep her on her toes.

"In other news," said Hollie, "I've lost the little crochet rabbit that was attached to my key ring. I must have dropped it at school yesterday. Please can everyone keep an eye out?"

"Hollie Linton, you are forever losing things," said Jada. "But, yes, I will."

Aden was leaning back on his chair so that it was only balancing on two legs. "Anyone want to hear about the rowing club party I went to? Approximately one guy for ten point five girls. The point five was our cox. She's tiny. Great night. All of us ended up in the river. And now I've got a cold." He sniffed dramatically.

"Aden, *please* be careful!" Ms Reid, our form tutor, came over, her hair a fresh shade of red, wearing one of her shapeless boho dresses. "I don't want to be mopping up blood from your cracked skull if you keep that up."

We liked Ms Reid. Not much fazed her, which we put down to her having three teenage sons and understanding our world better than a lot of other teachers. She could keep control of a class without shouting, she listened to feedback and her lessons made you see things differently.

"How were your weekends?" she asked the rest of us.

"Stan and I were getting over the trauma of the Big Tidy Up on Friday," I said.

Jada shot me a daggers look but I ignored her. I hadn't landed Hollie in it.

"Ah, yes," said Ms Reid. "I saw the photo Mr Ferris put on the staff Teams, and I was proud to see two of our form group getting involved."

Stan and I smiled angelically at her.

Ms Reid looked up at the clock above the door. "Okaaay. Time to head off for period one, folks."

Hollie reached across to my table and clutched my hands. "Amy, we're good, right? You don't hate me? That ridiculous meme will disappear soon."

I looked into her eyes, at the different variations of blue

25

and green that reminded me of a pendant my mum was particularly fond of, and I wished, like I had wished ever since I met her five years ago, that I were more like Hollie. She was infuriating, exhausting and totally endearing. You could never be annoyed with her for long.

"We're good," I said.

We had an enrichment session in the last period where we had to listen to a poor mum talk about how her daughter had died in a car crash because her friend was drink-driving. We were shown a video of her daughter in her prom dress, tragic and beautiful, and the room had been so silent we could hear the whir of the laptop beneath the soft music accompanying the footage.

Stan and I were quiet as we walked home together. Neither of us could wait until we turned seventeen and could start driving lessons.

"That was super-sad, but I hate how everyone assumes all teenagers are going to make bad decisions," I said.

Stan kicked a stone along the road and didn't comment. "Want to come back to mine and work on our colony?"

"Got a stack of work to do," I said. "And I said I'd FaceTime with Dom before he goes to swim training."

"Sure," said Stan. I caught something in his voice. He sounded down. Before I could ask if he was OK, he was heading off along the street. He grinned and waved at me – but something wasn't right.

I'd make sure I caught up with him properly this week.

I thought he'd fully recovered from being ghosted by a girl from Hinchford he'd seen on and off over the summer, but maybe he was still feeling sore about it.

When I got in, I took a mug of tea and some biscuits up to my bedroom, and made notes for a history essay on the Cold War until I lost concentration. I googled best-ever pranks. The toothpaste in Oreo cookies came up a lot. I thought about the time Harry had made Oreo cookies from scratch, right down to the lettering. Even Granddad had been impressed and it took a lot to impress him.

I sighed and put down my history book. Sometimes I was envious of Harry – he'd always known what he wanted to do. He even had a Plan B to make sure he got there and probably Plans C and D as well. He wanted to run a catering company. After A-levels, he was going to study business at uni while training in pastry-making alongside. Then he'd open his own catering company. If that didn't work, he'd have his training as a pastry chef – or *pâtissier* as he liked to call it – to fall back on.

And me? I wanted to go to uni but I wasn't sure what I wanted to study. I kept hoping there'd be a light-bulb moment when I suddenly knew which path to take. If I was honest, the step up to A-levels had been a shock, with all the work required now. Whenever Mum and Dad tried to get me to "focus on my options" I felt panicky and sick and would come up with some excuse to get them off my back.

My phone started ringing with the FaceTime tone.

Dom. My heart squeezed and I glanced at my face in the mirror above my chest of drawers to check there weren't any biscuit crumbs clinging to it. Then I answered.

"Hey!" I said, as soon as I could see Dom's face. I wished we were in the same room so much I felt a slight ache in my chest.

"Hey!" he said. He was in his large kitchen, doing something on the worksurface. He lifted a slice of toast. "How's it going?" He took a large bite of the toast.

I lay on my bed, against my pillows, and told him about the photo of the litter pickers going round and he smiled. "I'm sure it's not that bad."

"You have no idea," I said.

"Amy, you're gorgeous. Even in hi-vis, I'm sure."

"Hmm," I said, while banking the fact that he'd called me gorgeous. "I want revenge on Hollie, but she's the real evil genius. I've got nothing."

Dom laughed. "I'll help you get her back. You could use some outside perspective, right?"

"Absolutely," I said, propping myself up on one elbow, hoping he didn't mind me gazing at him. On top of being good-looking and charming, I loved how supportive he was. "Nothing too mean, though, that's not our style. Something funny."

"Go on, then. I need some information first. Her weaknesses. What's she into?"

"Art," I said. I'd known Hollie for so long, surely I could find a chink in her armour. "Curly Wurly chocolate bars, thrillers, Phoebe Bridgers, Taylor Swift, watching pranks on TikTok, and Liam Henderson."

Dom rolled his eyes. "She likes Liam Henderson? I don't know the guy but I've heard he's super-arrogant so she might be in for a shock if she ever meets him properly."

"I think she mostly just fancies him for his tennis whites," I said.

We talked about Dom's dog having fleas and we discussed the conclusion for his history essay and then a notification came through from Stan. *Call me*. I ignored it. Another pinged less than a minute later. *You've got to call me ASAP*. Then a third one appeared on my screen saying: *You won't believe this!*

"I need to go," I told Dom. "Stan is hassling me about something."

"No worries, I should take a shower anyway," said Dom with a yawn. Then he blew me a kiss and we hung up.


Stan was in his bedroom at his desk. I could see a couple of textbooks spread out on the bed behind him.

"What's going on?" I demanded.

"You won't believe what I just got my hands on," he said. He was hyped, eyes shining.

"Tell me!"

"I'm going to send you something. Open it on your laptop. I want to see your face when you do." Within seconds, I'd grabbed my laptop and was looking at a photo of usernames and passwords, written out in neat black biro.

"What's this?" I said, going slack-jawed as I realized exactly what it was – details for Liam Henderson's social media accounts. "What the— How did you get these?"

Stan laughed, the skin around his eyes crinkling. "Isn't it wild? You know Mum is a social media manager, right?"

"Yes…" I didn't know that was Stan's mum's job title, but I knew she gave talks about branding and had a few big clients whose socials she ran.

"I found out today that she's taken on a new client: *Liam Henderson!*" He shook his head to show his amazement.

I sit bolt upright in bed. "What? How did you find out?"

He was loving my reaction. "She mentioned it tonight when she got in. Liam's mum approached her a few weeks ago. It's not the usual sort of thing Mum does, but I think she felt like she couldn't say no to a neighbour. Liam's not interested in social media, so his mum has been running his accounts. But now his parents want to make him into a *thing*."

"Nice technical term there, Stan."

He laughed again. "They want to make him more high profile so he attracts as much sponsorship as possible. Mum's been given access to all his accounts and a load of photos. Hang on, I'll show you."

He sent through a few images, photos of Liam at different ages, holding a tennis racquet as a toddler, standing on the end of a diving board aged about five, looking like a professional skier aged about eight, and at the

30

Wimbledon Lawn Tennis Museum as a young teenager, looking unfeasibly excited by the prospect. "Of course, Mum doesn't know I'm doing this," Stan said. "She would totally kill me."

"These are rogue," I said. "Baby Liam looks a bit smug, doesn't he? Wow, your mum must be seeing all sorts of messages to Liam. Wish we could see. Don't suppose she'd let us have a peek?"

"'Course not," said Stan. "That would be unprofessional – but..." He paused. "We've got all the info we need to do it ourselves."

"She'd be furious," I said, but I felt a shiver of excitement. "Arghh. I really want to log in."

"Me too," said Stan. "We could do it together?"

I could smell bolognese from downstairs. It was Monday evening and I had homework. Mum and Dad were unlikely to agree to me going out after we'd eaten, but this was irresistible. "Could you come over here later?" I asked.

"Sure," said Stan. "Message me when it's a good time."

An hour later, full of spaghetti, I opened the front door to Stan and bundled him upstairs to my bedroom. "Psychology homework emergency," I called in case anyone was being nosy.

"Let me know if you want me to bring up a cup of tea," called Mum. "Kettle's just boiled."

"Thanks, but no thanks," Stan shouted down before I closed my bedroom door. There was barely any floor space

31

that wasn't covered with my clothes, books and general life detritus. We picked our way over to my desk and the two grey fabric gaming chairs I'd bought second-hand with birthday money after GCSEs and persuaded Mum to drive forty miles to pick up. They were my pride and joy.

I sat cross-legged in the one I always chose when I was with Stan. It meant I could swivel round and grab anything I needed from my chest of drawers.

"This is weirdly exciting," I said. "I didn't realize I was so nosy."

"I know," said Stan. He opened his phone and propped it up so we could see the photo of all the usernames and passwords.

"Hollie would die to see these," I said.

We barely glanced at the Facebook account. It was beyond boring. On messenger there were a few amateur journalists asking for interviews and someone trying to sell him a vintage collection of tennis racquets.

Instagram and BubbleSpeak were much more interesting. There were strange messages, lots of people asking for autographs, a mildly abusive one saying he hadn't deserved to win a tournament the previous year, and another saying he still had time to repent his ways and join a strange-sounding church.

"Nothing too riveting," said Stan, sitting back.

"Imagine if we added Hollie to his BubbleSpeak," I said. "She'd faint with pleasure."

"Let's do it," said Stan.

I looked at him. "Wait. Are you thinking … this could be our way of getting her back?"

He nodded, his slow smile kicking in. "Yeah. Let her believe it for a couple of days."

"Won't your mum be furious?"

"If she found out, yes. But she's got so many accounts to run she won't notice, and Liam Henderson isn't exactly top priority. She's always saying she's drowning in work." He frowned and I saw a look of worry cross his face. Then he said, "And if we send a Bubble message, obviously it'll disappear immediately afterwards."

"A message?" I nibble at my thumbnail, thinking. "Like what?"

Stan shrugged. "We could send Hollie a message from Liam."

I gasped, from excitement and nerves, and he raised an eyebrow.

"Or maybe not, then?" he said.

"I say yes. It's the perfect revenge," I said, picking up his phone. I found Hollie's account, and caught Stan's eye. "We're doing this?"

He nodded and I did it. *I added Hollie Linton to Liam Henderson's official BubbleSpeak.*

"Oh my god," I said, half-horrified, half-euphoric. "Let's send a message before we chicken out. She'll expect a photo, won't she?" I settled my chin in the palm of my hand for a moment and looked at Stan.

His nearly shoulder-length brown hair was the same

colour as Liam's, just a lot straighter and longer. "I've got an idea. Follow me. Bring your phone." I led the way downstairs and into the kitchen. Harry and his friend Cooper were in there, leaning on the kitchen counter and watching something on Harry's phone.

"Hey, Amy," said Cooper, looking up and ignoring Stan. "I just dropped by to give Harry some lessons on taking better videos. Helping him up his blog game. Taking it to the next level and getting all the laydeez." He snorted. "Joking. Harry doesn't stand a chance with the ladies."

I grimaced. Cooper had joined Harry's year in the sixth form. He had a neat side parting with hair that flopped in his face, and a fondness for tight jeans. He liked to start sentences with, "No offence but," before proceeding to say something offensive, and his resting face was a smirk.

"Shut up, Coops," Harry said easily, scrolling on his phone. "Like you're such a hit with the ladies yourself."

Cooper watched me as I switched the outside light on and undid the door to the patio. "What are you up to?" he asked.

"Psychology experiment," I murmured. "Don't worry, I won't leave the door open and let the cold air in. Gotta keep Dad happy." Dad was obsessed with not putting the heating on unless absolutely necessary.

Stan and I went into the garden. "We'll only be a minute," I told him as he shivered in his shirt. "We need a neutral background that Hollie won't recognize. Take a selfie which shows a tiny bit of your hair. At an angle. Super casual." I ruffled up his hair to make it less like a curtain and gestured to Harry and Cooper to stop staring out through the glass door at us. Stan snapped the selfie.

"What do you reckon?" said Stan as we reviewed it. There was a lot of fence and a tiny bit of hair and ear.

"Yes, let's use that," I said. "It's a real account – she won't be that suspicious. She'll think Liam's on his way to or from somewhere. Maybe." I took the phone and began to write – and delete and write again – a caption, with Stan looking over my shoulder.

"I think this works," I said finally. "*Hey Hollie, Dom told me I had to message you lol.*"

We looked at each other and I pressed send. We went inside, laughing.

"What's so funny?" called Harry as we headed upstairs, but we didn't answer.

Our revenge on Hollie was well and truly under way.

# CHAPTER 4

Hollie accepted the friend request right away and we could see she'd opened the Bubble. Stan and I sat in my gaming chairs looking at Liam's boring website and wondering if she'd reply.

She didn't.

It occurred to me that, as besotted with Liam as Hollie was, she was also pretty smart. The timing of this message from her super-crush was suspiciously close to the trick she'd played on us, so she might not believe its authenticity, and ignore it altogether. Stan and I looked at each other and shrugged. Maybe Hollie had outsmarted us.

Eventually, Stan's mum messaged to ask when he'd be home and I went downstairs with him to say goodbye.

"I'll keep checking the account," Stan said, as he tied the laces on his trainers. "I'll let you know if she replies."

"You'd better!" I said. "I'm one hundred per cent invested."

I waved goodbye as he did his usual gag of pretending to fall off the front step. This evening I actually laughed, perhaps because he did it with more animation than usual. The prank on Hollie seemed to have really cheered him up.

As I was on my way to the bathroom for a shower, Harry shouted from his room, "What are you and Stan up to, taking arty selfies in the garden? You aren't starting a blog or a YouTube channel, are you?"

I ducked into his room, which was far neater than mine. Harry had always been tidy, ever since we were little. I picked up one of his aftershaves, arranged on his chest of drawers next to a display of cufflinks which he collected and never wore, and sniffed it. "Eurgh. That's gross."

"Put it down," he snapped. "And get out of my room."

"Are you worried that you won't be the only blogger in the household?" I asked. I held up my fingers to do air quotes. "I mean, 'influencer'."

"I've got over twenty thousand followers," he said. "Seriously, Ames. Are you doing a gamer thing? I could help you, but I'd have to think about charging you."

"Really? You'd seriously charge your sister? Good thing we don't need your help," I said. Sometimes Harry was too entrepreneurial for his own good. "Just a little project."

I went off for my shower, listening to music on my portable speaker. I glanced at my phone as I dried myself.

There were six messages from Stan.

*Hollie's replied to "Liam"*

*Can't tell if she thinks it's real or not*

*Was selfie of her lol*

*Said "Hey Liam, how are u?"*

*Didn't want to save it. Would look creepy*

*Call me?*

Once I had my pyjamas on, I FaceTimed Stan. As soon as his face appeared, huge and serious on the screen, I said, "She really thought it was Liam?"

"No reason not to, I guess. But, yeah, I think so. She'd put some make-up on!" His face broke into a smile.

I did a victory wriggle. "When do we tell her?"

"Tomorrow evening?" He grimaced suddenly. "I'll have to make sure she never tells my mum, though."

"Yeah, it's Hollie, she wouldn't do that." It was the unwritten rule with all of our pranks – never land each other in it. "She'll be cool about it."

"You're right," said Stan. "By the way, Mum got sent some more recent photos of Liam which haven't been posted yet, as well as those old ones."

"So we could send another message with a photo?" I asked. "Something a bit flirty?"

Stan shook his head awkwardly. "Flirting is not my … strength. You know I'm not good at that."

"Aw, come on. Don't feel bad about what happened

with that rude Hinchford girl. Anyway, didn't you used to fancy Hollie back in the day? Work with those dormant feelings!"

"Amy!" he said, blushing. "You always say that, but it's not true."

"All right, all right," I said. It was an old joke between us, but I think there was a bit of truth in it, once upon a time. After all, most people did fancy Hollie. "How about we ask Hollie a question like, *Are you into tennis?* That'll mean she has to reply. Though obviously she'll probably leave it a while so she doesn't look embarrassingly keen."

"OK."

"And … I think I should tell Dom what we've done," I said. I ignored Stan's worried look. "He was going to help me come up with ideas to get our own back on Hollie, and we mentioned him in the first message, saying that he persuaded Liam to send the message. We shouldn't leave him out."

"OK, yeah, I suppose that makes sense," conceded Stan. "I'll message Hollie, you tell Dom. But remember: Mum must *not* find out."

"It's fine," I tell him. "I trust Dom."

When we'd ended the call, I hopped straight on to a FaceTime with Dom who had just got home after swimming training and was in his kitchen, making scrambled eggs. His hair was still wet and he looked gorgeous as usual.

"Are you on your own?" I asked.

"Yeah, why?" he said. "Got something you want to say?" He raised an eyebrow suggestively.

I laughed and told him what Stan and I had done.

"You're joking!" said Dom, eyes wide.

"Nope, and I don't think she's suspicious at all," I said.

"I'd love to have access to someone's account like that," said Dom. He stirred his eggs. "What a power trip."

"You won't say anything, will you?" I said. "Not to Hollie, not to anyone?"

"How much is it worth?"

"Seriously, you have to promise. Stan's mum will kill us if she finds out."

"All right, promise." He slotted some bread into the toaster and said, "Glad you came up with a good payback for her. She deserved it."

I nodded. He was right – and Hollie always came up with inventive pranks. This would show her Stan and I could be creative too.

"You look happy this morning," said Stan's mum, Karis, when she opened the door to me the next day, dressed in a smart black trouser suit and pale pink blouse. For a moment I imagined how angry she'd be if she found out what Stan and I had done, then I pushed the thought away. I'd never even seen Karis raise her voice. She was always calm, collected and perfectly put together.

"It's gorgeous outside," I improvised, looking around me. It was true. The autumnal air was crisp and the greenery in the front garden smelled fresh even if the trees were shedding leaves. His mum inspected the bright, cloudless sky and nodded.

"You're right, love. It *is* a nice day." She smiled at me and I saw that she also looked tired and was wearing a bit more make-up than usual. She looked thinner too and her dark hair was streaked with grey, as if she hadn't dyed it in a while. "It's good to appreciate the positives, isn't it?"

She then shouted to Stan that I was there.

Stan thumped downstairs with his backpack open, held up a hand in a wave, said, "Just need to grab some snacks," and disappeared into the kitchen.

"What's he like?" said Karis, holding up her hands theatrically.

I replied, "He does like his snacks. Especially those cheesy dipper things."

Karis smiled. Then, out of nowhere, she said, "You're such a good friend to Stan, Amy. I'm glad he has you in his life."

I didn't know how that was connected to my comment about the cheesy dippers, but I returned her smile and we waited in silence for Stan to come back. He headed out and I waved goodbye to Karis but she was already behind the door, closing it, glancing at her Apple watch.

Stan and I made sure we were talking to each other when we went into the form room, debating the pros and cons of a new video game he was thinking of buying, to keep up appearances that everything was normal. But then

Stan said morning to the others in such a wooden way I wanted to lean into his face and explain slowly what *acting natural* meant.

Luckily none of the others seemed to notice. Hollie and Jada were doing a Wordle and Aden was scribbling a late geography essay. They all grunted hello, and Ms Reid swept in, took the register and asked how many of us had lined up something for work experience week next term. Loads of people seemed to have organized something and I hadn't even started. I was usually more on top of things than this – but for some reason I couldn't face thinking ahead to the future. I put a note in my planner to make a start. One of Mum's colleagues in the X-ray department had a daughter who developed apps. Maybe she'd give me some work experience?

"I've got work as a runner on a documentary through my auntie's neighbour," said Jada. "The production company says I seem efficient, with a can-do attitude." She twirled her hands outwards. "Doesn't that sound like me?"

I flipped my planner shut loudly and we all murmured that it did.

"I'm thinking of asking the tennis club if they'll give me work experience, lol," said Hollie, and it took every gram of self-control for me not to exchange a look with Stan.

"What would you do?" asked Jada. "And I mean what, not who."

"Dunno," said Hollie. "Hoover the court? Pick up tennis balls?"

Aden was rattling his pen between his upper and lower teeth. He put the pen down and said, "That would be such a you thing to do, Hol, basing your work experience around the off-chance you might bump into a random guy you fancy. Would the great Liam Henderson look at the person collecting the tennis balls?"

Hollie fluttered her eyelashes at him. "He might look at *this* person, yes."

Ms Reid was going through key dates for work experience on the SmartBoard. "Now remember," she was saying, "this might not seem important now, but it could make all the difference to a job or uni application…"

"Besides, Liam Henderson isn't a random guy," hissed Hollie. She flung an arm round my shoulder. "Thanks to Amy's wonderful boyfriend, the great Liam Henderson sent me a cute message last night." She pulled me round so she could see my face better. "Did you really ask Dom to get him to message me?"

The moment fissured into two. I didn't particularly want to lie, not to one of my best friends. But this was a prank; I was getting Hollie back.

I feigned delighted surprise. "Ooooooh! I *did* mention Liam to Dom, but I wasn't sure he'd say anything. Oh my god. What did Liam say?" I allowed myself to look excitedly round at the others, and saw Stan beaming. I'd clearly nailed it. Maybe I was better at lying than I thought.

"You lot at the back," called Ms Reid. "Make sure you

download a work experience form from Teams by the end of the day."

We nodded enthusiastically and refocused on Hollie, who waited a couple of beats for Ms Reid's attention to switch to someone else. "He said Dom had told him to get in touch. Asked if I liked tennis."

"What did you say?" asked Stan, and I hoped Hollie didn't see me look surprised. He sounded so sweetly sincere. Stan had some acting skills after all.

"Yeah, and why didn't you tell me?" said Jada, which caused me a moment of pleasure.

"Or me?" said Aden. "This ranks way higher than any rowing club gossip."

"I've left him on read for now," said Hollie. She cast her eyes round us all to gauge our response and then seemed to linger on me. "Just playing the game."

# CHAPTER 5

"She doesn't believe it's Liam," I said as I walked with Stan to our first lesson.

"You think? Why wouldn't she?" said Stan.

"She's smart. Maybe she'll end up catfishing us back," I said. "That would be a Hollie move."

"True," said Stan. "I guess we just wait and see."

I saluted him and we parted company at the top of the stairs, him going to computer science, me to history.

After our lessons, he was waiting for me in the corridor, moving from foot to foot, and as soon as he saw me, he practically dragged me away from the group I was with. "Need to speak to you," he said and took me to the far end of the corridor, next to an empty classroom.

"Hollie DMed Liam on Instagram!" he hissed. He showed me his phone. It was strange seeing the message, blunt and to the point: *Hi Liam, did you send me a Bubble yesterday?*

"Whoa, interesting," I said. "Did you reply?"

"Not yet. I wanted to speak to you first. What d'you reckon – do we reply now or wait? Or…"

I chewed my bottom lip. "Or we tell her the truth," I said.

Stan nodded. We were silent for a bit. Would it feel flat to stop it now?

"Let's keep going for the moment," said Stan.

"All right," I said. "We'll be with Hollie at break so we'd better reply now." We'd be late to our next lessons if we took too long working out what to say. I took the phone from his hand and typed: *Yes, is that ok? I prefer BubbleSpeak to Insta though.* I showed it to Stan, he nodded, and I pressed send.

Stan took his phone back and deleted the DMs. "Can you imagine if Mum or Liam saw them?" he said, with a silent-screaming face.

I made sure to buy a cereal bar from the café at break, like I did most days, before slumping down on the sofa, even though I'd been desperate to join the group as soon as the bell went. "What have I missed?" I said.

"Jake Morley's dyed his hair blue," said Aden. "Have you seen it?"

"It's quite a violent blue," said Jada. "His skin tone is struggling."

"I swear I've developed an allergy to geography," said Aden. "I'm serious. Every time I set foot in the classroom, I sneeze."

"Oh, and breaking news, Ames, your favourite person has got the lead part in *The Wizard of Oz*," said Hollie to me.

I knew exactly who she was talking about. "Good for Kristen," I said sarcastically. "I'm sure she'll be totally chill about it, as always."

Kristen was Dom's ex-girlfriend and we'd hated each other long before I started seeing Dom. She'd accidentally cycled into me one morning about three years ago, cutting and bruising my leg, and hadn't stopped to say sorry. I was so angry I'd reported her at school and, after the nurse had patched me up, she came to find me to tell me I was a snitch. She was also famous for always getting the lead in the school plays and behaving like she was a West End star.

I caught Stan's eye. He knew what I was asking: *Has Hollie replied to Instagram or BubbleSpeak yet?* He shook his head, so subtly that only I would have noticed.

"How well does Dom know Liam?" asked Hollie suddenly.

"Hardly at all," I answered truthfully.

"Does he know if Liam messages a lot of girls?" asked Hollie.

"I really don't know," I said. I was grateful to see Harry walk past, even if he was with Cooper. "Hey, Hazza-Chops!" I called. "I forgot to ask: you'll make some things

47

for our charity bake sale, won't you? Pleeease? Date to be confirmed."

The two of them swaggered over as if they were doing us a big favour. Harry could be a show-off around Cooper. "Sure," he said. "A tray of brownies and some cupcakes?"

"Hell, yeah," said Hollie. "Thanks, buddy."

"I'll make a blog out of it," Harry said. "I gained five thousand followers after my Halloween bakes post."

"Impressive," said Jada drily. I glared at her. Only I got to make fun of my brother.

Later, at my house, after we'd checked our fortress in *Colony Survival*, Stan looked at his phone and stiffened. "I'm logged in as Liam and there's a notification!"

I grabbed his phone and entered his password.

There was a photo of Hollie – she'd straightened her hair and had eye make-up on. The message said: *I don't play tennis but I* 😍 *watching. My sport is dance lol.*

"Wow. She believes it's Liam," I said. "She wouldn't have done her hair and make-up like that otherwise. We've reeled her in, Stan! Let's reply. We need a different photo."

"Laptop keyboard?" suggested Stan. "Say he's drowning in homework." He took a photo of my keyboard on his phone and wrote: *Disgusting amount of h/w. Dancing def a sport.*

Hollie replied immediately with a photo of her dog-eared copy of *A Streetcar Named Desire*.

*Meant to be doing an essay too. Yh dancing keeps me fit.*

"Ew, she's flirting," I said. "Now I feel like a voyeur."

"Oh, god," said Stan, cringing.

Hollie was typing something else. *You got any matches coming up I can watch?*

"Is she asking for a date?" said Stan, almost dropping the phone.

I picked it up and started typing: *Yeah. You should come and watch me play sometime*

Hollie typed back: *Sounds fun!*

Stan and I looked at each other. Suddenly I was worried this had gone too far. "Argh," I said, placing his phone face down on my desk. "I'm going to leave it there. I can't cope any more! Should we tell her now?"

Stan looked at the phone and the little icon of Liam. "Let's sleep on it and decide," he said.

When Stan opened his front door the following morning, he was eating a potato waffle and looked tired. "Went to bed too late," he explained. "I started playing *Raft* and it was a massive time suck."

"Perilous sea journeys aren't the most relaxing thing to do before you go to bed," I said.

"Possibly true," he said and started to tell me how the game had gone, which meant that we hadn't spoken about Hollie and BubbleSpeak before we heard someone shout at us from behind and we turned to see Jada. I sighed.

"Wait for me," she said. Jada dressed to stand out and today was no different. Under her big orange furry coat she had on floral leggings. The sort of floral leggings that were marketed to the over-fifties but on her looked very cool. "Traffic on the main road's terrible. I had to get off the bus and walk. Did you hear the tennis player is still messaging Hollie? I'm here for it."

"Oooh," I said. I pulled my phone from my bag to see what Hollie had said on the group chat, but there was nothing. She must have contacted Jada separately.

Normally it would be *me* she would message about something like that.

"I'm sure she'll tell you all about it later," said Jada, smoothing her straightened black hair.

But when we got to our form room, Hollie was preoccupied with finishing a sketch for art and spent break in the art room too.

In the middle of our psychology lesson, Stan and I opened a new Bubble Hollie had sent to Liam, propping Stan's phone up inside a textbook so we wouldn't get caught. She'd taken it in the art room in her free period, standing against one of the blue-green walls which matched her eyes. It was a beautiful shot. If Liam was really chatting to her, he would totally fall for her right now.

*Let's meet up this evening!* was the caption.

"What do we say?" I whispered.

Stan took a surreptitious photo of the edge of the desk and the nondescript beige floor and typed. *I'll be at the outdoor court in Pennington Park at 6.* He pressed send before I could stop him.

"Why did you do that?" I hissed.

"I wanted to make her happy," said Stan.

"She won't be happy when Liam doesn't show," I said, shaking my head, then jumping when the psychology teacher called my name to answer a question.

# CHAPTER 6

Stan and I reached the sofas first at lunchtime and sat down to wait for Hollie.

We waited. And waited. I brushed cat hair off my sweatshirt and told Stan how I was training Hector to shake a paw. Stan nodded absently, eyes on the door of the café. We were too keyed up to bother with conversation after that.

"We should tell her the truth," I muttered.

"Yeah," said Stan, his leg jiggling nervously. "Or maybe we just let her go to Pennington Park and get annoyed and leave."

I pushed my lips together as I thought about it. That would be the coward's way out, but it was pretty tempting.

Suddenly Hollie rushed in, Jada behind her. Hollie ran over and said, "OMG, listen: I wanted to be sure before I told you guys, but I have a date with Liam Henderson. A date! With Liam Henderson! *Tonight!*"

"What was that?" joked Aden, striding over and plonking himself down on the sofa next to Hollie. He flashed one of his dazzling smiles at her, but I thought I saw annoyance flit across his face too. "I think there are still a few people in the café who didn't hear you." He held his shoulder and rotated his arm. "Ouch, I think I've twisted my shoulder from my gym session yesterday."

I looked at Stan. This was bad. People here might actually know Liam or know someone who knew him.

"A date? Where are you going?" Stan asked, his voice quiet. I nodded as if I wanted to know too.

"Pennington Park," said Hollie. "To see him play tennis. Time to watch a beginner's guide to tennis in two minutes on YouTube!" She twisted her ponytail round and round, let it go, then started again. I realized Hollie must really like Liam because there was no way that she would normally think standing around on the court watching some guy play tennis was a good date. "What am I going to wear?"

"Come to mine before if you want me to do your hair and make-up," said Jada. Then, as an afterthought, she added, "Amy, you can come too. If you want."

"I don't want to look as if I'm trying too hard," said Hollie. "Girl-next-door-yet-fabulous." She held out her hands. "I've even lost my hairbrush I always have in my bag! You'll be able to sort me out, won't you, Jada?"

"No problem," said Jada, crossing her floral-legging legs. I could have sworn she gave me a smug look.

Hollie dropped her head into her hands and gave a dramatic wail. "Ohhh, I've wanted this for so long and now I feel super-nervous. That's not like me at all." My stomach twisted uncomfortably. Hollie lifted her head and caught my eye. "What if he's just messing around? I know he said he was single in that interview but that was a while ago. Amy, can you double-check with Dom to see if he's got a girlfriend?"

"He hasn't," said Stan quickly.

Hollie whipped her head round. "How do you know?"

Stan blinked and a blush crept up his neck.

"Stan was at my house when I was FaceTiming Dom and I asked him," I said. "It's good to know, right? After all, we hardly know anything about the guy."

"You know what, Hol," said Aden, still moving his shoulder around. "I don't think you'll like him when you actually meet him. He's invited you to watch him hit a ball around for god's sake. And in those videos you made us watch, he seems like a brat."

"Don't burst her bubble," said Jada. "Hollie can make up her own mind, can't she? And isn't life about seizing opportunities?"

Aden tore open a Snickers bar and shrugged. "Just saying."

"Thanks for having my back," Hollie said. "Are any of you free to walk with me tonight to the park? You can disappear when it's going well, lol. Meet by the Tesco Express on the way into town?"

"Sure," I said, looking at the others who were nodding too.

"I'm so happy. Come here, y'all," said Hollie. "Group hug."

I couldn't look at Stan. I felt like too much of a traitor.

We didn't have a chance to speak on our own until we walked home. As we turned right out of the school gate I said, "Why didn't we say anything?"

"Because it would have been like kicking a puppy," said Stan. "We should have known how Hollie would fling herself into this."

I nodded, anxiety hovering in my throat. "We've got to cancel the date, obviously."

Stan nodded. "Liam can message to say he's not feeling well and then he can ghost her later," he said. "And she can think he's the jerk he actually is." He sounded almost angry and I wondered if he was thinking of his own experience of being ghosted. I was still so annoyed with that girl – couldn't she have at least told Stan she wasn't feeling it any more but to have a good life, instead of just vanishing?

I put my hands in my jacket pockets – it felt cruel but there was no other option that I could think of. "Your place or mine?" I asked.

"Yours," said Stan. "It's cosier there."

We sent the cancellation message from my bedroom, not bothering with a photo because it didn't matter any more. *Sorry Hollie. Won't be at the park. Am not well L*

I sat back in my chair. The whole thing had got out of hand and I was relieved it was over. "Maybe we never tell her it was a prank," I said.

"Yes, because if Mum ever finds out, she'll ignite." Stan stood. "I should go. Need to pick up milk on the way home."

"What a responsible person you've turned into," I teased as I went to the front door with him. "I thought your mum was always trying to get you to do the shopping with no success."

"People change," he said.

"Let me know if Hollie replies," I said, as Stan did his familiar lurch off the doorstep. "Or are you OK with me going into the account myself?"

"I guess. Just be careful," said Stan. "Leave no trace." As soon as he'd gone, I video-called Dom, and told him what we'd done.

"So we decided to cancel," I finished breathlessly. "I think it's gone far enough."

"Good call," he said, stirring sugar into his tea.

"*How* much sugar?" I queried, leaning closer to the screen.

Dom laughed and angled the phone away so I couldn't see what he was doing, before turning it back as he took his first sip of tea. "Mmm, delicious!" We talked about our days and Dom told me all about some swimming

56

competition he was training for. I zoned out and focused on his deep brown eyes.

"Got to go," he said finally. He pretended to kiss me through the phone and I was still laughing after we ended the call.

I saw Hollie had written on the group chat: *He cancelled. Says he's sick.*

Everyone sent sympathetic messages, including me and Stan, and I felt another surge of relief as I went into the kitchen to find Harry trying out salted caramel profiteroles. To focus on something else, I helped him style them for his blog. He specialized in extreme close-ups – the crispy surface of a sugar-encrusted pudding or the sheen of an iced bun. His fans loved it.

After Dad came home from his shift as a sound engineer, and we'd eaten, I took a break from homework and watched a home makeover show with Mum. During a slow part of the programme in which a woman was making built-in cupboards from pieces of wood she'd found in a skip, I logged on to Liam's BubbleSpeak, feeling like a spy.

There it was, a message from Hollie. Torn between curiosity and guilt, I opened it.

*Hope you're better soon! Lmk when you want to reschedule!*

Hollie was super-keen and didn't seem to mind that he knew it.

Towards the end of the TV programme, in the lead up to the big reveal of the house makeover, the group chat started popping.

Jada: *Check this out. Hilarious.*

She'd attached a link to a reel of a couple of refuse workers carrying bin bags dripping with something disgusting to a truck, then retching, set to music, with Stan's head and mine superimposed on top of theirs.

Mum turned to me. "D'you have to play music out loud, Ames?"

Aden: *Who made that? Lollll*

Hollie: *OMG* 😂 😂 😂

Jada: *Dunno but whoever did is a genius*

I didn't think it was possible to dislike Jada any more than I already did. And why were Aden and Hollie going along with her, agreeing that the horrible reel was hilarious?

Stan: *I'm going to find out who did this*

I typed quickly and furiously: *It's not funny*

Hollie: *Learn to take a joke Stamy*

What? Stan and I had taken plenty of jokes in our time but this wasn't funny. Why would she slap us down like that? Was she trying to impress Jada?

Mum nudged me. "Don't miss this bit."

I watched the house owners gasp at the transformation of their home, and Mum and I told each other what we liked and didn't like, and as the credits rolled, I saw Stan had private-messaged me and written: *But can Hollie take a joke?*

*Wish we hadn't cancelled the date now*, I typed.

"Amy? Shall we watch another one?" Mum asked.

I looked up. "Er ... no. I should do some homework."

*Reschedule it for tomorrow?* suggested Stan. *See how she takes the joke.*

Mum stood up and searched about for her own phone, muttering about calling Granddad.

*Yeah, maybe we should*, I wrote.

Stan: *How about*: "*Should feel better tomorrow. Wanna meet then, same time, same place?*"

Those words from Hollie − *Learn to take a joke* − annoyed me even more as I thought about them. Stan and I were allowed to say if we thought a joke had gone too far. I typed back: *Go for it!*

By the time I'd gone upstairs and opened my history book, Hollie had already replied with: *Yeah ok!*

The next morning as we all sat in form, I waited for Hollie to start talking about meeting up with Liam again. She let Jada go on about what a shame it was that last night's date had been cancelled, but that was it − no mention of the new date.

I glanced at Stan, confused, and he frowned back. What was going on?

We waited all day, but Hollie said nothing. Instead, she was preoccupied with losing her favourite pen with hedgehogs on it, and a new skateboarding dog on TikTok who was even more of a pro than the one we loved who'd learned to go round corners. She obviously was going to keep this date to herself, and I found myself getting annoyed. I found it hard to even look at her. I was one of her oldest friends and from her perspective, she wouldn't even have the date without Dom's involvement. Why not tell me? Was she keeping it between her and Jada?

"Here, Amy, look at this," she said, showing me a video of a rabbit doing the Hokey Cokey.

"Why d'you think I'd like that?" I snapped.

Hollie gave me a curious look. "Excuse me," she said in an unapologetic tone. "I was under the impression that we both found dancing rabbits amusing."

I shrugged and busied myself playing *Subway Surfers* on my phone.

"D'you think she's going to go to the park?" I asked Stan as we walked home. "I feel as if she would have said if she was."

"I doubt it," said Stan.

"Or maybe now she's worked out that it's not real, but doesn't want to lose face?"

Stan sighed heavily. "Maybe."

We walked the rest of the way listing the homework we had. Stan told me that he'd been invited to a party by someone at his computer science taster day. My stomach jolted. Stan was making friends without me? Then I got a hold of myself. Of course he was – and it was a good thing.

"Go you, Stanley Maloney! Making friends outside of Markham High."

"Anyone ever tell you how patronizing you can be?" he said, laughing as he nudged me almost into a bush.

60

We'd reached his house. "You want to come and see what the zombies got up to last night in *Colony Survival*? My dad's not here so we can use the big screen in his office."

"Go on, then."

We eased off our trainers, grabbed a couple of packets of crisps from the snack cupboard and I skidded the length of the highly polished kitchen floor in my socks, jumping on to the carpet in his dad's office. Stan's house was a little bigger than mine even though they had one less person in it. It was always immaculate, with the exception of his dad's study, which was usually a sea of papers and cups of cold coffee. He did something in finance which involved driving round to various offices. Today the study was tidier than I'd ever seen it. "Look at that! Your dad's had a massive sort out," I said.

"I preferred it how it was," said Stan.

"I'd forgotten how much I like this screen," I said. I settled back in his dad's office chair and spun round for old times' sake while Stan brought in a chair from the kitchen. We used to love spinning around in the office chair when we were little, and his dad wasn't bothered as long as we didn't run over any of his random paperwork on the floor. Stan's dad always seemed absent-minded but sweet, a bit like Stan.

"I wonder what Liam's house is like inside," I said. "Weird to think it's on this road."

"Mum's been there," said Stan. "She had a meeting with Mrs Henderson the other day about the account. She

61

said there were huge photos of Liam everywhere. Like, life-size."

"Wow. How is it possible that I am both surprised and not surprised by that?"

The houses got progressively fancier nearer to Old Markham where there was a delicatessen, flower shop, bakery and expensive restaurant. The *really* posh houses, like Liam's, were on the green. We knew which was his house – most people who lived in Markham probably did – but it was behind a high fence, with gates which opened automatically, showing a passer-by the sweep of the drive and the huge bay windows and the front door which looked as if it should be part of a church.

"You want to stay for curry?" asked Stan as we did our psychology homework together. "Mum made loads at the weekend. We've got curry for days."

"Yeah, thanks. You know I love a Karis curry. I'll just check no one's started cooking for me at home."

As I finished my call with Mum, who was fine about me staying to eat at Stan's, I heard a text message ping. I scanned it quickly. "Mr Peaty's had a parcel left outside and he wants me to bring it in," I said.

"That's nice of you," said Stan.

"It all helps my bank balance," I said, putting on my trainers. "Maybe I'll be able to afford interrailing in the summer?"

Stan tilted his head thoughtfully. "I didn't know you wanted to travel," he said.

"Well, maybe I do," I said. But I wasn't sure if I did. The future felt so hazy to me.

I walked to the front door. "I'll be ... forty-five minutes, maybe?"

It took me more like an hour because I was too lazy to walk and once I'd started waiting for a bus I couldn't give up because it would have turned up as soon as I'd started walking, and when I arrived at the flat, Hector was being needy and wanted to sit on my shoulder for a little bit. It meant that by the time I got back to Stan's it was past seven and he was dishing up the curry and apologizing for overdone rice.

"I wonder if Hollie went to the park," Stan said, as we ate in the living room in front of *Gogglebox*.

"Oh!" I'd totally forgotten about the fake date. "I guess we'll find out tomorrow."

"We could check the app?" suggested Stan. "See if she has a go at Liam for the no-show?"

I shook my head. "Let's not." I was starting to feel a bit icky about the whole thing.

We'd moved on to Liquorice Allsorts by the time Karis came home shortly after eight.

"Oh, hello, Amy," she said, coming into the room with her coat still on. She looked exhausted. I offered her a Liquorice Allsort although there were only the bobbly ones left.

She shook her head and sat down on the armchair near us, in a daze.

"Are you OK, Mum?" Stan asked.

She shook her head. "Emergency vehicles everywhere. A poor girl got attacked in the park, apparently. Someone posted about it in the road's group chat."

"What park?" I asked, alert with dread.

"Pennington," said Karis.

The shock winded me, and the room blurred. I heard Stan gasp.

*No,* I thought. *No, it couldn't be.*

Before either of us said anything Karis's phone buzzed with a text. She read it. I saw her eyes widen and the whole room seemed to dip.

"Oh no," she said softly. She had tears in her eyes. "I'm so sorry, you two. That was Jess next door who heard from her friend who lives near the park. I don't believe it. She says the girl who got attacked – it was your Hollie. Hollie Linton, and … it's not good news … she died at the scene."

# CHAPTER 7

I couldn't stop shaking. Nausea came and went in uncontrollable waves, but I wasn't sure if my legs would get me to the bathroom if I needed them to. The most vibrant person I knew, the friend who'd made secondary school fun – my funny, silly, brave, beautiful friend – was gone.

*Hollie had been attacked.* I doubled over, winded, as if someone had also attacked me too with a punch to the stomach.

My brain couldn't take in the information properly. Someone had done this thing. To Hollie. My Hollie.

I heard Stan say the word *dead* but I couldn't go there. Couldn't allow my brain to understand it.

*It was our fault.*

After Karis had given us tissues and left the room to call Mum to let her know what had happened, I said the words out loud.

"We did this," I whispered. "We're the reason Hollie is dead."

Oh my god. If everyone knew … Hollie's parents, Emma and Paul … and Archie, her little brother. What would Mum and Dad say? Everyone would hate us. How could I explain this to Aden, and Jada – to *Dom*? Oh my god.

*Hollie, I'm so, so, so sorry…*

Stan wiped his eyes with the cuff of his jumper and blew his nose on a tissue. "No. We're responsible for her being in the park, and she might have been hanging about…" He shook his head as if to dislodge the vivid scene he was imagining. "But it's not our fault she was attacked."

I could see it too – Hollie, with make-up on, dressed to look casually gorgeous, loitering in the park. The light would have been fading. She likely wouldn't have bothered with a jacket because it would have ruined her look. She would have been surprised that Liam wasn't there. Someone else had approached her. Frightened her. And then…

My stomach turned over. I found myself staring at my socks. They were white, tinged with blue from being in the wrong wash, the colour of veins.

"Should we say something?" I asked quietly. "To explain why she was there? Or won't it make any difference?"

"We didn't kill her," said Stan. His voice was cracking. "We were here." He buried his face in his hands.

Karis came into the living room, and said, "Pop your shoes on, Amy. Your mum's coming over to walk you home." She was talking to me as if I was six again.

"Speak to you later, Stan," I said, as I stood up to go. In the hall, I pushed my feet into my trainers and did the bows in a double knot, my fingers numb. Stan hugged me awkwardly, as though unsure if I wanted him to. I couldn't have said either way.

"When I was your age, a friend of mine died too," said Karis. She squeezed my shoulder. "She was in a car crash half a mile from her own house, on the way back from a music lesson. Life can be unbearably cruel and it's hard to make sense of it."

I hated myself for being envious of her story; at least she hadn't been involved in any way. It was remote, a terrible accident. Whereas I was horribly mixed up in Hollie's death.

The doorbell rang, and Mum was there, hugging me. I breathed in her comforting smell – her perfume and the faint aromas of cooking – and rested my head on her shoulder as she spoke in a low voice to Karis about how awful it was and how you didn't expect something like that in your own neighbourhood and—

"I'm so, so, sorry, Ames," she said, squeezing me to her. "It's just unimaginable. And I can't even think what Emma, Paul and Archie are going through right now. It's the most awful, awful thing. But what was Hollie doing in a park on her own in the dark?" she asked. "I don't get it."

Karis shook her head. "I'm sure the police will find that out."

Still feeling numb, I pulled on my jacket and scarf, and hung my backpack over one shoulder and we stepped out into the cool evening air. Our footsteps were loud on the pavement and we walked more quickly than normal, hyper-aware of our surroundings.

"There was an email from school already. They're calling it an incident for now," said Mum. "Students are expected in tomorrow but there'll be people to talk to if that's what you want. There will be a lot of speculation about what happened, Amy, but it's important to wait and hear from the police. Now let's get you home." She gave a faint smile. "This all must feel unreal to you. It does to me."

I nodded, and dropped my neck down into my scarf, my hand tucked round my vibrating phone in my pocket. Social media was ablaze with news, thoughts, opinions and emotion. Notification overload.

As soon as we stepped through the door, Dad appeared in the hall. He wrapped his big, thick arms around me and hugged me long and hard, his beard tickling the side of my face in a comforting way. "I'm sorry, Ames," he said. "I can't believe it. Hollie was so full of life. Such a lovely person."

"Yes, she … was." I heard the sad hollowness in my voice. *Was?* Was that it – we were saying "was" now for Hollie?

"For something like this to happen, and in our town… It's unthinkable. Do you know why she was in the park? Was she using it as a shortcut on the way back from somewhere, d'you think?"

I shrugged. I wished Stan and I had taken a moment to decide jointly what we were going to say about this. I was grateful, monstrously, guiltily grateful, that all our messages on BubbleSpeak had been automatically deleted after being read.

Harry came downstairs, white-faced, looking serious for once. "I was on the art trip — we heard on the way back. Oh, Ames. Poor Hollie."

"It's made the local news," said Mum, pointing at the TV screen through the open living-room door. Dad must have been watching it. The four of us moved into the room and sat down, sitting forward. I read the moving text at the bottom of the TV: *Seventeen-year-old-girl killed in park attack named as Hollie Linton.*

Seeing those words on TV made it horrifyingly real. She was gone. The girl I'd hoped would be my friend for ever was gone. I wanted to lie on the carpet and howl.

"People are saying online she was struck on the head from behind," said Harry, reading on his phone, and Mum's hand flew to her mouth.

"I went to sort out a parcel for Mr Peaty," I said, suddenly remembering. "I was probably out at the same time as the murder happened." My stomach heaved and I clutched it with one hand and my throat with the other.

"I think we should turn it off now," said Dad, reaching for the remote. Mum nodded.

The screen went mercifully black.

"Do you want me to sleep in your room, Amy?" asked Mum. "In case you wake in the night?"

I shook my head, tears finally spilling.

"They'll catch who did it," said Mum. "Not that it's any comfort right now."

"I let her down," I said.

"Nonsense," said Dad. "You didn't know what she was doing. There was nothing you could have done."

"Someone else in your group might know," said Harry.

I should message all of them. And Dom. I hadn't even looked at my phone, still buzzing in my pocket.

"I'm going to bed," I said. I looked at Mum. "I'll be OK."

"Steer clear of social media," Dad said. "It'll be upsetting. Wait for the facts, OK, Ames?"

After I'd done my teeth and crawled into bed, I looked at my phone. The messages were overwhelming. Hundreds of them – from friends, people I hardly knew, even one from Granddad who must have heard from Mum. Dom had sent a heart emoji and: *Are you OK? Want me to call?*

I sent a heart emoji back and said: *Thanks but I'll only cry.*

*That's OK x*, Dom had replied. He called but I let it ring out.

*Sorry*, I messaged.

Dom: *Speak tomorrow. Love you xxx*

Me: *Love you too xxx*

Stan had sent a hug emoji, just to me. I looked at it for the longest time. At the hands either side of the flushed face, and the upside-down "V"s for eyes. It seemed a childish thing to send after what had happened.

After what we'd done.

The group chat for us five – a new one since September when Jada became part of our group – was full of shock and horror from Aden and Jada. Stan had written: *No words.*

I thought about all our messages, still going through to Hollie's phone. Where was it now – lying in a box at the police station as evidence?

I added: *How can she be gone? I want to reverse time*, and then I turned my phone off. I lay in the dark listening to Mum, Dad and Harry talking in low voices. One of them locked the front door. It made a clunk and then there were soft padding footsteps coming upstairs, followed by silence.

I was up early, while everyone else was still sleeping, and went over to Mr Peaty's. I lay on the sofa and watched the news with Hector lying on my stomach. Hollie was mentioned in local news. There was no footage of the park, but a photo of her flashed up which her parents must have provided. It had been taken in the summer. She was tanned, more beautiful than ever, and smiling with her teeth showing. Usually she tried to smile with her mouth closed, even though her teeth looked fine. I could almost feel her next to me, rolling her eyes that her parents had chosen that photo.

Aden sent a message into the group chat: *Anyone else going to school? Need the distraction*

Stan: *Mum wants me to stay home but she'll be cool if you're all going in*

Jada: *I'll be in. Flat's too cold to stay home even if I wanted to*

I typed: *I want to see you all so I'm coming in* and there was a flurry of virtual hugs.

When I called for Stan on my way to school, he opened the door straight away as if he'd been waiting for me. His face was hollow and there were dark rings under his eyes, but he looked pleased to see me. He asked me if I'd slept and I said, "Sort of," and he said, "Same."

I'd kept surfacing from one confusing, frightening dream for a few moments before plunging into another, where people were creeping up on me from behind and Hollie appeared out of nowhere and clung to me, dragging me into a dark corner of the park where I couldn't see anything but I could hear footsteps getting closer.

"You seen the online stuff?" Stan asked after we'd walked in silence for a while. "Liam's name is being thrown around."

I'd only glanced at it but I knew what he was referring to. Liam's name had cropped up a few times. Rumours that he and Hollie had been meant to meet the previous night – so perhaps they had rearranged the date and something had happened between them.

I knew where that had come from, of course. Aden and Jada knew that there'd been a cancelled date on Wednesday evening. They must have said something. Why wouldn't they?

They had both put up Instagram posts, pictures of all of us together, with heartfelt captions. Only Stan and I hadn't. It probably looked strange. Except sometimes people did avoid social media in situations like this. Didn't they?

Stan muttered, "Do you think Liam will get in trouble? What if the police interview him?"

I bit my lip. "I'm sure he'll have been playing tennis or with his family. If he's got a decent alibi they'll drop that angle and no one will have to know about the messages."

"You're right," said Stan. "Listen, let's not say anything about the prank to anyone. It won't be connected to the murder other than it being the reason Hollie was in the park."

I hesitated. But he was right. Yes, we sent Hollie to the park — but that was all. It would only confuse the investigation. And if people knew...

"Agreed," I said. "We don't want everything to get twisted." I thought back to Monday evening when Stan had rung me, so excited about having access to the accounts, and nausea surged again. I wished more than anything I could go back to that moment. Wished we could have decided not to send a message from Liam's account. Come up with a different way to prank Hollie.

We were nearly at school and we'd both unconsciously slowed down. Now we stopped and looked at each other.

"Do you think the police will want to talk to us?" I asked nervously. "We were Hollie's best friends."

"Even if someone specifically asks, we'll say we have no idea why Hollie was there," reiterated Stan. He caught my arm. "OK, Ames?"

"Yeah, OK."

Aden and Jada were waiting for us by the school gates. Aden was stooped, his shoulders rounded and his hands bunched into his rowing club hoodie pocket. Jada was blowing her nose, her hair tied up tight on her head with a plain elastic rather than one of her usual bright accessories.

We hugged each other in turn.

"I can't speak," Jada croaked. "I haven't stopped crying. I can't believe someone that incredible is just … gone."

"I know," I said. I indicated the others. "We'd known her a long time." It came out wrong. Jada was staring at me as if I was trying to trump her grief. Perhaps I was.

We walked through the gates together: Hollie's squad, a person down.

"Do you think Liam rescheduled the date for last night?" asked Jada. "Weird coincidence otherwise, right – same park, same time?"

Stan and I were saved from having to answer by someone called Izzy from Hollie's art class coming over, sobbing hysterically, wanting to hug us.

"Come on," said Aden, squeezing my hand with his

calloused one. "Let's go in. It's not going to get any easier the longer we wait."

In our form room, everyone was talking in low voices about Hollie and what had happened. They agreed the attacker would be caught soon. Hussein, who was a police cadet and liked everyone to know it, said there was bound to be heaps of forensic evidence and there was CCTV all over Markham.

"You've all seen *Hunted* on TV," he said, twirling a pen between his fingers as if he was in the squad room himself. "It's impossible to stay hidden with technology around us. They'll catch whoever did this, it's only a matter of time…"

Every moment, we were painfully aware of Hollie's empty seat.

Ms Reid came in with swollen eyes.

"You will all have heard this very sad news," she said quietly. "This will be a difficult day for everyone. The school have brought in extra counsellors for anyone who needs to talk – they'll be here for as long as they're needed. Staff will be struggling too but we'll get through this together. If anyone wants to talk to me, please come and see me in the history department office at break or lunch. My door is always open."

I imagined telling Ms Reid everything in her cosy, cluttered office. How our prank had turned deadly. But I couldn't.

*

It was hard to concentrate in economics but our teacher went at a slower pace, giving us small chunks of information at a time because we couldn't take in much when our heads were elsewhere. Towards the second half of the lesson, the door opened and in came Ms Mackie, from the pastoral care team.

"Amy," she mouthed, beckoning me with her finger. "Come with me. Bring your bag."

The rest of the class watched as I scooped up my bag and walked to the front, sweat prickling under my arms.

"What is it?" I said, as soon as we were outside.

"I just want a word," she said. She gave me a tight smile which matched her pulled-back ponytail. Ms Mackie could be kind or she could be sharp, depending on what the issue was. "In my office."

As we went down the staircase, I saw Stan leaving his computer science classroom on the ground floor with another person from pastoral, being led towards a meeting room. He looked hunched and miserable, as if he wanted to disappear.

Miss Mackie pushed open the door to her office and said, "Amy, let me introduce you to a detective working on Hollie Linton's case, DS Stuart Haig."

# CHAPTER 8

"Hi, Amy," said DS Haig. "Why don't you take a seat?"

The officer was dressed casually in black jeans and a grey hoodie, a big man without much hair and plenty of lines at the corners of his eyes. I wasn't sure if this meant he frowned a lot, enjoyed a laugh or had never used sun cream round his eyes. He was sitting behind Ms Mackie's round meeting table, but when I came in, he half-stood and leaned forward to shake my hand, and then thudded back on his chair. He indicated that I should sit on the chair opposite him, while Ms Mackie slipped behind her desk and sat like a statue.

DS Haig's voice was deep and authoritative. "Amy, I'm very sorry about your friend Hollie. A tragedy. We're doing all we can to discover who could have done this terrible thing." He cleared his throat. "I have a question or two for you, if that's all right. Firstly, I'm hoping you can shed some light on why Hollie might have been in Pennington Park yesterday evening. Why was she there, do you know?"

I thought fast. The police had probably found Hollie's phone. If they'd been able to unlock it, they still wouldn't have seen who she'd been communicating with on BubbleSpeak – the messages automatically deleted after being read. But I was certain they could send a phone off to a special lab and uncover everything on it eventually.

Stan and I had agreed not to say anything about our prank. But if I lied now, could I get done for withholding evidence? Did I need my parents to be here for this, or a lawyer?

"She didn't tell me she was going to the park," I said at last. That wasn't a lie, exactly, but it wasn't the truth either. I sucked in my top lip and waited, aware of how warm the room was.

"You don't sound very sure," said DS Haig.

"She didn't tell any of us," I insisted, looking at my knees, at the tiny rip in my jeans which was probably thanks to Hector's claws.

"Was she meeting someone?" DS Haig asked, as if he hadn't heard what I'd just said. I said nothing. "Who was she meeting, Amy?"

My skin felt hot and itchy and I could feel my head begin to pound with the effort of lying.

I needed to tell the truth, I realized. This was too important.

I swallowed. "I don't know who she met, but I do know why she was in Pennington Park in the first place," I said in a small voice and DS Haig sat quietly, his eyebrows raised, waiting. "She thought she was meeting a boy she fancied. She'd had a message from him. Only it wasn't really from him – we were just pretending. As a – a prank."

Ms Mackie let out an audible gasp.

"Who's *we*?" DS Haig asked, honing in on that first.

Oh god. "Me and my friend Stan," I said, barely audible. "Hollie had signed us up for litter picking as a joke, so this was us paying her back." I swallowed. "I'm so sorry."

"Who was this boy you were pretending to be?" DS Haig's voice seemed gentler now he'd cracked me.

I thought of Stan being interviewed in a room nearby. I imagined him hunched over, his hands on his thighs, sweating. If he stuck to his lie – and I told the truth – would he get into even more trouble? This was excruciating.

"We pretended to be Liam Henderson. He goes to Ivy Green. We … used his BubbleSpeak account to send Hollie a message."

DS Haig was taking notes now. I felt Ms Mackie's horrified eyes on me. She led assemblies every September about being responsible on social media.

"Tell me about this account."

I explained how Stan and I had gained access, how we'd used it to chat to Hollie, sending messages from Stan's phone, how we'd cancelled the first date, then rearranged it for last night. I told him we hadn't gone to the park. "We didn't think anything bad would happen there," I said. "We thought if she went at all, she'd soon get fed up, go home and think that Liam was a loser. When Stan's mum told us what had happened, we were devastated. Beyond devastated." I was full-on crying now.

Ms Mackie came over with a box of tissues. She handed it to me without making eye contact and went back to her desk. I blew my nose and attempted to pull myself together.

DS Haig said, "Thank you, Amy. Excuse me a minute, will you?" He stood up and left the room. Ms Mackie tapped on her laptop in the silence left behind.

When DS Haig returned, he said, "Just a few more questions, Amy, and then you can go. Whose idea was it to set up this fake date? Yours or Stan's?"

I squeezed the fingers of my left hand so tightly they hurt. "Both. It started off with us wanting to see Liam's messages," I said, looking him in the eye. "Then we thought it would be a laugh to message Hollie from Liam's account because she was so obsessed with him … and then things escalated. Hollie wanted to meet him – watch him play tennis – and we sort of went along with it. Then we cancelled it—"

"Why did you cancel?" asked DS Haig.

"We weren't sure it was a good idea," I mumbled. "But then – well, we ended up rescheduling for last night."

"Whose idea was it to reschedule?"

"I don't remember," I said.

DS Haig stopped writing for a moment. "What changed, Amy? What made you go ahead with the date? Were you angry with Hollie?"

I wondered how much he knew. Did he have access to our group chat, where Hollie said Stan and I should learn to take a joke?

"I wasn't angry," I said. "Definitely not angry." I couldn't let him think that.

"You and Stan just wanted to get back at Hollie for signing you up for the litter picking?"

"Yes," I said. My armpits were slick with sweat now.

"So, revenge?" He held my gaze.

"Kind of – but that makes it sound worse than it was."

"I see," said DS Haig and he kept writing in his notebook for a while. When he'd finished, he said, "Who chose the location of Pennington Park?"

"I can't remember," I said. "There are tennis courts, that's why we picked it – because Liam plays tennis. With floodlights. It wasn't supposed to be a horrible location."

"And yet it was, for Hollie," said Ms Mackie coldly. DS Haig glanced at her and she dropped her gaze to her laptop.

"It didn't feel like a bad choice at the time," I said quietly. "But I regret it now. Of course."

"So you don't remember who chose the location?" pressed DS Haig. "Whether that was you or Stan?"

I shook my head. I knew it had been Stan. But I didn't want DS Haig to get the wrong idea.

"OK. Final question," said DS Haig. "Who else knew about this fake date?"

"Only me and Stan. My boyfriend, Dom Martin – he's at Ivy Green, knew we were pretending to be Liam, but he didn't know about the date or the location or anything."

"OK … and Liam Henderson himself had no idea?"

"I don't think so. I heard that he doesn't check his official social media," I said.

DS Haig ran his hand over the thin fuzz on his head. "Thank you, Amy. That's all – for now. I'm going to give you my card with my direct phone number on in case you remember anything else, or something crops up later. Ms Mackie will be phoning your parents to fill them in but you are free to leave now."

I took the card and pushed it deep into my bag, letting my shoulders drop, unaware until then how much they were aching. "Do my parents have to know?" I asked Ms Mackie.

"It's our duty to keep them informed," she said. There was no mistaking the tone of her voice. She thought what I'd done was despicable.

And maybe she was right.


There were twenty minutes left of my economics lesson but I didn't want to go back. I wanted to wait for Stan.

Had he ended up telling the truth? Or had he lied and been found out?

I walked outside, heading for the low wall near the car park where people sometimes sat when the benches were full. I'd perched here with Hollie at various times since Year Seven. I wrapped my arms around myself in the cold breeze and closed my eyes.

I missed her so much already. I'd forgiven her for saying Stan and I had to learn to take a joke. That felt a million years ago. Besides, it was probably true.

Hollie had definitely been able to take a joke – she'd laughed her way through life and everyone had loved her for it. Teachers often found her exasperating but they were drawn to her too. She exuded warmth and energy.

And now she was gone.

I opened my eyes at the sound of footsteps on the concrete. Stan. He'd seen me and was coming over. His face was hard to read but I could tell he was upset. "How did your interview go?" he asked.

"I told them everything," I said.

"I know. I thought we'd decided not to say anything." His tone was accusatory.

"I couldn't lie. I just couldn't. What did you say?"

He let out a breath. "I started out saying I didn't know anything. Then your officer came in and said that you'd told them…" He swallowed. "So they know I lied. It was awful, and Mum is going to kill me. I'm probably their prime suspect now."

"I'm sorry," I said. "The police would have found out we were behind it eventually," I said. "But it doesn't mean everyone else will find out."

Stan seemed to deflate then. "I suppose so. They took my phone. I won't get it back for weeks." He looked at me. "Did they take yours?" I shook my head and he kicked a stone in front of him. "That's not fair. We're equally responsible."

"I guess the messages were all sent from your phone," I said. "But don't worry, Stan. I told them it was both of us."

We stayed side by side for a few minutes, not talking, and then suddenly Jada was in front of us.

"Give me the truth," she said, stabbing me in the chest with a finger. "Did you two lure Hollie into the park last night by pretending to be Liam?"

"I don't know what you're talking about," said Stan weakly.

"I heard a rumour from someone whose cousin goes to Ivy Green that you were catfishing Hollie," Jada said loudly. Her hair had come undone and her eyes were blazing with anger. "Go on. Let's start with that. Did you pretend to be Liam in those messages?"

I wondered with a heart-lurch if Dom had told someone at Ivy Green that we'd been catfishing Hollie, starting the rumours. Perhaps it didn't matter who had leaked it. Everyone would know mine and Stan's horrible secret now. There was no going back.

"It was supposed to be a bit of fun," I said. Instead

of feeling guilty, I felt angry. Jada didn't understand me and Hollie, didn't understand our history. "We've been playing jokes on each other for years; her, Aden, me and Stan. Things to make each other laugh. You wouldn't understand."

Jada's eyes were ablaze. "Did you set up a fake date?"

What was the point of lying now? I nodded and cringed simultaneously.

"So you lied to her, tricked her into the park at night, where she died? How could you? You disgusting pieces of garbage," shouted Jada. "She was meant to be your friend!"

I flinched. A teacher opened a window and leaned out. "Stop that," she called.

Jada looked at us, hurt and hatred written across her face. Then she said, "I hope you rot in hell," and turned away from us, thumping back towards the school building in her Doc Martens, giving us the finger behind her back.

That was when I saw Aden, standing near the school entrance. It wasn't the end of the school day yet. He must have left his classroom early too. His gaze met mine questioningly.

"Let's get out of here," I said to Stan.

We let ourselves out of the gate with our sixth form cards and walked home without talking. At the petrol garage we slowed down and Stan said without looking at me, "See you tomorrow," and we went our separate ways.

*

I slammed my front door behind me. Home was quiet. My phone vibrated as I went into the kitchen. It was Mum.

*School rang. Sounds as if you've got caught up in something awful. Hang tight. We'll talk when Dad and I are back xx*

I ignored all the other notifications on my phone which had arrived since I left school, took a deep breath and typed a message to Dom.

*Did you speak to the police?*

He replied immediately, as if he'd been waiting for me to get in touch.

*Yes, before school. I had to, Amy. My parents told me that withholding information is a crime.*

I supposed his parents would know, being lawyers. He messaged again.

*Liam must have got told about the catfishing because he's been going on about it. Police have been at school. Did you set up a meeting in the park as part of your prank? How are you? Call me?*

That was that mystery solved, then. I went to the bathroom and washed my face, removed my mascara, smudged from crying, while I thought about how to reply without sounding too self-pitying. I decided on:

*Will tell you everything but not now. I'm devastated about Hollie. I never meant for any of this to happen.*

He replied: *Of course. Stay strong. Got swim training in an hour. Please call me later x*

Did Dom want to speak to me so he could pass on gossip to his friends? We'd only got together in the summer. How well did I actually know him? To distract myself I started to make a hot chocolate. My phone vibrated again while I heated the milk in the microwave. I ignored it until I'd managed to achieve the perfect hot chocolate temperature and all the powder had been stirred in. It was soothing making it, but after I took a sip, I realized I didn't want it.

I decided to find some comfort telly and headed into the sitting room, checking my phone as I went. It was a BubbleSpeak notification – a friend request from Liam's official account.

I took a deep breath. I accepted it and braced myself for an angry message. I'd take it on the chin – I deserved this.

The message came through – but it didn't make sense:

*Hey Amy, will you notice me now?*

# CHAPTER 9

"Is it true?" asked Harry, bursting through the door a few minutes later. He had patches of red on his cheeks and some of his hair was stuck to his face with sweat. He must have jogged home. "Ames, it's all round the school that you sent Hollie to the park last night. Is it true?"

I couldn't speak. I could only weep.

Harry held his hands up quickly. "Sorry. Sorry. I didn't mean to make you cry." He came and hugged me. I rested my head against his broad chest. "It's not your fault," he said, handing me a piece of kitchen towel to blow my nose on. "Everyone knows you guys used to prank each other. How could you know it would end up like that? I heard Jada had a massive go at you. She'll understand when she calms down. Everything will be fine, I promise."

"Mum and Dad are going to be furious," I said miserably. "And ashamed of me. They're talking to me when they're both home."

"I can be there too if you like," he said, squeezing my shoulder.

I nodded and wiped my eyes on his T-shirt. "Thanks, Harry." Then I pushed him away gently. "Ew, you stink! Where's your deodorant at?"

He grimaced and went to have a shower. I was grateful for him though when Mum and Dad were home from their shifts. He sat with me for solidarity at the kitchen table for The Conversation with Mum and Dad.

"We just can't understand it," said Dad. He looked tired and bewildered. "You pretended to be someone else? As a joke?"

I looked at Harry for help.

"It's called catfishing," explained Harry. "It's why you should always be careful when you get messages from someone new…" He trailed off. Obviously Hollie hadn't been careful. "She shouldn't have gone off to meet someone in the park on her own," he said, almost to himself.

"She should have been able to go to the park on her own at six p.m. without being attacked," I said in a small voice.

"You're right," said Mum. "Of course she should. This isn't Hollie's fault or yours."

"It still sounds to me as if you escalated the prank thing in an irresponsible way," said Dad.

Mum nodded. "It was a lapse in judgement," she said. "And you're going to write to Hollie's parents and tell them how sorry you are."

I knew she was right, but the thought of writing to them made me feel sick. I'd been to Hollie's house loads of times and I couldn't even imagine how her mum, dad and little brother were coping. Or what they must think of me now.

"*And* you're going to apologize to Karis," said Mum. "She could lose work over this."

I nodded, swallowing down tears.

"Let's eat now," said Dad and stood up to look in the oven where the pasta bake was drying out. "I think we've all said enough."

"Wait," I said, suddenly remembering. "I want to show you a message I got earlier. From Liam's BubbleSpeak account. I screenshotted it." I pulled it up on my phone: *Hey Amy, will you notice me now?*

Mum said, "What's that supposed to mean?"

"I don't know," I said. "But I don't think this is Liam somehow."

Dad tutted. "Unbelievable that someone would mess around at such a tragic time."

"It's definitely from Liam's account. Who else knows the password?" asked Harry, peering at the message.

"I don't know. Karis. Liam's parents."

"It's not going to be them, is it?" said Harry. "Could they have given it to anyone else? Could Stan have given it to someone else?"

"Whatever you do," continued Mum, "don't reply. I've heard about this. People copycatting when there's been an incident. They get a thrill from it."

"D'you think it *could* be Liam?" I asked. "Teaching me a lesson or something by making me feel uncomfortable?"

"We'll report it in the morning," said Dad firmly. "Let's not speculate. Like Mum says, it's probably someone being silly and winding you up – but we'll talk to the police just in case."

We ate the pasta bake in silence, punctuated by Dad moaning about the evils of social media and Mum trying to lighten the mood by telling us about the X-ray department, where she worked, being repainted. Staff were voting on a choice of white or off-white for the walls. "Do you know what I said?" she asked, looking round the table at the three of us.

"You said you didn't care?" I muttered.

"Yes, that's exactly what I said. I'm just grateful the department is having an overhaul."

"I'd have gone for white," said Harry. "More hygienic-looking for the patients."

"Maybe the patients like a less clinical look," said Dad.

"I'm with Mum," I said. "I honestly don't care."

As soon as I could, I escaped upstairs. I took DS Haig's

card out of my bag and put it in the top drawer of my chest of drawers, under my socks. I crawled into bed and called Dom.

"Hi, I've been waiting for you to call," he said, his voice echoey. I hadn't bothered to check if he was free to talk and from the white shiny tiles next to him and his wet hair it looked as if he was in a changing room at the swimming pool. "Hang on, I've just got dressed. I'll go somewhere more private." My phone screen blurred as he walked through doors and into an empty corridor in the sports centre where he sat on the floor. I saw a glimpse of trainer shoelaces not yet tied. "Tell me how you are." He said it in a kind way, and I felt the pressure on my chest ease ever so slightly.

"Not good," I said, followed immediately by, "I mean, it's a lot, lot worse for the Lintons. It's just…" I held back a sob.

"It's OK," said Dom. His face was anxious. "People aren't blaming you."

"They are," I said. "Some people so are."

"I guess they are," said Dom. "They think you went too far with a prank, but they don't understand the history you guys had. It will blow over."

"Will it?" I said, hating my neediness.

"Of course. People need someone to blame. Once the attacker is caught, the focus will shift."

"There must be loads of CCTV around Pennington Park," I said. "Someone will have seen something."

92

"You'd think so," said Dom, "but it's been twenty-four hours and no one's been arrested yet."

My heart sank. How could someone commit murder in the middle of a town like Markham, where everyone knew everyone and nothing ever happened, and there be no suspects whatsoever?

"Or maybe the police are playing mind games," said Dom. "Maybe they do have a suspect, but they're waiting for them to incriminate themselves."

I took a deep breath. "I got a weird message from Liam's BubbleSpeak." I read it out to him.

Dom gave a low whistle. "That's wild. I don't like the guy, but I don't think Liam is the sort of person to do that."

"It was horrible whoever sent it," I said. "As if someone's singled me out."

"Ignore it, Ames," said Dom. "It'll be some lowlife who's found the password or somehow hacked into the account getting a kick out of creeping you out."

"I'm not creeped out," I said, but as I said it, I knew that I was.

"Stay strong." Dom looked up and said, "Hey," to someone walking down the corridor. "I'd better go. I'll check in with you later, OK?"

I nodded, grateful he was on my side.

When we ended the call, I went online and saw news footage of Hollie's parents, Emma and Paul, talking about Hollie's attacker needing to be caught quickly. I couldn't watch it to the end. Emma, who was the most fashionable mum I knew, looked rough, as if she hadn't slept or given her clothes a millisecond of thought and Paul just looked ... broken.

On Instagram, a boy in my economics class had posted a photo of Hollie and written: *Pranks can have dire real-life consequences.* I put my phone face down on my bed.

Finding a notebook, I started to compose a letter to Hollie's parents. I got as far as *Dear Mr and Mrs Linton* – Emma and Paul felt too casual for what I had to say – then couldn't see the page for crying. The Lintons had always been kind to me, inviting me to their many events and looking as if they were pleased I was there. There was always something on the Linton horizon – a huge Halloween party, a convoluted and hilarious Easter egg hunt, their own festival in the summer with Hollie's dad's band playing in their garden. They were fun-loving and energetic and many times I'd secretly wished I was a Linton.

I left my letter half-composed. I'd try again another time.

I thought about Karis and how we'd let her down too. I'd known her ever since I could remember. I'd been on heaps of days out with her and Stan and sometimes Stan's dad – to theme parks, swimming pools, Bird World, museums where she'd bought me things in the gift shop, the cinema, burger places. She'd even come with Stan and cheered for me when my football team were in the borough final in Year Nine.

I made up my mind to apologize right now and get it

over with, otherwise I'd be avoiding Stan's house until I did. I stood up to make the call, leaning against my window sill, looking out at the damp garden. At the end of the summer, Hollie, Aden, Stan and I had sat around our fire pit, laughing hysterically at Hollie's impression of her little brother Archie having a meltdown. So many things would remind me of her for ever.

My stomach churned as I heard the ring tone.

I could do this.

Karis answered the landline cautiously. "Hello?"

"Karis, it's Amy," I said quickly.

"Oh, right. Hello," said Karis. Her voice was thick, as if she'd been crying, and I felt shaky in the silence that followed.

"I'm phoning to say I'm sorry about what happened," I said.

More silence.

"I feel so bad," I added. "We didn't think about the consequences of our actions. I mean, obviously we never imagined anything like this, but still…"

"It's a nightmare," said Karis.

"I'm sorry," I repeated.

"I know you are," said Karis finally. I heard her blow her nose, then she said in a brighter tone, "Thank you for apologizing. I'm sure Stan would like a word with you. I'll just get him."

There was the sound of footsteps and then Stan said in a flat voice, "Hey."

"You OK?" I said.

"Been better. My mum's in bits," he said. "The police were round asking her questions."

"I'm sorry," I said. Would I ever stop being sorry?

"How about your parents?" he asked.

"It was rough but they were OK. Listen, something weird happened. I got a Bubble from Liam's account which said: *Hey Amy, will you notice me now?* It was really creepy."

"Wasn't me because I don't have a phone, remember?" he said.

"I worked that out," I said patiently. "But have you given Liam's password to anyone else?"

"Of course not. It's some randomer trying to wind you up." He thought for a minute. "Unless it was Liam?"

"I guess," I said. "Seems a bit out of character, from what Dom says. Bit weird, isn't it?"

He made a *mmm* noise. "Everything is weird. Do you know anyone selling a phone?"

"Nope," I said, "but I'll ask Harry. He'll know if anyone in Year Thirteen's selling one."

"It's got to be cheap," said Stan.

"I'll let you know," I said. We ended the conversation, and shortly afterwards a message came through on the group chat.

Aden: *Amy, Stan – I heard what happened. I know you'll be beating yourselves up. It's not your fault, guys*

Jada: *Hard disagree. H's death is on you. You put her in danger*

Me: *It was a prank. We had no idea this would happen. I wish I could go back and not have sent the messages but I can't*

96

Me: *FYI Stan doesn't have a phone at the moment. If you know anyone who's selling one hit him up*

Me: *I feel terrible*

Jada: *You should*

Aden: *Hollie wouldn't want us to fall out*

Jada: *Too late for that*

I shoved my phone under my pillow and didn't look at it again until I heard the FaceTime ringtone. It was Dom. He was on the sofa in his living room, his dog nuzzled into him.

"Hi, Amy," he said. "I need to tell you something."

My stomach somersaulted. Was this it – were we over? He'd been thinking it over and decided it would be best if he wasn't dating me right now? I braced myself.

"What is it?" I said, trying to sound calm, wishing I was on the sofa next to him. Maybe the conversation would be easier then.

"Kristen called just now. She asked me if I'd go to her grandma's funeral on Monday."

I blinked. "Why would she ask you?" I said before I could think better of it. "You split up with her ages ago. Why wouldn't she ask one of her friends?"

"I knew her grandma really well. We hit it off," he said, sounding taken aback. "Kristen just wants me there as a friend, Ames. Are you OK with it?"

"I guess," I said, but my stomach hollowed at the thought of Dom sitting next to Kristen during the service, comforting her afterwards. Putting his arm around her...

"And I wanted to check if it was still OK for me to come round for pizza tomorrow night?" asked Dom, clearly keen to change the subject. "Last time I had a home-made pizza was years ago when we had to make them at school."

"Yes, 'course," I said, forcing myself to sound cheerful, but cursing past-Amy for trying to show off with talk of home-made pizza. The last time I'd made them was years ago too, and mine had looked like burned roadkill. "I'm looking forward to seeing you."

"Me too."

At the very least, it would be good to have a relatively simple project to keep my mind off everything else. I hung up, and shoved my phone back under my pillow.

On Saturday I woke up to a GIF from Dom of a man munching pizza in double time and a message from a number I didn't recognize. It turned out to be Stan telling me he had a new phone, thanks to his neighbour.

I added Stan's new number to the group chat and saw that Jada had left it. I looked up her socials. She'd unfriended me on everything, but I saw she was organizing a candlelight vigil for Hollie at Pennington Park the following evening: "for anyone who loved Hollie Linton".

Before Dad left for his parkrun, he came into my room. "Let's speak to the police about that message. We don't want to sit on it in case it helps them."

I wasn't ready for this so early in the day but Dad was on a time schedule, so I put my dressing gown over my pyjama

T-shirt and shorts and fetched the card with DS Haig's number on from my chest of drawers. We sat on my bed together and Dad called the number on his phone. As the dialling tone rang loudly on speakerphone, I told myself that at least I was getting this over with.

DS Haig picked up. He was professionally neutral when Dad told him about the message which helped. I couldn't tell whether he thought it was useful or a waste of time.

"You've done the right thing letting us know," he said. "Amy, I'm going to give you an email address for you to send that screenshot to."

I tapped the address into my phone as he spelled it out, then attached and sent the screenshot.

"Thank you," he said when he could see it had arrived. "It's probably someone trying to wind you up – but the team will take a look at it." He ended the call swiftly, in a manner which suggested he was super-busy.

I wondered whether they would suspend Liam's official account. Or monitor it at least. Did they think someone else with access to the account had known Hollie would be there that night? Or did they think it had nothing to do with Hollie's murder?

I went back to sleep for a while after Dad left for the park and when I woke an hour later, I checked Liam's account. I was sure Karis would have reset the password – but I tried it, on a whim. It still worked. I was in.

There were unopened messages. I felt immediately uncomfortable and went to log out – then stopped.

One of the messages was from Kristen, of all people.

What was going on? I tapped it open before I could think twice.

She'd taken a selfie in a kitchen, holding a mug of tea or coffee. A Wimbledon tennis mug, to be specific. Talk about a try-hard.

*No, I don't know Amy well. What she and Stan did was terrible and I'm sorry it's impacted on you. Good luck with your next tournament. I'll be cheering you on x*

I stared at the message. It sounded as if Liam had been chatting to Kristen about the murder. But why would Liam suddenly be using his official BubbleSpeak account after what had happened?

Or was it someone else using his account?

I went back to the list of contacts. Five girls had been added in the last twenty-four hours, including Kristen.

I tapped on another message, from one of the recently added girls, Sara, who was in Year Thirteen and occasionally sang in assemblies because she had an amazing voice. Her message was short and to the point: *It's not appropriate to be messaging me on here after Hollie Linton's death. I'm deleting you.*

I messaged Stan back on his new number. *I think your mum needs to change the password to Liam's account.*

He replied as I was eating a bowl of Weetabix fruit and nut minis. *She was told not to do anything with the account by the police. Why did you go in there?*

I ignored that.

Me: *Why can't Karis change it?*

Stan: *Guess it's evidence*

I stopped chewing. That word *evidence* was scary. Stan and I might have to go to court about this, I realized. To give evidence about how our silly joke had ended with Hollie dead.

Stan sent through another message: *Promise me you won't go into the account again. Mum could get into even bigger trouble*

Me: *Don't worry*

I mashed my last mini Weetabix into the milk remaining at the bottom of my bowl, watching as it turned to mush.

And then another message came through from Stan: *I need to tell you what happened last night.*

# CHAPTER 10

I sprinted to my room, to the gaming chair next to my chest of drawers, and FaceTimed Stan, who picked up instantly. He was in the swivel chair in his dad's newly neatened study.

"What happened?" I asked without preamble.

Stan picked up a glass paperweight from his dad's desk and tossed it from hand to hand. "Liam's mum came round late last night and she yelled at Mum, like, *really* yelled. She said Mum had been slack with her online security and deserved to lose all her clients." He took a shaky breath. "Mum has already sent emails apologizing. She doesn't know what else to do. If this gets out, she'll lose work."

"Your poor mum." I imagined calm, gentle Karis being yelled at by Liam's mum. "What did your dad do?"

Stan shook his head. "He wasn't here. I came downstairs when I heard the shouting and Mrs Henderson started laying into me. Said I'd cost Liam thousands in sponsorship deals and we'd both pay."

"Sounds awful," I said.

"It was," said Stan. "I hate the Hendersons. No, I don't. I *loathe* them." His voice wavered with emotion. "Hey, do you want to come round later? We could hang out."

I hesitated. He sounded upset and I felt guilty – it wasn't fair that Stan and Karis were bearing the brunt of this when it had been my fault too. "I wish I could, Stan," I said gently, "but I have plans."

"Are you seeing Dom?" He shrugged. "Silly question. Of course you're seeing Dom."

I was seized by a sudden longing for it to be summer again, after our exams, when I saw Stan most days, and we hung out with Hollie and Aden. Before Jada, before Dom. It had felt uncomplicated and easy. I didn't want Stan to slip away from me, but I wanted to be with Dom too. I wanted to be with him a lot.

"Yeah, I'm making pizzas with Dom later."

"That's OK, there's a thing with the computer science lot I can go to." Stan smiled faintly, then said, "Hang on. You mean *Harry's* making pizzas for you to pretend you've made?"

I grinned at him because he knew me so well. "No,

I'm *actually* going to make them myself. The dough and everything."

"Fun!" said Stan. "Hope they don't explode this time."

"They didn't explode last time," I corrected him. "They caught on fire. It's completely different."

I could tell Harry was itching to help me make the pizza dough but told him I was fine on my own. I propped my phone against the kitchen wall tiles and went through an online tutorial while he sat at the kitchen table allegedly revising for a business studies test.

"I like this bit!" I called to Harry as I kneaded the dough for a second time and thumped it around on the work surface.

"When did you get so aggressive?" he asked.

"It's helping with all my feelings about Hollie and … all the online stuff."

"Fair," said Harry. "People are the worst." He came over to the fridge and found a can of diet coke at the back. He held it up. "Want to split it?"

I shook my head. Only half an hour until Dom would be here. "You could chop some mushrooms and red pepper for me if you like?"

"Now you're talking!" said Harry, grabbing a chopping board. "Much better than revising." He looked over at my dough. "Time to let that rise now."

I placed the dough back in the oiled mixing bowl, flicked the tea towel across it and put it next to the oven to double in size, then washed my hands. Over Harry's obnoxiously loud pepper munching, I said, "I think there might be something going on with Stan, but I'm not sure what."

Harry frowned. "Um, one of his best friends was just killed. Of course there's something going on with him."

"I know, but I think there's something else … I don't know. I'm not sure what I'm saying, really." I grabbed the hand towel off the hook to dry my hands. "Does he seem different to you?"

"Er…" Harry paused over the chopping board. "He's got more angsty, maybe? I dunno. Stan's so quiet you never know what's going on inside."

Harry's friendship group was looser than mine, a bunch of amiable but casual friendships – with the exception of Cooper, who I wished Harry would shake off.

"Have you spoken to Stan about it?" asked Harry. "Asked if everything is OK? That's, like, the obvious thing to do, isn't it? Unless…" He trailed off.

"Unless what?"

"Nothing," said Harry, focusing on chopping a mushroom as small as possible.

"Tell me – that's an order."

"Maybe now you're with Dom he's realized he fancies you," Harry said.

"God, Harry. No, we're friends. That's the sort of thing Cooper would say." I thought about it. "He's never really had a proper girlfriend. If anything, I think Stan always had a silent crush on Hollie, just never properly admitted it to himself." Hollie's face flashed in my mind, and it was like a punch to the gut. *Oh, Hollie. I miss you.*

Harry took a gulp of diet coke. "If you say so," he said.

The first thing Dom said when he saw all the pizza toppings was, "Wow, those peppers are cut so tiny and even," and I had to confess that Harry had helped me.

We spent ages on our pizzas, as if we were back in primary school. I made a big "A" on mine and used little strips of pepperoni to make rays coming out from it. When it came out of the oven it wasn't quite as impressive as Dom's spiral pattern.

"You're a natural," I said, squeezing some garlic and herb dipping sauce into a bowl for our crusts.

"Yeah, I should so specialize in pizza art," said Dom, landing a kiss on my neck. I swivelled round and kissed him on the lips and he put his arms round me. I breathed in the clean smell of his Nike sweatshirt and smiled at the knowledge that he was happy to let his pizza go cold for this.

It was just a moment of letting go, and then I was back in the real world, back in the nightmare of grief and regret that my life had become.

But it was good to have Dom here with me tonight.

We ate in front of *Gladiator* in the living room. Dom was horrified I'd never seen it before, telling me that I was lucky he was around to get me up to speed with the best movies of all time.

When we'd eaten as much as we could, we put our

plates on the floor and I leaned against Dom, tucking my arm around him, finding bare skin under his sweatshirt and T-shirt to touch. He found the corresponding skin by my waist under my top and we stayed like that a while. We were on our own and it felt nice. Mum and Dad had gone out for dinner, probably realizing I needed some time with Dom, with everything going on, and Harry was at the pub for someone's eighteenth birthday.

"I've actually never been to a funeral before," said Dom when the credits rolled.

My stomach lurched. I hadn't even thought about the funeral. "I wonder when it will be," I said.

"Oh." Dom looked stricken. "Sorry, I didn't mean Hollie's. I was thinking of Kristen's grandma's."

I felt a prickling of discomfort.

"I hope I don't cry," said Dom. "I want to be strong for Kristen."

"I don't think it matters if you cry at a funeral," I said. I'd never been to one either. "I think everyone expects it."

"Kristen's grandma was fun. Very theatrical," said Dom. "She was an actress, so no surprise."

"Kristen's going to be Dorothy in *The Wizard of Oz* at school," I said. "The parts were announced last week. She's already started wearing a pin badge with sparkly red shoes." Whenever Kristen landed a part in a show she got hold of an enamel badge with a motif of it. Last year she wore a badge of a glittery hairspray can for *Hairspray*, the year before a plant for *Little Shop of Horrors*.

"Yes, she told me," said Dom. "That's awesome."

Kristen told him? When? And I didn't want him to think it was *awesome*. I wanted him to see how annoying she was. He saw my face. "Don't be jealous, Ames."

"Of you chatting with her, or of getting a part in *The Wizard of Oz*? You're right, I'd have loved a chance to shine." I started singing 'Follow the Yellow Brick Road', really going for it, to make it into a joke. As he laughed, I wondered whether he was right. Was I jealous? I thought about how I'd felt seeing Hollie develop a close friendship with Jada.

Was it me? Was I the problem?

# CHAPTER 11

I woke early on Sunday and went to feed Hector, then came home and finished my letter to Hollie's parents. It didn't convey everything I'd wanted it to – how could it? – but it was done and I hoped they'd see how heartfelt it was. I put the letter in an unsealed envelope, so that Mum and Dad could read it before I posted it. They were friends with Emma and Paul – or they had been. I wasn't sure whether that would change now.

After that I settled down to do my homework. I had so much but I couldn't concentrate. After an hour, I unhooked a coat from the downstairs cupboard, grabbed my fluffy pale green scarf, and went outside into the cold misty morning, not knowing where I was going until I turned right out of my house.

In the direction of Pennington Park.

There was no mistaking where the attack had happened – flowers, tea lights, and a couple of teddy bears had been left there, and the bench itself where Hollie must have waited was still cordoned off. It had rained and everything looked sodden, and some of the messages on the cards had run. Hollie would have commented on all the single-use plastic round the flowers but she'd have loved them. She wasn't a teddy bear sort of person. I could hear her voice in my head saying, "Look at the face on that one! Looks as if he's swallowed a wasp."

Everything had been propped up against a little fence next to the bench. I had a vision of Hollie sitting there waiting for Liam that night, and I shivered.

I looked around, taking in the tennis courts and the surrounding park. There were just a few dog walkers, and kids playing, closely watched by their parents. It was hard to believe that nobody had seen or heard anything – but this spot was a fair distance from the entrance and if the floodlights hadn't been on, it would have been quite dark as well as secluded. The enormity of what Stan and I had done hit me all over again and it came out as an involuntary wail. I stood with my eyes closed for a long moment and murmured, "I'm sorry, I'm sorry, I'm so sorry, Hollie."

When I felt more composed, I took a photo of the scene

which I sent to Stan with a message: *Felt the need to be here.*

He replied: *Yeah, I took flowers down yesterday afternoon.*

My fingers hovered over the reply box. Why hadn't Stan asked me to go with him? I reminded myself that I hadn't thought to ask him to come with me today. I walked back to the flowers and scoured the tags, looking for Stan's writing among the rain-damaged messages. I found a message from Aden first, attached to a yellow rose in a jam jar, legible because he'd written in biro and it hadn't smudged in the rain. He hadn't put his name but I recognized his handwriting.

*To my best friend. I wish I could take it all back. RIP Hollie x*

*I wish I could take it all back.* What did that mean? Some silly fight, perhaps, and he'd never had the chance to make up.

Stan had left a bunch of sunflowers – Hollie's favourite colour was yellow. His note was smudged and unreadable apart from his name with the large *S* and the much smaller *tan*. Jada had left a vase of flowers and a long note, with one remaining readable line, *Your light will live on.*

I rolled my eyes – it felt so dramatic and performative, Hollie would have laughed at it – and then caught myself. Jada was just being herself and at least she'd done something. I'd done nothing except write a shame-filled letter to Hollie's parents. I looked around, wondering whether there was something I could leave. The park was autumnal, brown leaves in sodden piles or dried out, skeletal. A few metres from the bench there was a bush with dark green foliage and small pink flowers. The tiny branches were surprisingly hard to tug off but I gathered a few of them, tied them with my hair elastic, and left them next to the sunflowers. I'd come back for the candlelight vigil this evening with the candle from my room which Hollie had loved the scent of.

I walked out of the park and my phone vibrated in my jeans pocket. I wanted it to be Dom, telling me he'd won his swimming race, and inviting me to his. That might help me take my mind off this, if only for a short while. Instead, it was a Bubble from Liam's BubbleSpeak.

I hesitated. The app was evidence. The police might even be looking at it right now. But I wasn't doing any harm by looking, was I? I opened it.

*I want to be closer to you, Amy.*

I sucked air too quickly into my lungs and it hurt. Whoever the creep was who'd messaged me earlier, they were back. I took a screenshot and walked faster, loosening my scarf, phoning Stan. He picked up as I passed Greggs.

"What's up?" he asked.

"I got another Bubble from Liam's account. I'm sending it to you."

"Ew," said Stan after he'd seen the screenshot. "That's incredibly stalkery."

"It's weirding me out," I said. "Who could be sending it?"

"No clue," said Stan. "Could be Liam, could be

112

someone else with access to the account using it to message girls. But whoever it is…"

"Yeah?" I said.

"What if they're the person who went to meet Hollie?"

I went cold. I had been wondering that myself; I just hadn't dared say it out loud. But he was right. That person would have had access to the account, seen the fake date being arranged.

"I hate this," I said.

"Are you on your own?" asked Stan. "Keep walking. I'm coming to meet you."

"You don't have to … but thanks." The tension in my neck and shoulders eased.

He reached me as I was on the bridge over the River Mark and we hugged. "You OK?" said Stan, searching my face as he fell into step beside me.

I nodded. He looked pale and tired himself – maybe he was hungover. "How was your thing last night with the computer science lot?" I asked, my pace slower now I wasn't on my own any more.

"Everyone had questions about Hollie and what the police had asked me. They all knew about the catfishing." He said it lightly but I could hear the stress underneath.

"Oh."

"It'll be like that at school tomorrow too," he said. "Bound to be."

I'd blocked school out. The thought of it now turned my stomach. "We'll go to the vigil tonight, though, won't we?"

"Yes, of course," said Stan.

We walked in silence for a while, hands in our coat pockets, the Sunday sounds of Markham around us – groups of cyclists swooshing past, a little kid squealing about a lollipop outside the newsagent and a couple of chatty family groups converging on the footpath that led to the river.

"I think we should meet with Liam," Stan said eventually.

"Really?" I said. "You think that's a good idea?" Stan was the least confrontational person I knew. He shrunk and hid behind his hair whenever people looked directly at him.

"I just think we should clear the air," he said. "Ask if he's the one messing with you, sending messages from the account."

I nodded slowly. "Perhaps we should try to defuse the situation. Explain what happened and tell him that it wasn't your mum's fault. Apologize to him," I said.

Stan gave a slight shrug, not committing to an apology. "He plays tennis at the Canbury Club on Sundays," he said. "It was in the notes my mum got sent."

I nodded. That made sense. "OK. How will we get in? We need a member. Shall we ask Aden?" I said. "I'm sure he won't mind. We've been there often enough with him."

When I said *we*, I meant Hollie, Stan and me. The club was about as exclusive as Markham got, but they did open their doors to non-members for events if you were vouched for by a member. The last time we'd been was for a quiz night. The questions had all been aimed at the old people and were impossible, but we'd been happy enough with the amazing buffet that had been included in the tickets Aden had got us. To Hollie's disappointment, Liam hadn't been there.

"Aden might not want us around," said Stan, and I bit my lip. Surely not? After all, Aden had stood up for us on the group chat. He didn't want us to fall out. "I bet the pin code for the back gate that leads to the tennis court is still the same as last time we went in that way," said Stan. "It saves going through the reception area."

"All right, let's go," I said, indicating that we should cross the road if we wanted to change direction.

"Now?" Stan's forehead creased.

"Now."

We got there in twenty minutes, flushed from the walk and the anticipation of what we were about to do. The pin code still worked and the gate opened smoothly, and we did our best to walk confidently towards the courts, like we came here all the time. There was an indoor court but the weather was good enough for Liam to be playing outside. We heard the thwacks of balls being hit before we saw him. He was by the net practising volleys with an older woman – his coach, maybe.

"Check out that polo shirt," murmured Stan.

Liam's dark green shirt was Fred-Perry logoed on the front and in white lettering on the back it said: *Henderson the Hero*. Modesty obviously wasn't Liam's thing.

We circled the courts once until we were standing out of sight under a tree, observing a duck make its way to the little pond outside the café. We watched as Liam and the woman came off the court. Liam was wiping his face on a towel, a huge tennis bag over his shoulder. The woman was on her phone. She mouthed something to him and strode off and Stan seized the moment.

"Hey, Liam! It's Stan Maloney."

The famous Liam Henderson swung round slowly, his top lip lifting in contempt. "Haven't got anything to say to you," he said. He had a loud, carrying, arrogant voice. "I'm bloody raging at what you did." He looked at me as if I was something unpleasant. "Are you Amy? The other one who messed with my account?"

"Yes," I said. I talked fast, before he could walk off. "Listen, I'm sorry we used your official account. Our friend Hollie had just pranked us so we were pranking her back. She fancied you big time."

Liam nodded ever so slightly as if this was totally normal.

I kept going. "We never meant all this to happen. Obviously. But it had nothing to do with Stan's mum and … well, we're really sorry."

Liam shrugged. "Whatever."

He started walking briskly towards the main entrance and we kept up with him.

Stan said, "We can't put right what we did and that's something the two of us will have to live with, but can you ask your mum to back off? My mum feels terrible about what happened."

Liam stopped to cram his face towel into his tennis bag. He made a scoffing sort of noise. "She's furious and with good reason." He stood straight, much taller than either of us. "If this affects my brand, I'll *mutilate* you. Don't do anything – or say a single thing – to embarrass me again. Get it?"

"Of course," I said quickly. "You – you haven't been messaging us from that account, have you?"

Liam looked at me with renewed scorn. "Why would I be texting *you*? I don't want anything to do with you – or that account."

"Does anyone else know your social media passwords?" I asked.

"No one. Aside from my mum and that idiot's mum," said Liam, jerking his head at Stan. "And I guess you two. Now go away, or I'll tell the reception staff you're harassing me." He looked us up and down. "Who even let you in?" He rolled his eyes and walked off.

We watched him go.

"Hollie would have loathed him if she'd met him," I said. "Dom was right, he's horrible. But I think he's telling the truth. It's not him sending the messages. He just wants this whole thing to go away to protect his precious *brand*." Stan nodded.

"Wait for me here," said Stan. "I'm going to the toilet and then we'll go home for a Stan Special hot chocolate at mine."

117

"Squirty cream and chunks of real chocolate on top?"

"That's the one," he said, as he went towards the clubhouse.

I waited by the back gate. After a few minutes I got a Bubble from Liam's account. I wanted to wait for Stan before I opened it but he was taking for ever and in the end curiosity won.

*Enjoying the Canbury Club, Amy? Not somewhere you usually go. But you fit right in. And you look stunning in that green scarf* 💚

# CHAPTER 12

I spun round to see who was watching me, instantly nauseous.

An elderly couple was strolling towards the pond, the man walking unsteadily and leaning on the woman's arm. Two men were laughing as they approached the courts, tennis racquets in their hands. One pretended to swipe the other one's head with his racquet.

Stan came out of the clubhouse, lightly jogging.

"Sorry!" he called. "The main toilets were out of order."

"I got another Bubble," I said, and as soon as he was close enough, I showed him my screenshot. "The stalker vibes are ramping up." I said it lightly but I was shaking.

"I shouldn't have left you," said Stan, looking around. "If they know what you're wearing and where you are, then that means..."

"They must be watching me right now." I swallowed. "Did you see Liam in the clubhouse?"

Stan shook his head.

In the distance I thought I saw a couple of people I recognized. Two boys kicking a football around on the immaculate grass. Both tall and moving easily, like professional athletes. "Is that—" I began.

"Aden," said Stan. "With his brother."

For a moment, the horrible thought crossed my mind – could it be *Aden* messaging me, trying to creep me out because of what I'd done to Hollie? No. Aden was one of my best friends. Besides, he didn't have the password to Liam's account.

We walked towards them. Aden looked up and saw us and kicked the ball with the side of his foot to his brother, Rory, to motion that he'd stopped playing. Rory, who was in Harry's year at school, picked it up and did a series of keepie-uppies. He was broader than his younger brother, his choice of sport rugby rather than rowing.

"Hi," Aden said. His face was questioning. "What are you two doing here?" he asked.

"Came to speak to Liam," I said. "We knew he'd be here."

"And did you?" he asked.

We nodded. "It's all calm between us now," I lied.

120

"That's good. I'd heard he was making trouble for you." Aden glanced back at Rory, then moved closer and lowered his voice. "Listen, I wanted you two to know that Jada's angry."

"We worked that out," I said.

"Like, really angry." He cleared his throat. "Don't know if you heard but she's organizing a vigil in the park this evening?"

"Yes," I said. "We'll be there."

Aden exhaled. "Jada says you aren't welcome." He winced. "She'll calm down eventually and realize she's overreacting, but it's probably better if you stay away this evening."

There was a collapsing feeling inside me. Our friendship group had been obliterated by what had happened. By what we had done.

"One more thing," Aden said, shoving his hands in the pockets of his joggers. "Jada said she got a message yesterday from Liam's BubbleSpeak account. It said she was *a bad person, like Hollie and every other Eng lit girl.* Um … that wasn't you, was it?"

"Of course it wasn't," said Stan at the same time as I said, "No, who do you think we are, Aden?"

"You haven't been back into the app?" he queried.

My heart thumped.

"No," said Stan emphatically.

Aden assumed Stan was speaking for both of us and nodded. "OK, cool." He frowned. "But I don't think Liam would have sent it. He doesn't know Jada. Like, not at all. She's new to our school. She can't be on his radar."

"Someone else is messaging from that account," I said. "I've had messages too. We've no idea who's sending them."

"That's messed up. Seriously messed up," said Aden.

"I reported it to the police," I said.

"Jada did too," said Aden. "Let's hope they find out who it is and pay them a visit sharpish."

"I don't know how easy it is for the police to monitor BubbleSpeak accounts if the messages get deleted," Stan said. "Mum says there are all sorts of laws and permissions around it and social media companies don't always respond quickly."

"Unbelievable," said Aden.

"And depressing," I said.

Rory called over, "I'm going in for a drink, Aid." He picked up the ball with a swift, easy movement. "You coming?"

Aden nodded at his brother, and said to us, "See you tomorrow, then."

If it had been any other time, he'd have asked if we wanted to come to the café with him and Rory. But not now.

Monday was always going to be bad. Everyone at school knew what Stan and I had done, Dom was spending the day with Kristen at her grandma's funeral, and Hollie was

122

dead and nobody had been arrested for her murder. Dom had been comforting about the messages I'd received and said I shouldn't open any more Bubbles from the account. I saw his point but the compulsion to open them was strong.

"Isn't it better to know what the messages say?" I'd said.

"If it was me, I wouldn't want to know," said Dom.

Maybe he had more self-control than I did.

I'd seen photos online of the previous evening's vigil. About fifty people had shown up and it had looked both beautiful with the candles and the flowers, and hideously ghoulish. Despite Harry warning me not to, I watched all the online footage of it I could find. Jada had worn a gold coat. *Gold.* She'd looked like a high priestess as she held a pillar candle and read a poem about love continuing beyond death in her clear voice, which seemed designed to make people cry more than they already were. Aden had stood next to her, wiping his eyes with the sleeve of his rowing hoodie. I thought I'd seen a glimpse of Hollie's mum at the edge, being consoled by a friend. They had a minute's silence and two girls from dance club had sung an out of tune duet.

Part of me was relieved I didn't go. I'd written an Instagram post saying that Stan and I were staying away so that we weren't a distraction, but we would never forget our beautiful friend. There had been some supportive messages underneath saying that nobody thought we were to blame and a few horrible ones that said that there would be a special place in hell reserved for us, and it was those that stuck in my head and made me cry myself to sleep. It took all my strength to walk into the form room.

Aden was still at his regular spot at the back but he was reading a book, which I had never seen him willingly do before. It was the book on critical analysis in poetry that had been kicking around at the back of the classroom for weeks. He loathed poetry. Jada, sitting at the front with Sabine from her English lit class, gave us a hard stare as we walked in.

Ms Reid wasn't in yet. I'd been dimly aware of heavy traffic as we'd walked to school, so she'd probably been caught in that. I wished everyone else had been delayed too.

Stan and I took our seats, heads bowed. And then the questions began.

"How long were you two catfishing Hollie for?" asked Sabine, and as I looked up I saw her glance at Jada. The question had probably been fed to her.

"Did you follow her to the park? Did you see anything?" asked Jake, who had always been one of the most excitable people in our year. His blue hair was less blue today but he'd given himself a new fringe.

"What did the police say to you?" asked Hussein. "You know you would have been entitled to have a lawyer present, don't you?"

"Are you going to be arrested?" asked Jake. And on and on. Jada watched us from the front, her face stony, as we answered as best we could, heat building in our faces.

"Are you still sending messages from that account?" Jada

asked when everyone else had finished. "Because I got a weird message."

"No," I said emphatically. "Please believe us. I've had weird messages too. I've reported the account to the police."

"You must be on first-name terms with the police by now," said Jada, then looked away as if any response I gave wouldn't be worth listening to.

Hussein said, "Come on, everyone. Stan and Amy aren't stupid enough to continue messaging people from that account, are they? Someone will be having a laugh." He looked horrified for a moment. "Not having a laugh. I mean, wasting police time. Wanting attention. Classic behaviour. You get lots of hangers-on around high-profile cases like this."

Jake said, "You think you know it all, don't you, Hussein? Being a police cadet doesn't make you an actual officer, you know."

"I'm confident I know more than you," said Hussein. He sat back in his chair, arms folded over his rounded stomach.

"Morning, folks," said Ms Reid, bustling into the room with many bags. "Sorry I'm late. I have a lot of notices so I'll dive straight in." She located her glasses in one of the bags and connected her laptop as she spoke. "What I have to say this morning is important and it comes directly from the police in charge of Hollie's case. Please be careful around social media. How many workshops and assemblies do we need to have on the subject before you understand how dangerous it can be?"

We nodded sombrely.

"OK, moving on, Hussein has asked if I could put his photos of last night's vigil up – I'll have it set up tomorrow on slide-show mode for when you come in. Now, I know some of you will want to attend Hollie's funeral and her parents have contacted the school to let us know that it will take place a week on Thursday at two p.m. Everyone in the sixth form is invited and you may leave school early to attend. More details as I get them."

"I doubt the family want Amy and Stan there, and I agree," said Jada loudly and a couple of people murmured their support.

There was a silence. I felt sick.

"Stay behind after the bell to speak to me, Jada," said Ms Reid at last. "One final thing – Markham Council have warned that there's currently a problem with rats in the local area due to the refuse strike last month. They request that students dispose of any unwanted food in the correct way and don't go dropping it in the street." Ms Reid peered over her glasses. "I hope none of you would do that anyway."

I put my head in my hands at the thought of a rat population explosion.

The bell rang and Ms Reid called out, "Take care out there, folks. Jada, let's talk."

At lunch, Stan, Aden and I ate in our usual place on

the sofas in the café while Jada sat on the other side of the room with her AirPods in, watching a film on her phone. I wondered what Ms Reid had said to her – told her to leave us alone, probably. It wouldn't change anything.

At first we sat in silence and then Stan said, "What are your best memories of Hollie?"

"That time she made us do a mud run," said Aden. "Remember when she tripped over and just stayed there, so we lay down next to her and made mud angels."

"My shower after that run lasted at least an hour," said Stan. "I remember when we went to the snake sanctuary in Year Seven and she was the first one to volunteer to hold a snake and was completely calm while she held it but then…"

"As soon as she'd given it back, she ran round that hut squealing," finished Aden. "Didn't a teacher have to remove her because they said she was scaring the other reptiles?" He gave a half-laugh. "What about you, Amy?"

"I keep thinking of the things I wouldn't have done if she hadn't persuaded me," I said. "That hideous roller coaster at Thorpe Park, the bands she made me go to see at festivals, that time she insisted we have a barbecue in the snow, made us run for the charity committee…"

"She was good at imitating people," said Stan. He had one leg resting on top of the other and his foot was wiggling. I wanted to tell him to stop. "Remember when she tapped me on the shoulder and told me to tuck my shirt in and I thought it was Ms Arnold?"

"And practical jokes," said Aden. "Though that time she changed the auto-correct on my phone was a pain."

"Lol," Stan said.

"You mean unicorn," I said because Hollie had changed the auto-correct so every time Aden typed "lol" his phone had changed it to "unicorn". And "rowing" became "badminton".

"Watching you litter-pick in those hi-vis jackets was fun," said Aden, and then we fell silent because we all knew what had happened after that.

"I never got to go clubbing with her," I said. "Not to a proper club. I expect she'd have embarrassed me somehow on the dance floor. All those inappropriate moves of hers."

"For sure," said Aden. "I wished she'd got to take her driving test. She was so hyped about that, wasn't she? All those road trips she was going to go on."

"She'll never be a children's TV presenter," said Stan.

"Or a dog trainer," I added.

"Or start her own events company," said Aden. "Or anything."

I couldn't do it any more. I told the others I had to return a book to the school library, and left them to laugh about the parody personal statement Hollie had begun writing a couple of weeks ago. *I'm pretty much the greatest person you'll ever meet* had been her opening line.

When we were younger, Hollie and I had sometimes gone to the library and done one of the jigsaws, gossiping quietly as she sorted the edge pieces and colour graded them while I picked out the shapes. I'd always been able to see the subtle differences in jigsaw pieces. It was something we did when the boys were busy. Before Jada came along.

Now I picked a jigsaw we'd once done together — a relatively easy five-hundred-piece puzzle of a thatched cottage. I wouldn't be able to get much done before my next lesson. I just wanted to touch the pieces, feel the shapes. I understood, suddenly, why I liked doing jigsaws. I liked the neat way everything slotted together, the way that order emerged out of chaos. I found a free table and picked out some edge pieces from the box.

A girl from lower down the school came over and leaned against my desk. When she opened her mouth I saw a brace on her upper teeth. They had different colours on each section and that's what I was thinking when she started to speak: that when I had braces I was only allowed to choose one colour. "I don't know how you have the front to behave as if nothing's happened," she said loudly. "You should be locked away for what you did."

The room was silent, alert to what was unfolding at my table. Mrs Hartridge, the librarian, came over. "What's going on here? Kyra? Amy?"

I said nothing, head bent. "Her catfishing was the reason Hollie was murdered," explained Kyra. "She should be expelled. Get her to leave."

"I don't know what you're talking about, but the library is open to everyone," Mrs Hartridge said. "Go and sit down, Kyra."

I kept my head down over the jigsaw, holding one piece in my hand, feeling the smoothed edges with my thumb. It felt hard but it was made of cardboard. If I wanted to, I could make it bend.

Other people's conversations rippled towards me. Fascinated. Curious. I pictured myself standing up, telling them it wasn't like they were all so perfect either. Last year, a girl had pretended to be Ms Reid, notifying a boy that he had a history detention. The boy's mum had actually phoned Ms Reid to complain about the detention. Everyone had laughed about it.

Other people had done exactly what we'd done – pranked someone by pretending to be a boy or girl they liked. The only difference was that their prank hadn't ended in a death.

The bell went and I stayed at my table, waiting for everyone else to leave before I did. Kyra walked past and swiped the jigsaw box on to the floor with her hand. Five hundred pieces dispersed across the carpet tiles as she disappeared.

I went to student services instead of lessons. The person who came to the window was Ms Hadley. There was sympathy in her eyes.

"Hello, Amy," she said. "What's up?"

"I don't feel well," I said. "I think I need to go home."

"Would you like to speak to a counsellor?" Ms Hadley asked. "One of them has a free slot now. She's very easy to talk to."

I knew I should say yes, but I felt so tired. Too tired to talk. All I wanted to do was go home and lie on the sofa, so I shook my head.

"I can't force you, Amy," said Ms Hadley. "But remember – they're here if you need them. Let me know when you're ready and I'll fix it. You go home, then, and switch off from everything. Let your brain rest as well as your body." I began to walk out, but she called my name again. I stopped.

"Amy?" Ms Hadley said gently. "This wasn't your fault. I hope you know that."

I nodded and walked on.

As soon as I was outside, I messaged Stan to tell him not to wait for me after school, and I walked home, letting myself into the empty house. I ate a slice of Harry's lemon cake while I made myself a mug of tea, then took the tea into the living room where I put on the first season of *Grey's Anatomy*. Hollie and I had watched nineteen seasons of it together.

Thoughts crowded into my head. Hollie, watching TV with me on this sofa. Liam's hard angry face at the tennis club. Stan's mum, her voice hoarse with crying. Dom with Kristen at the funeral, his arm round her. Was he regretting splitting up with her? I'd heard that she'd been devastated when he had. Maybe she still was. Then I remembered. She'd messaged Liam.

Or the person she thought was Liam…

A Bubble came through on my phone from Stan: *Hope*

*you feel better soon.* He'd sent a random photo of the letter box on the way home to show where he was. For some reason it made me feel lonelier. There was a distance between us. I could feel it but I didn't know why.

I sent Dom a selfie of me with *Grey's Anatomy* in the background and wrote: *How was the funeral?*

No reply.

I didn't follow Kristen on social media but now I stalked what I could of her. She still had photos of her and Dom on Instagram, but most of them were of her dressed up for parties or in shows. There was one of her enamel pin badge of the sparkly red shoes, captioned: *#BigNews.*

My mind kept returning to Liam's account. Why had Kristen and those other four girls been added after Hollie's death?

I was in Liam's account before I registered logging in. And there... There was a notification from Kristen.

I tapped before I could pull back. She was replying, but I couldn't see to what. And her message said: *Yes, OK.*

# CHAPTER 13

My head pounded with thoughts. What was Kristen agreeing to?

She must know to be suspicious of the account. She knew – Jada had been shouting it from the rooftops – that strange messages were being sent from the account. Kristen wasn't foolish enough to meet anybody on her own. Or was she?

I would forget I'd ever been in the account. Or should I text Dom and tell him? Or—

The front door banged.

"Hi!" called Harry. He came into the living room. "Ah. *Grey's Anatomy*. Isn't that what you and Hollie were obsessed with for, like, ages?"

I nodded. Hot tears suddenly coursed down my cheeks and I fumbled in my pocket for a tissue.

Harry plonked himself down next to me and said, "Sorry! I know things have been rough today. I heard a Year Ten girl had a go at you in the library."

"How come you know?" I asked. If he knew, the whole school probably did.

"One of Coop's friends from maths was in there."

"Cooper has friends other than you?" I joked weakly. "Yeah, it was a girl called Kyra."

"Coop informs me that Kyra did dance club with Hollie. He's doing the lighting for the dance show," said Harry. "Hollie and Kyra were supposed to do a fancy duet together." He stood up. "How about another tea?"

"Yes, please. I like it when you're nice to me." I sniffed, starting to feel a bit better.

"Well, I do have an ulterior motive, Ames."

I smiled cautiously. "What?"

"Tell Granddad I'd like money towards a KitchenAid mixer for Christmas. Mum told me he's planning to get me a car tool kit. Why he thinks I'd like that when I've failed my test twice and don't even own a car, I don't know…"

Mum was on a late shift so we ate as soon as Dad got home. Harry had thrown some jacket potatoes in the oven and I opened some cans of baked beans and grated some cheese. Harry being Harry grilled some bacon and snipped it over.

After we'd finished, Dad pushed his plate away and said,

"Amy, I need to tell you something that won't be easy to hear. Mum wanted to be here too but it's better that I tell you sooner rather than later." My heart squeezed. What was coming? Dad took a deep breath. "Emma and Paul Linton have been in touch with us via email. They got your letter and they said to thank you for that, and they do understand this wasn't your fault. But they've also said they'd like you to sit out the funeral."

I stared at him. "Sit out?" I said, confused.

"They'd rather you didn't go," clarified Dad.

"But why?"

"That's mean," said Harry.

Dad grabbed my hand. "I'm sorry, Ames. They're trying to do the best thing for their family. It's too difficult for them to have you and Stan there and it will cause a lot of talk. They need some time. We've got to respect that."

"I'm not going either, then," said Harry. "They probably don't want me anyway."

I stood up, my chair making a screech. "It's OK. I thought they'd probably say that. It's for the best." I wanted to break into howling sobs and I didn't want Dad and Harry to witness it. "I think I'll go to bed. I'm wiped out after today."

Dad stood up to hug me but I pulled away, desperate to be on my own, to let out the emotion that was building up and pressing on my ribcage. I ran a bath, the water thundering into the tub drowning out my sobs. I lay in the water until it went cold, letting the remaining tears run freely and then I went to bed shivering, curling up into a ball.

I thought I'd never sleep but when I opened my eyes it was morning. Pale grey November light. I reached for my phone on my bedside table. My heart missed a beat when I saw the number of notifications. Stan alone had sent me twelve messages and called four times. Dom hadn't called but had sent ten messages. There were countless social media notifications. Something had happened while I'd been asleep. I tapped on Stan's messages first.

*Another murder.*

*Call me.*

*Please call me when you get this.*

*Amy, why aren't you answering your phone?*

*Are you OK?*

*Please, please call me.*

*It's Kristen.*

*She's dead.*

*Her body was found by the river.*

*Please call as soon as you can. I'm on my own at home and I can't deal.*

*OK, I'm calling your mum to check you're all right.*

*Your mum says you're asleep. Call me when you're up.*

My bedroom door opened and Mum came in, searching my face to see if I'd read my messages. My tears told her I had. She rushed forward to hug me, stroking my hair.

"Oh, sweetheart, I'm sorry. Another young girl," she murmured. "What's going on?"

I had to gulp for air, to quell the panic.

"A girl called Kristen," said Mum. "Do I know her?"

"I might have talked about her," I said, pulling up the shoulder of my pyjama T-shirt to wipe my cheek. "She's in my year at school. She's the girl Dom went out with before me."

"Oh," said Mum, looking shocked. "Yes, that's it. It's absolutely tragic. From now on, I'm not letting you leave the house alone. Not until they catch this person. Two girls at your school, girls you knew. This whole thing feels too close."

I nodded. Mum was right.

It felt horribly close.

# CHAPTER 14

I locked myself in the bathroom to get away from Mum's panic, wishing I was somewhere else. At Granddad's cosy little flat on the coast, maybe, or on holiday. With the promise of a carefree day ahead, sending photos to the group chat to make the others laugh. All five of us.

Could I have prevented this murder? It couldn't be a coincidence that Kristen had been messaging Liam's account the night she died. Whoever was behind it must have arranged to meet her and then—

And I had done nothing. I could have messaged Dom again last night – told him I'd seen a Bubble from Kristen on Liam's BubbleSpeak. He could have called her, warned her. I sent Dom a heart emoji. Then I typed: *So sorry* and sent that too. It felt cowardly not to at least call him, but I didn't know what to say. It was all too big and sad.

He replied straight away with: *Devastated*. I wondered what time he'd said goodbye to Kristen yesterday. If she'd said anything about her plans for the evening. If he knew anything…

I splashed water on my face and got dressed in joggers and a T-shirt but then I got back into bed. I couldn't face school and it seemed lots of people felt that way when I went online. In our group chat – that had dwindled to three people now – both Stan and Aden said their parents wanted them to stay home until there was more information about how Kristen had died.

I told myself I hadn't let Kristen down. The police had. They should have been monitoring Liam's BubbleSpeak and working out who was behind it. Why hadn't they? I threw my phone to the end of the bed then picked it up again. I knew I shouldn't but I had to look.

But I couldn't get into the account. I tried again. I'd been locked out. Someone had changed the password. Access denied. It was the same with Instagram and Facebook.

The police must have finally shut it down.

When I went downstairs Harry was in the living room with Dad, watching the local news. Dad got up to give me a hug. "Your mum couldn't swap her shift," he said. "I'm going to work from home today. I'm so sorry, love."

Harry said, "Sounds as if hardly anyone's gone into school."

I looked at the TV which was live broadcasting from Markham town centre. "Have they arrested anyone?"

"Not yet," said Dad. "They will. You can't have two dead teenagers and no arrests. The police will be investigating people known to them. Hauling them in, checking their alibis. Lots of work going on behind the scenes. Then they'll swoop. Can't afford any missteps." It sounded as if he was convincing himself as much as us. "There's a police press conference in a minute..."

"I need to speak to the police again about Liam's BubbleSpeak account, Dad," I said. "I'm not the only one getting messages from it. Jada did too and ... so did others. I have a really bad feeling about it."

Dad beckoned me over to the sofa, "Of course." He was distracted by the TV. "We'll do that. Let's see what the police are saying at the press conference first."

A reporter who had been interviewing an elderly man said they were going to cut to the press conference and we saw an empty table with a dark blue cloth over it. I drew my knees up to my chest. I wondered if I would see the detective who interviewed me at school, DS Stuart Haig, and then it flashed up on screen that Detective Chief Inspector Mark Gorling would be speaking about the Markham Murders.

The Markham Murders. Of course. They already had their tabloid name.

DCI Mark Gorling was dressed much more smartly than DS Haig had been. He was older, and balder, and wore a dark suit, white shirt and plain burgundy tie. The skin on his head shone under the TV lights.

He started by giving his sympathies to Kristen's family and explained that Kristen had been found next to a bench on the riverside by a member of the public walking their dog late the previous evening. "Kristen had been hit by a blunt instrument and died from head trauma. No weapon was found at the scene of the crime." The detective looked straight at the screen. "Kristen was a young girl doing no harm. I cannot stress enough how important it is that the person who did this must be caught."

A reporter asked a muffled question and the detective nodded.

"Yes, we are actively pursuing the line of inquiry that Kristen's death is linked to that of Hollie Linton's last week, although it's too early to state this definitively. We urge members of the public to be careful when they are out in the evening and to be aware of their surroundings, and we would like to give out a number that people should call if they know anything or have seen anything that might be pertinent to this investigation. We will be issuing a photo shortly of Kristen taken in the clothing she was wearing when she died."

He reeled off a phone number which also appeared across the bottom of the screen and ended with, "Thank you very much," and a quick, decisive nod of the head to indicate the briefing was over.

The journalists in front of him stepped forward with

large microphones and one said, "Can I ask if—"

But DCI Gorling was gone and one of his minions said, "No more questions. Thank you."

"I'm going to stick my neck out and say the murderer is a man who hates women," said Dad, rubbing his forehead.

"I don't think you're sticking your neck out," I said bitterly. "It's an obvious conclusion, and it's always, 'Take care when you're out at night,' and never, 'We need to do more to protect women.'"

I hugged my knees more tightly, thinking about the riverside bench. Hollie had been killed by a bench too. It sounded like a copy of Hollie's death.

"I'm going to bake the things you lot wanted for the charity cake sale," said Harry at last. "I need something to take my mind off this."

The cake sale. I remembered Hollie standing up in the café, taking a vote on sweet vs salty popcorn. It would be awful to do it without her. "I think that'll be cancelled," I said.

"I'll bake the brownies and cupcakes anyway and freeze them," said Harry. "I'll be in the kitchen if anyone wants me."

I wanted some distraction too. All I could think about was Kristen answering that message. The person she thought was Liam. Heading out to meet them in the evening…

"So what exactly are we telling the police about Liam's BubbleSpeak?" asked Dad.

I took a deep breath. It was time to be completely

honest.

"Dad," I said, "there's something I need to tell you."

He turned to me, eyes wide and serious. I forced myself to go on.

"I went into Liam's account yesterday after school and I could see Kristen had been chatting with the person using the account. I think she might have gone to meet them last night. I went to have a look this morning and I've been locked out." I cringed, waiting for him to be angry that I'd been into the account.

There was a pause then Dad said calmly, "Did you save the messages or take screenshots?"

"No. The messages deleted after viewing. That's what the setting was."

"Wasn't there a way of saving messages?" Dad liked to boast that the only social media he used was LinkedIn as if that was a good thing.

"Yes, but the other person would know. Same with a screenshot. I could have taken a photo on my iPad but I didn't. I … didn't want to be involved. I was scared enough."

Dad, who'd been rubbing his beard, froze now. "Have *you* had any more messages from that account?"

"I've had three. I did screenshot those." I read them aloud. *"Hey Amy, will you notice me now? I want to be closer to you, Amy. Enjoying the Canbury Club, Amy? Not somewhere you usually go. But you fit right in. And you look stunning in that green scarf."* I looked at Dad. "That last one had a red heart emoji at the end."

"We need to tell the police about this, Amy." He exhaled loudly and placed a hand on each side of his head as if he was holding it together. Almost to himself he added, "Both girls were in your year. Friends. Close to you."

I didn't correct Dad about the friends thing. I hadn't been friends with Kristen – but we were definitely connected. Through Dom.

Dad seemed to gather himself. "Look, we'll phone DS Haig again. Maybe this information is something they can use."

We sat on the sofa together and I had a terrible sense of déjà vu, phoning this number on loudspeaker on my bed after I received the first message.

An answering machine clicked in, then DS Haig's recorded voice, and then the bleep came and I wasn't quite prepared. Perhaps the team were too busy answering calls on the helpline number for him to pick up.

"Hello," I said in a wobbly voice. "It's Amy Mathews again. I rang before because I'd had a message from Liam Henderson's official BubbleSpeak. I've had a couple more, plus, um – I went back into the account yesterday around... Dunno the exact time. Maybe four o'clock. I saw that Kristen was messaging the person using the account. All she said was, *Yes, OK*. I didn't think it was important but now I wonder if it's connected to her death. Maybe she went and met that person by the river. I can't get into the account any more and I don't know whether it's been locked by the police or someone else…"

I stopped and looked up pleadingly at Dad. He said in a voice that was too loud, "This is Amy's dad, Simon Mathews. I'll leave my number so that you can reach her through me if you need to."

I gave him a tight smile. I was relieved to have made the call, pleased he was here to help if the police called back.

Then I had a terrible thought. What if the police thought *I* had something to do with Kristen's murder? I remembered all the messages I'd ever sent Hollie about how much I disliked Kristen. The police had Hollie's phone and would be going through the contents. Another nasty thought wormed into my brain. What if people said I'd been jealous of Hollie too, of her friendship with Jada, and angry at the prank she'd played? That maybe I had a motive for both murders? My breathing was suddenly hard to keep even.

"It's OK," said Dad, rubbing my back briefly. "I'm proud of you for making that call. I'd like you to be careful around everyone, even your friends. Just pull back for a bit if you can – until the investigation turns up something concrete."

Why would he say that? "Dad, my friends aren't anything to do with what's going on. Not in any shape or form." My voice had risen higher than I'd wanted it to.

"All right, all right," said Dad quickly. "I suppose I'm only saying be aware of everything and everyone." He squeezed me to him – his way of apologizing, I guessed.

"I need to go and feed Hector," I said. "Mr Peaty'll be

back soon."

"I'll come with you," said Dad. "I don't want you going there on your own today."

"It's only up the road," I said, although I liked the idea of him coming.

"It's a non-negotiable offer," said Dad firmly. "Unless you're at school, you're not going anywhere without someone else, preferably your brother."

"Do you know how sexist that sounds?" I said. "I did self-defence classes in Year Seven, remember?" The classes had been run by an instructor who'd told us the most gruesome stories of injuries he'd witnessed in various fights. His main advice, if we found ourselves in a threatening situation, was to forget the moves and run. I'd giggled through most of the classes with Hollie or laid down on the crash mats in imagined poses of people having been knocked out.

"Hmm," said Dad. He clearly wasn't in the mood for a debate. "Put some shoes on, Ames. We'll leave in five minutes."

I was ready before Dad and sent Dom another message saying: *Thinking of you. Not at school today if you need to be with someone*

He replied: *Thanks x*, but that was all.

Outside it was cold, quiet and sombre. The whole neighbourhood must have known what had happened yesterday evening by now and there was no one around. Our two pairs of trainers made light, rhythmic noises on the pavement as we walked in step. I put my arm through Dad's, something I never normally would have done, and felt simultaneously sad and lucky.

At the flats, I unlocked the main door, watched by the gardener, who Dad glared at.

"Is he always hanging around, staring at you?" he asked.

"Nope," I said. "You don't have to be paranoid, Dad."

The main door slammed with a heavy click behind us. We walked up two flights of stairs and I unlocked the door to Mr Peaty's flat. Hector was there waiting for us when I pushed the door open, miaowing and curling round my legs. I gave him a quick tickle under his chin and went into the kitchen to open his food pouch as he made his I'm-so-hungry noise. I washed out his water bowl and refilled it while Dad looked around the room – at the three black-cat ornaments on the kitchen window sill and the notes on the fridge, held on by black-cat magnets: a reminder that the boiler's annual service was due, bin collection dates and a Post Office receipt.

Dad wrinkled his nose. "Does this flat always stink?" he asked.

"Yep," I said. "Hector poos on the living room carpet as a protest when Mr Peaty goes away, and I can't leave the windows open." I grabbed a poo bag from the kitchen table. I was pleased Dad finally recognized that my main source of income was hard-earned. He usually referred to it as a "cushy job".

I left him in the kitchen, looking out of the window

to see if he could see our house from there and went into the living room. I'd tied the bag in a knot ready to throw it in the communal bin outside when Dad called me from the kitchen. "Amy, it's DS Haig on the phone. He wants to speak to you."

# CHAPTER 15

I left the poo bag by the front door, washed my hands and took the phone from Dad.

"It's me," I said, my voice squeaking which made me cough. "Amy, I mean."

"Hi, Amy, good to have your message," DS Haig said. He sounded slightly impatient, and it made me anxious. "I understand you went back into Liam's official BubbleSpeak account last night, is that right?"

Dad was watching me and I'm sure he wanted me to put his phone on speaker. Instead I walked back into Mr Peaty's living room and sat on his squashy grey leather sofa, avoiding the cream throw that was covered in black cat hair. "Yeah."

"Can I ask why?"

"I was curious." There. That was the truth. "Someone's been sending me messages. I know Jada got one too. That account is still active. Five girls have been added." I was aware of Dad leaning against the door frame now, listening in. "Then I saw the message from Kristen and now she's…"

"I see," said DS Haig. "Do you have any suspicions of who might be sending the messages, Amy?"

"No," I said. I felt my voice rise with frustration. "I thought the police would have been checking the account. Do *you* have any suspicions?"

"I can confirm it's part of our investigation," said DS Haig. He said it stiffly, almost defensively.

"But not a big enough part," I said. "You thought it was just the reason why Hollie was at the park. Jada and I both told you we got messages from the account but you didn't do anything about it. You didn't make it a priority when you should have." I glimpsed Dad's shocked face and dialled down my anger. "The two deaths have to be connected. Hollie and Kristen were murdered in the same way, and they'd both been interacting with Liam's BubbleSpeak…"

There was a pause.

"I can't comment on an ongoing investigation," said DS Haig, and his voice was softer now, "but what I can say is social media companies sometimes make things difficult for us, especially new ones not based in the UK. There are legal hoops we have to jump through, and it takes time for us to be granted access to messages that have been sent, particularly those that have been encrypted. It's not as straightforward as you might think and it can be exceedingly frustrating for us too."

I sniffed, wishing I had a tissue. "The account's had the password changed now," I said. "Was that the police?"

Another pause. "No," said DS Haig. "That wasn't us. That would be altering evidence."

"You need to issue a warning about the account. So that girls know not to reply to messages from it."

"Yes, we'll definitely be doing that," said DS Haig. "Can I ask if Kristen was a friend of yours?"

"She was in my year at school but I didn't know her very well," I said carefully.

"No particular link with you? You didn't do any extra-curricular activities together or…"

I swallowed. "I… She was my boyfriend's ex," I said. "Not that it matters."

Out of the corner of my eye I could see Dad shift in the doorway.

"OK," said DS Haig. "Thanks, Amy. You've been very helpful, and I promise you we are working hard with all the resources we have. This account is absolutely a priority." He should have added the word *now* at the end of that sentence. "I'm hopeful there'll be a breakthrough soon. Please do give me another call if there's anything else you want to tell me. Anything at all."

"Thank you," I said. I waited until I heard him

disconnect his line before ending the call and then I let out a breath.

Dad came and gave me a hug. "Good work, Amy," he said. "Shall we go home?"

"Actually, Dad," I said, "I'd like to go to Stan's."

Dad checked the time on his phone. "All right, I've just about got time to take you round to his before my zoom call. If we walk fast."

This new life of being escorted everywhere was wearing thin already, but I bit my lip and choked out, "Thank you," while messaging Stan to ask if I could come round.

He replied: *OK.* Not exactly enthusiastic, but he was probably still reeling from the news about Kristen.

I noticed a dead plant by Stan's front door as we waited for him to open it. Karis was usually really into gardening, so this must be a sign of how upset she was.

"Meet my bodyguard," I said, indicating Dad as Stan opened the front door.

"Call me when you want me to come round and pick you up," said Dad. "I mean it."

I waved goodbye to him as he walked to the front gate then jogged along the pavement, hurrying back for his meeting.

Stan hugged me and said, "Hollie and now Kristen. What's going on?"

"I can't believe it," I said as I went inside. "Kristen and I never got on, but I never wished her dead."

He looked at me, startled. "Of course not. I never thought you did," he said. "I was the only one here when my notifications blew up. It was scary and then I couldn't get hold of you. I was worried something might have happened to you too."

"I was in bed, asleep." I followed him into the kitchen, glancing into his dad's study. It was still super-neat, nothing out of place. Then I stopped. "Oh no."

"What?"

"Just remembered I left a poo bag in Mr Peaty's flat." I groaned. "Oh, well, if it wasn't in the bag, it would still be on the carpet."

"That's gross," said Stan, but he grinned and for a brief moment things felt OK. "Do you want a drink?"

"I'll make myself a tea." I always made my own tea in his house.

"OK." He opened the door of the washing machine and said, "I'll hang this stuff up and then there's this new game I've bought. *Alien Heist.* You'll love it."

"Since when have you helped with the washing?" I asked. Stan's mum did everything round the house. "Have my lectures on gender roles finally hit home?"

He shrugged and took the basket of washing into his dad's study where there was an airer waiting, and I sat in the swivel chair and watched him hang up a row of socks. The care with which he was doing it – each one hanging straight – was mesmerizing.

"Start the computer," he said. "I won't be long."

I input the password which had remained unchanged the entire time I'd been using this computer – *Maloney1234!* – and said quietly, "I spoke to DS Haig this morning." I turned to face him; he stood holding a wet shirt of his mum's, staring at me. "Don't be angry, but I went into Liam's BubbleSpeak last night. I saw that Kristen had messaged whoever is pretending to be Liam. I think she might have gone to meet him."

Stan's mouth dropped open.

"This morning, when I heard the news," I continued, "I tried to get back in, but the password had been changed."

"What did DS Haig say?" Stan asked, still clutching the shirt.

"Reading between the lines, they hadn't made the account a priority but they have now – and BubbleSpeak aren't being helpful about letting them see old messages." I hesitated, then asked the question I had to ask. "*You* didn't change the details, did you?"

"No way. My mum's whole career is up the spout because of this. I wouldn't do anything to make things worse." His face was red. Angry. He took a breath. "Listen, Amy. It's great you've given the police this lead. But – enough now, OK? Stay away from that account. It's not safe to get mixed up in this any more than you are already."

"You're right," I said. "I don't know why I kept being drawn back in, but I'm locked out now anyway. The police can handle it." I turned to the computer. "Shall we play *Alien Heist*, then?"

But I couldn't focus. My brain couldn't take in the rules of the game. Stan tried not to get irritated as I kept dropping banknotes and blowing up the helpful aliens. Whenever my phone vibrated, I grabbed it.

I hoped each time it would be Dom.

"Can't you look at your phone after we've finished the game?" snapped Stan.

"I don't want to miss anything," I said. That was true too. I was on enough platforms and group chats that I'd hear about anything to do with Hollie or Kristen. Even though I knew that most of it would be rumours and gossip, I wanted to be in the loop. Speculation was all over the place. It was impossible to know what to pay attention to and what to ignore.

One piece of information doing the rounds was a news article showing that a girl had been murdered two months ago in Southampton. Someone posted her photo – blonde, pretty – and said she looked like Hollie and Kristen. I showed Stan.

He glanced at it and shook his head. "She looks nothing like them, apart from she's young and white," he said, going back to the game. He'd taken over my avatar, who was currently trying to find a secret door in an underground vault. "Although … Hollie and Kristen were actually similar types, weren't they? I mean, yes, they both had long blondish hair, but they both had quite loud personalities. They were lively, didn't really mind who they upset. People noticed them."

"You're right," I said. "And they were both risk takers. They went to meet someone on their own without telling anyone else." I found another article about the girl in Southampton and saw that her ex-boyfriend had been convicted of her murder. "That other girl," I said. "She's not linked." I read out some of the article to him.

"Shows how much unhelpful information is out there about Hollie and Kristen," said Stan. There was an on-screen explosion and he crashed out of the game.

I looked at my phone again to tune out his irritated muttering. There was a message on our group chat.

Aden: *Want to hang out tonight? Talk things through? My parents are fine for me and Rory to have people at ours. Usual suspects welcome.*

I felt pathetically grateful that he'd sent it to me and Stan when there were probably people who felt we shouldn't be there.

"Let's go," I said. "I hate that we weren't at the vigil in the park."

"I'm not sure," said Stan. "People might give us a hard time."

"We can't hide for ever," I said firmly. But I was thinking that maybe I could ask Dom. I really wanted to see him.

Stan tilted his head in a resigned pose. "OK," he said, without looking at me. "If you think we should go, we'll go."

"Cool," I said, messaging Dad for a lift home and Dom to see what he thought.

When I was back home watching *Grey's Anatomy* and ignoring Dad, who was teasing me because I'd told him about the poo bag on Mr Peaty's mat, Dom replied saying he'd be up for coming. Next came the negotiations about how to get there and if Harry was going to be with me. In the end, Harry wanted to stay home and work on his blog and Mum said she'd give me and Dom a lift there and back.

I messaged Dom when we were outside his house and it took several songs on Mum's 'Relaxing Music for the Car' playlist before he appeared, looking crumpled and drained, carrying a jacket which was probably wrapped round a bottle of spirits. I stepped out of the car and gave him a big hug. We settled in the back seat together and I took his hand. He squeezed mine and I squeezed back.

"I'm so sorry about your friend," said Mum, making sympathetic eye contact in the rear-view mirror as she drove. "When did you last see Kristen?"

I froze – what if Dom didn't want to talk about Kristen? – but he answered easily enough. It was almost as if he'd been waiting to let it out.

"I was with her at her grandma's funeral yesterday. That was at twelve," said Dom. "We went to the golf course for the wake afterwards and – well, she was in a strange mood. I thought it was because she was upset about her grandma. I mean, she *was* upset about that. They were really close. But now I'm not sure if there was something else going on. The police came to talk to me – they're saying they think she went to meet someone later that evening. No one knows who."

"Really?" said Mum. "Like Hollie. Maybe she thought it was a date with someone she knew…"

*Oh, god.* The last thing I wanted was Mum letting slip that I had seen the message from Kristen on Liam's account. Dad had told her all about it.

"Let's not talk about it any more," I said hurriedly. "This is hard for Dom, Mum."

"Of course," said Mum. "What you both need is a quiet night with your friends."

When she dropped us outside Aden's we could hear Rory's techno music thumping from inside and Mum raised an eyebrow. "Maybe not so quiet!" she said. "Let me know when you need picking up."

"Sorry about the interrogation," I said to Dom, as we walked to the front door.

He shrugged and gave me a light kiss on the cheek. "No worries. It's nice that she asked."

I gestured to the house as I rang the doorbell. "Let me know when you want to leave. Anytime is fine."

"Thanks. My head's all over the place right now."

"Mine too – I left a bag of cat poo in Hector's flat and Mr Peaty's back tonight."

I was hoping to make him laugh a bit, but he just smiled at me absently. The door was opened by Jada. She'd bleached the tips of her hair and she was wearing a lavender crop top with army combat patterned leggings. The crop top had the word *Raging* across it. My outfit of plain white top and wide legged jeans couldn't have been more dull in comparison. I'd ditched my pale green scarf for a navy-and-white stripy one. I wasn't sure I'd be wearing the green scarf again anytime soon.

"Oh, it's you," she said with disdain and walked away, leaving the door ajar.

"That's Jada, right? I thought she was one of your friends," said Dom as we went inside.

"She was. Sort of," I said. I took a deep breath. "She blames me for Hollie being in the park that night. And I guess she has good reason to."

Dom squeezed my hand. "Stop that – it's not true. And anyway, Kristen being by the river had nothing to do with you," he said, and I felt a twinge of guilt. Maybe I *could* have prevented Kristen's murder, if I had shown someone that message. Dom didn't know it, but I *was* more connected to both murders than he realized.

The hall was empty apart from two girls from our year on the stairs. One was crying and the other was comforting her.

I hesitated, not sure whether to go right to the kitchen where I could hear the sound of people talking loudly, or left to the big living room where the music was coming from. It seemed to have been turned down since we'd got out of the car. But I wasn't going to choose the room ahead, a smaller living room, because Jada was standing near the doorway, holding court about how she'd want her

159

own funeral to be. *She's enjoying this*, I thought, and then pushed the thought away. Just because Jada liked being centre stage didn't mean she wasn't devastated by Hollie's death.

Aden emerged from the living room.

"Hi!" he said, an open bottle of wine in his hand. "I wondered who was at the door." He was unsteady and reached out for the banister. The two girls shifted along their stair. "Dad's away. Mum's back at eleven-thirty so make yourselves at home until then. Let me know if you see my phone. Lost it somewhere. Retracing my steps."

"Thanks, Aden," I said as he wandered into the toilet. I reached for a bottle of beer in my tote bag and offered it to Dom, but he unwrapped his jacket to reveal half a bottle of expensive-looking whisky.

"Nicked this from my parents' stash."

We went into the kitchen for a bottle opener for my beer. The back door was open and I could see a few people smoking and vaping. Most people in the kitchen were Rory's friends from Harry's year, sporty and loud.

"No word of a lie, I felt something weird was up yesterday evening but I couldn't put a finger on it," said Rory, sitting up on the kitchen counter, playing with a bottle opener. I didn't want to ask him for it while he was in full flow. "I was walking back from your house." He pointed at a girl who looked startled, and I wondered whether this was meant to have been a secret. "I wasn't that far from the riverside where Kristen was found. If I was a girl with long blonde hair I might not be here right now."

"Did you see anything?" one of the girls asked, and he shook his head.

"Nothing out of the ordinary but I definitely sensed a bad atmosphere," he said seriously.

It seemed that everyone had an opinion on the murders, wanted to insert themselves into the story somehow.

Dom had poured his whisky into a plastic cup and he took a gulp of it and I pounced on another bottle opener sticking out from underneath a bag of Doritos.

"Hey, you two," said a voice behind me. I wheeled round to see Stan. He must have just arrived, as he was still wearing his black puffa and cold air was coming off him. He gave me a hug and shook Dom's hand, clasping him on his shoulder, like I'd seen his dad do when he was greeting people.

"You all right, Dom?" he said.

Dom shook his head. "Not really. It's destroying me, not knowing how the investigation is progressing. It doesn't look as if the police are trying hard enough. Why aren't they out there doing door-to-door interviews? Or arresting someone?" He poured himself another whisky. "I was so wound up I called the helpline but it's an answerphone. What's the point of that?"

"Amy can give you DS Stuart Haig's direct line," said Stan. "The two of them are on first-name terms the amount of times she's spoken to him." His slight laugh didn't land.

I tensed.

Dom's forehead creased. "Why d'you keep in touch with DS Haig?" he asked.

"Telling him about the messages from Liam's BubbleSpeak account," I said. I was desperate to move the conversation on, but Stan carried on, oblivious.

"At least the police will take the account seriously now, though. Thanks to you, Amy."

"What changed?" asked Dom. He was looking at me hard. "Why will the police take the BubbleSpeak account seriously now, Amy?"

"I… Er…" Everything in my head was grey and insubstantial. All my words had floated out of reach. I realized that the others had gone quiet and were listening, alert for drama. "I'll tell you later," I said to Dom. I saw Stan wince – he hadn't meant to drop me in it. Or had he?

"Tell me now," Dom demanded, his eyes on mine.

I lowered my voice. "I went into Liam's account yesterday," I said quietly. "I saw Kristen had sent a message."

"What?" He seized my shoulders. "What did she say?"

"Just: *Yes, OK*. It could have been about anything…"

His expression was somewhere between shock and anger. "But it could have been about meeting up."

"I guess … yes." I bit my lip. I waited for the inevitable question.

"And you told the police straight away, right?"

"I told them this morning," I said, my voice barely a whisper.

He made a strangled noise of despair. "You waited till this morning. When it was too late. You could have warned Kristen, saved her, but you didn't. And now she's dead."

He lifted the bottle of whisky to shoulder height, threw it hard at the kitchen wall and walked out.

# CHAPTER 16

The noise was ear-splitting. I stepped over the glass and the pungent smelling urine-coloured alcohol to go after Dom. He was at the door, fumbling with the lock.

"Leave me alone," he said, eyes brimming with tears. "I can't be around you right now."

More and more people came out of the living room, staring and whispering. "Please. Let's talk," I cried. "I want to explain properly."

"We're done," he said, and he let himself out of the house, slamming the huge door behind him.

*We're done.* Did he really mean that?

I leaned my forehead against the door. When I returned to the kitchen, Jada was picking up pieces of glass and Stan was soaking up the whisky with a roll of kitchen towel. The smell stung the back of my nose. I didn't make eye contact with either of them.

"You should probably go home too," Jada said icily.

"No. I'm going to help clear up," I said. I found a dustpan and brush, crouched down and searched out the smaller pieces of glass she'd missed.

Stan had stopped helping and vanished, I realized.

Aden loomed above me, calm in his drunken state. "Tell you what. We'll pick up the worst of it, dry it off then get the vacuum cleaner out." He stared at the wall, discoloured with whisky splashes. "Not sure about the wall. Does whisky evaporate?"

Rory's crowd had cleared off into the garden where I could hear them talking in voices they'd have considered quiet but I could hear the odd phrase.

*Waste of whisky. Looked like a good brand too.*

*Bet Amy is being watched by the police.*

*She knew Kristen was messaging someone on Liam's BubbleSpeak and she didn't say anything?*

*No wonder her boyfriend hates her.*

*Is it me or do you think she's really intense?*

I carried on picking up pieces of glass, not caring that one of them had cut my index finger. I deserved it. Each shard of glass that was no longer on the floor was a tiny way of making amends. Jada found the vacuum cleaner and I located a clean cloth, dampened it, then rubbed the wall. People were ignoring me now, fetching

165

themselves more drinks, looking in the cupboards for snacks.

"Hey, it's not your house," Jada told them, pausing the vacuuming. "Go up to the petrol station to buy what you want."

"We might get attacked," Lou from my history class said in a whiny voice.

"Go in a group," said Jada, slowly to show how stupid she thought Lou was. She saw me looking at her. "You're making that stain worse," she snapped. "Here." She took the cloth from me, handing me the vacuum cleaner.

As I fastidiously went over each section of flooring in the kitchen, Jada found something to spray on to the cloth and dabbed the wall carefully.

Eventually, the kitchen was as back to normal as we could make it. The stains on the wall were paler but still noticeable. I returned the vacuum cleaner to the utility room off the kitchen, grabbed my bottle of beer from where I'd left it on the work surface when I went running after Dom, and went to find Stan.

He was in the smaller living room, on Aden's family computer, looking through a news report about Kristen's murder. I could see from the open tabs that he'd been on other news sites and been looking up serial killers.

"Hey," I said, standing alongside him and he jumped. "You threw me under the bus back there," I said bitterly. "Why did you have to tell Dom I'd been in touch with the police again?"

"I thought you'd have told him you'd been into the account," he said, eyes on the screen. "Why didn't you?"

I couldn't think of any answer to that.

I slid open the door that led into the garden. A low brick wall edged the flower beds and I sat on it where it curved round under a tree, where I wouldn't be seen from the house. It was dark and cold, but I understood why Aden and Rory hadn't put their garden lights on. This wasn't a party. I took a gulp of beer and messaged Dom, sending it before I chickened out. *I'm sorry, I know how this must seem to you, but I can explain. Let's talk?*

My phone vibrated and my mouth went dry, expecting an angry reply from Dom, but it was a notification from someone in my economics class group chat, posting an official statement from the police about their progress on the murders.

I scanned through it. The most important part seemed to be: *There was little sign of a struggle, which is consistent with Hollie and Kristen being struck from behind. We are also considering the possibility that they knew their attacker. We again urge the public to come forward with any information they think could help us with the inquiry.*

I shivered and pulled the sleeves of my sweatshirt down over my hands, imagining Hollie and Kristen waiting for Liam, being confused when someone else turned up. Was it someone they were initially pleased to see? Both girls would have left as fast as they could if they hadn't felt comfortable. They wouldn't have tried to be polite. Hollie and Kristen spoke their minds. So was the killer someone they knew?

Rory's friends drifted back inside, and soon I was alone in the garden, listening to the sounds of music, now a more mellow playlist, and the clattering from the kitchen, the shouts, the occasional muffled laughter. It sounded … ordinary. But it didn't mean that people weren't grieving. It was the clamour for life, knowing that it could be cut short in a heartbeat.

The trees rustled above me and a bird hopped about in a bush. It was cold but I couldn't face going inside. I wanted to put off phoning Mum for a lift and admitting that Dom had gone home early.

Someone came out through the main living room door. I recognized the silhouette. Aden. He thought he was alone – I could tell by the slump to his shoulders, the absence of his usual purposeful walk. He wasn't pretending any more.

He was a few metres away from me when I said, "Aden, I don't want to make you jump but I'm here."

He leaped backwards with a yelping sound, then squinted at the flower beds. "Hollie?" he said hoarsely.

I flinched. "No, it's Amy."

"Amy!" He stumbled towards me and sat on the wall nearby, almost falling backwards on to the flower bed. "Too much to drink. Everything is spinny. Spinny and sad."

I put my arm out but he righted himself. "I know," I said. "Nothing will be the same again."

"We were the OGs," he said.

"Yeah, you and Hollie, me and Stan," I said. He nodded. He didn't mention Jada, the newcomer. Had he felt jealous of her too?

Aden began to cry, and the terrible sadness of everything hit me in the throat and I couldn't speak. "I ruined everything," he said quietly. "I did, didn't I?"

He wasn't making any sense. I was the one who had ruined things, not him. "You didn't do anything," I said.

"I wish she was here," he wept, dropping his face into his hands. "I wish I could take it all back." It echoed what he'd written on the card attached to the yellow rose. *I wish I could take it all back.*

"Me too," I said.

"I can't put it right now," he mumbled through his fingers.

I shifted closer. "Put what right? What are you talking about, Aden?"

He removed his hands and sat up and seemed to notice me for the first time all over again. "Amy. I don't feel well. I think I'm going to—" He projectile vomited on to the grass and I leaped back to avoid being splattered. "I'm sorry," he said. "I'm so sorry for everything. Don't come near me." He started to cry again, his head in his large hands, an almost inhuman, heart-breaking noise.

"It's OK," I said softly. I stood up. "I'll be back." I jogged into the kitchen. No one was in there and I saw on the oven clock that it was 11.37 p.m. Aden's mum would be back soon. Most people had gone. I looked in the small living room. It was empty. In the larger one, Rory was on the sofa entangled with Lou, the girl who hadn't wanted to go and buy snacks. Two boys were watching football on TV.

Stan had gone. Without saying goodbye. He'd seen me go into the garden. I hadn't been hard to find.

I went back to the kitchen, swiped the roll of kitchen towel, poured a glass of water and went back outside where Aden was leaning forward as if he might be sick again. I handed him a square of kitchen towel to wipe his mouth, then the water.

He took a sip, groaned and said, "I want to go to bed." He put the glass down, stood up and swayed. He was so much bigger and heavier than me but I grabbed his arm and led him inside.

I'd been in his bedroom many times with the others. It was at the top of the house, up two flights of stairs and that wasn't going to be easy. At first he leaned on me and I struggled to stay upright too. He kept stopping and sitting down to hold his head, and then he crawled up the final few stairs.

I turned his bedside light on and he flopped on top of the duvet, his face falling heavily on one of his pillows.

"I'm scared," he said out of the corner of his mouth. He sounded like a little boy.

"It's OK," I said, sitting down beside him. "I'm here. I'll wait until your mum comes home."

"Promise," he said, and I said, "Promise," and I patted him on the shoulder, like Mum used to do if I woke from a nightmare. He closed his eyes and I looked round his room.

There was a photo of the four of us Blu-tacked above his desk. It was one Karis had taken several summers ago when we were at a BBQ at Stan's house. We were all biting into hot dogs at the same time. The sun was in our eyes and we looked relaxed and happy. Hollie and I were wearing matching crop tops we'd bought in Markham Market earlier that day.

There was another photo, curled at the edges, lying on his bedside table next to the lamp and a cereal bowl with a pool of yellowy milk at the bottom and a spoon in it. I picked the photo up.

It was Aden and Hollie on what must have been their first day in Year Seven. The day Stan and I first met them.

The two of them were standing poker straight outside Hollie's front door, in immaculate uniform. Hollie's smile was broad and infectious. Aden, shorter than Hollie then, was more solemn. His hair looked as if it had been dampened down instead of being allowed to do its own thing. "Cute hair for your first day at Markham High, Aden," I said, but he was asleep.

I heard the front door open and close a few minutes later, and then I heard voices. It was Sally, Aden's mum, turfing the stragglers out.

I waited until it sounded like the door had shut behind

the last of them, then I went downstairs and met Sally in the hall. She was holding her black leather jacket, her ponytail still sleek and high on her head after her night out, and looking round at the discarded bottles and cups.

"Oh. Amy. Didn't know you were still here," she said. "Where's Aden?"

"He's had a lot to drink," I said, not bothering to lie. "I helped him to bed. I think – I think maybe you should keep an eye on him."

Sally's face changed. She didn't look annoyed – she looked sad, worried. "Right. Thanks, Amy. It's been a difficult time for all of you... Hollie's friends, and Kristen's. You shouldn't be having to deal with this; you're just kids. My friends and I couldn't talk about anything else all evening. I expect it's the same all over Markham." She hung up her jacket, faced me again and said, "Rory says Aden holds it together at school, but he's falling to pieces at home."

*Falling to pieces at home.* I hadn't realized that.

I said, "It's horrible," and she nodded sympathetically.

"Thanks for keeping an eye on him, Amy," she said. "Perhaps I shouldn't have gone out tonight, with his dad being away."

"No, no," I said, trying to reassure her. "It was nice of you to let everyone meet up here. I think it really helped."

That was a lie; it hadn't helped with anything.

I realized as soon as the door had shut behind me that I hadn't phoned Mum for a lift and she'd erupt like a scalding drink in a microwave if I walked home on my own. It felt too awkward to knock on the door again, so I walked to the end of their drive and sat on their wall and messaged Mum quickly. If anyone approached me, I would run back to the house.

The street lamps were on but only every other one and with a weak energy-saving orangey light. I was alert to every noise. The cars on the main road, a dog barking, someone up the street chucking a full bin bag into a plastic dustbin, and then my phone. It was Mum replying: *Be right there xx*.

There was nothing from Dom.

I looked at his Instagram and saw he'd posted a photo of Kristen with a heart and RIP for the caption. It was a good photo of her – she was relaxed and smiling directly into the camera.

My phone pinged again – this time with a BubbleSpeak notification. From Liam's official account.

My heart thudded in my ears. I shouldn't open it. I knew that. Completely knew that. But maybe this would be a confession, something I could give to DS Haig. It would eat me up from the inside if I didn't tap on it. If I never knew what it said.

I opened it.

*Haven't you worked out that I'm doing all this for you? But next time remove the cat poo. That was disgusting.*

# CHAPTER 17

When Mum drew up in the car I opened the door before she'd fully stopped, desperate to get inside. To be safe.

"You all right?" she asked, touching me on my arm, concerned. Her hand was warm and grounding. I felt less like I was going to throw up. I breathed her perfume which lingered on her coat. I could see she was wearing her fleecy pyjamas under it. "Where's Dom?"

"He left early. Wasn't feeling good," I said. I clipped in the seat belt, and felt my phone through the fabric of my tote bag where I'd put it. The weight of it sent a flood of anxiety through me. I could see the words again in my head. *I'm doing all this for you.* The reference to the cat poo.

"Was it nice to be with your friends?" asked Mum,

starting the car, and she looked so desperate for the answer to be yes that I nodded.

"I'm shattered now, though," I said.

"Yes, it's not great to be out this late on a school night," said Mum. "Speaking of which, I've been in touch with Karis, and I think you and Harry should go in tomorrow. He'll walk you to Stan's and the three of you can walk in together. We're worried about you missing too much school, and you'll be safe there. Lots of adults."

I closed my eyes, and Mum said teasingly, "It's not that bad walking to school with Harry, is it?"

"No, no. It's fine."

I shivered and Mum turned up the car heater. Who knew that I'd left the cat poo in Mr Peaty's house? Dad, Mr Peaty by now, if his plane had landed on time and he was home. I'd told Stan and Dom about it too. Nobody else knew.

Out of all of them, Stan was the only one who had the password to Liam's account, as far as I was aware.

Stan.

I thought back to the night of Hollie's murder. I'd left Stan on his own when I went to sort out Mr Peaty's parcel. Pennington Park was only minutes from his house. He'd also told me that he'd been on his own in his house when Kristen died. He didn't have an alibi for either murder…

*No.* I shook myself. What was I thinking? Stan was my best mate and he wouldn't hurt a fly. He had no reason at all to kill Hollie and Kristen.

Later, in bed, I scrolled through all the news stories about the murders. It had emerged that a crucial CCTV network in Markham hadn't been working, which meant that the murders hadn't been picked up on camera. Some people were saying that this missing CCTV was widely known. Meanwhile Markham Town Council said temporary CCTV cameras were being put up as a matter of urgency.

In the end I closed my eyes and I fell into a dream where I was running for an exit in Aden's garden, but I couldn't reach it because I was being circled by Dad, Mr Peaty, Aden, Dom and Stan and none of them would look me in the eye.

"Going via Stan's house adds on at least ten minutes, maybe fifteen," said Harry the following morning, annoyed that he was having to leave the house earlier than he usually did. "I haven't had time to gel my hair."

"It depends how slowly you walk," I said.

"Remember why you're doing this, please, Harry," said Mum, as she stood by the dishwasher, eating her muesli. "Anyway, it's good for you to get the exercise."

"Rude," said Harry.

Mum rolled her eyes. "That's not rude. Dad and I are paying for the gym you wanted to join and you hardly go."

I put my trainers on while they bickered. I stared out of the window. It looked bleak outside, damp and cold.

Harry grumbled all the way down the road about Mum being out of order, and did I think he'd put on weight, and was it insensitive to keep posting on his blog when Hollie and Kristen were dead? I answered in monosyllables and let him waffle on as I pulled my navy-and-white scarf up to fully cover my ears.

There'd been no message from Dom overnight. I'd woken up at five that morning and it was the first thing I'd checked. I felt awful every time I remembered how he'd looked at me before he threw the whisky at the wall. As if I was someone he didn't recognize.

I knocked on Stan's front door the way I always did: three decisive taps. He opened it within seconds and I caught a glimpse of Karis in her work suit. She was scuttling into the kitchen as if she didn't want to be seen from the front door. I felt hurt.

"You didn't say goodbye last night, Stan," I said, once we were walking.

"Couldn't find you," he said.

"You saw me go into the garden. That might have been a good place to start looking."

"Are you two always this tetchy with each other in the mornings?" Harry asked. "Geez, Stan, don't let her push you around." He stuck in his AirPods and walked in front of us.

"You OK?" asked Stan, finally, after we hadn't spoken for the length of an entire road.

"As OK as I can be," I said. "Given that one of my best friend's been killed and the killer might be sending me messages. Oh, and I've been dumped. So, yeah, not great."

Something darted into the bushes near us and I gave a small scream. "Was that a rat?"

Stan said with a quick smile, "Think it was a squirrel. Dumped?"

"I think it was a rat." I glared at him. "It's not funny, Stan. You know I hate them. And, yes, dumped."

"I'm sorry," he said. "I really am, but I don't get why you're so cross with me all the time at the moment."

I held up my hands. "Forget it, Stan. Let's just get to school."

We walked the rest of the way in silence. I felt stiff and unnatural, and my thoughts were frantic. I was desperate to tell someone about the latest message, but what was the point? The police were supposedly doing all they could. When school came into sight, we saw several vans. Then we saw the TV cameras. School staff were in hi-vis jackets, directing students. A path had been made using crash barriers either side, to funnel us towards the school gates and I could see staff ushering students inside.

"Keep your heads down," said Harry, taking out an AirPod and swivelling round to speak to us. "Unless you want to be on TV."

As we walked down the narrow path, we passed a reporter doing a live broadcast. She talked about "the brave few coming into lessons" and it was true – there weren't that many of us. At this time of the morning there would normally be a swarm of students descending on the gates.

Us sixth formers were sent straight into a special

assembly which was being given by the head, Ms Arnold. Dressed in a dark trouser suit and white shirt, her bob set firmly in place with lots of hairspray, her make-up immaculate, she stood tall at the front of the room. I looked around. Aden was absent but Jada was there, sitting with her arms folded, looking straight ahead.

I thought about what a mess Aden had been the previous night, crying that he had *ruined everything*. What had he meant? Nothing – he had just been drunk, I told myself.

"We'll make a start now, if that's everyone," said Ms Arnold when nobody else had slunk into the hall for a few minutes. "I want to say I appreciate you coming in after such terrible news. Our thoughts are of course with Hollie and Kristen's families. They were shining lights in our school community and we will grieve their absence." She paused for a moment, then said, "However, it is *imperative* that your education continues in spite of these senseless acts of violence. This is a crucial time for your studies. As I've said before, counsellors will be at the school for as long as they are needed. We have brought them in from other schools in the trust. I urge you to make the most of them." She took a breath and looked us all squarely in the eye. "Now, you may have noticed the media outside."

*Er, funnily enough, yes*, I thought.

"I do not want any of you to speak to them," continued Ms Arnold. "There is no value in adding to the speculation and gossip around these poor girls' deaths. Let the police do their job – that's the best thing you can do for Hollie and Kristen."

We all nodded.

"Now, the police have asked me to pass on this important message: please do not" – she paused and looked at us to check we were listening – "I repeat, do *not* have anything to do with any social media accounts purporting to come from Liam Henderson. Be extremely careful about social media in general. Do not arrange to meet *anyone* based on a message on, er" – she glanced at her notes – "BubbleSpeak or any other social media platforms. I can't stress enough that you need to be absolutely sure who you are communicating with online." She shook her head and her bob swung stiffly. "I mean, goodness, Year Twelve and Thirteen, we have had enough talks and workshops about online safety."

We shifted in our seats. Message received. Stay in school, keep quiet around the press and don't engage with any online accounts.

There was more. "The governors have also discussed a memorial or commemoration for Hollie and Kristen. If you have suggestions about how we as a school community can commemorate the lives of Hollie and Kristen, please speak to your form tutors and they will pass feedback to me." Ms Arnold squared her shoulders. "Finally, I would like to say that the long shadow cast over the school by these tragedies will not define us for long. Good will triumph over evil. I know that all of you will demonstrate our school values of responsibility, resilience and empathy, continuing to work hard and keep our school community safe and caring. Thank you for listening."

We all looked around, uncertain whether to clap or not. Ms Reid shook her head slightly – it was a no to the applause.

At lunch Stan and I sat on our usual sofa in the café, purportedly revising for a short psychology test that was coming up next lesson. Instead, Stan was looking at news sites on his phone, totally engrossed. After a while I picked mine up too. I was scared in case there was another Bubble from Liam's account but desperate for a message from Dom.

There was nothing, other than a stream of information and gossip about the murders. Kristen's time of death had been established as around nine-thirty p.m. and some people were posting what they'd been doing at that time.

Aden's brother Rory had jumped in with his story again, writing on his Instagram that he had been walking through Markham then. *It was a Monday night so you'd think it would have been quiet*, read his post. *But the community centre was showing a movie that let out just before the murder. Someone must have seen something...*

Someone else had posted a link to the latest police briefing. I put my AirPods in and listened to DCI Mark Gorling say, "We are satisfied that there are sufficient similarities between Hollie and Kristen's murders to say with confidence that we are looking for the same perpetrator. Hollie Linton's murder weapon is thought to have been a small tree branch, found near the body, and for Kristen Sorrenson's murder, a small hammer-like object is believed to have been used. This small hammer has yet to be recovered."

A new hashtag was circulating: *#FindtheHammer*

Ms Reid came into the café and said in a loud voice, "Hi, everybody. Listen, I can't help but notice that very few of you are making use of the counsellors we have on site. So, I thought I'd come to you instead. I was wondering whether any of you would like to chat? We could share some memories of Hollie and Kristen. Come and join me."

She dropped on to the sofa next to me and Stan. Everyone looked at each other, but gradually several people came over, including Jada. Stan and I budged up. Harry and Cooper, who had come in to buy chips, squeezed next to Jada and Sabine, with Kristen's friends pulling up chairs and other people standing around.

Jada started. Of course she did. She was the self-appointed Chief Mourner of Hollie. "Hollie was a very special person. I knew that as soon as I started here. Warm and funny. So flipping pretty too."

"Yes," echoed Cooper. "She was beautiful inside and out – especially out."

I looked at Harry and rolled my eyes. Cooper was an embarrassment. Harry ignored me.

Kristen's friends talked about Kristen's talent for singing and acting. How warm and supportive she was.

I didn't recognize these versions of Hollie and Kristen. They hadn't been saints – they'd been real people who had died.

"What about you two, Stan and Amy?" prompted Ms Reid. "You were such good friends with Hollie."

"She made us laugh," I said. "She was always up for anything." Those things were true but they sounded like clichés. Tears brimmed in my eyes. "It's really hard – knowing that we sent her to the park that night…"

"Nobody is blaming you," said Ms Reid firmly. "Absolutely nobody."

People looked away awkwardly.

"I miss her a lot," said Stan. He looked at his trainers. He sounded wooden, as if he was reading from a script.

The bell went and people began to move. "Keep an eye on each other," Ms Reid murmured to us as everyone dispersed. "You all need your friends right now."


After school, I asked Stan if I could go back to his and he said, "Sure. Whatever." I shook Harry off at the gate, telling him that I was sure Mum wouldn't mind picking me up from Stan's on her way home from work.

Stan and I walked the long way round to his house because of the road being cordoned off for the press. Outside the petrol station, newspapers were lined up in the clear plastic display boxes. Hollie and Kristen's faces looked back at us from front pages. *Markham Murders – Killer Still Out There.* Another had *CCTV Failure in Markham* as a headline.

"I'm not sure I agree with Ms Arnold about how it's better to be in school," I said. "But then … home can feel claustrophobic."

"I'm definitely better at school," said Stan.

As we approached it, his house looked dreary, with no lights on, no cars in the drive and the dead plant by the front door, and I could see why maybe school felt better for him at the moment. At least I had Harry around when my parents had to work long hours.

Stan flicked on some lights and I made myself a mug of tea in the kitchen as he poured himself an orange juice. I thought of Karis this morning, ducking out of sight.

"How's your mum doing?" I asked.

"Not great. Clinging on to work by her fingertips," he said.

"Does your dad hate me too?" I asked.

Stan's shoulders slumped as he sat at the breakfast bar. "My parents don't hate you, Amy."

"They used to think I was wonderful," I said sadly.

"I'm sure yours used to think I was wonderful too."

"They still do!" I insisted. "Doesn't that make your heart sing?"

He raised a smile.

"Strange question coming up, Stan," I said, seizing the moment. "Did you tell anyone that I'd left cat poo in Mr Peaty's flat?"

"Er, no," said Stan. He looked confused. "Why would I have done that?"

"The catfish knew about it. They mentioned it in a message, to scare me."

"You're still getting messages?" asked Stan. "Why are you opening them?"

"I knew you'd say that," I said. "I have to. Someone's watching me, Stan. Like they were at the Canbury Club."

Stan pushed back his hair and I saw worry in his eyes. "That's weird."

"Super weird," I said.

He placed the carton of orange juice back in the fridge, then said, "Let's have another go at *Alien Heist*."

"No. Let's talk about this. I'm scared, Stan. You're supposed to be my friend. You're supposed to talk things through with me and be on my side." I looked down at the mug I'd made my tea in; it had a crack near the handle. It was my favourite mug in the Maloney household – not just because it had cartoon cats on it, but because it was the perfect shape for a cup of tea. Now, it felt scarily fragile, as though it might break in my hands.

"I *am* on your side," said Stan, with a flash of an emotion I couldn't name. Frustration? Irritation? "I'm always on your side, Amy."

"Why does it feel like you're shutting me out, then?" I demanded. "We're going through something bad together here. That should bring us closer, not push us apart."

Stan's whole body tensed. "Amy, has it ever occurred to you that people deal with things in different ways? I can't always act how you want me to, OK?"

"Right, I get it," I said angrily. "You just want to hide away and pretend all this – this horror – isn't happening. Mature."

"I'm not hiding," said Stan. He shoved his glass in the dishwasher and slammed the door shut. "I'm trying to get through each day as best I can without losing the plot. It's hard."

"And it's not hard for me? I've had *threatening messages*. I could do with some empathy. I thought I might get it from you, but clearly I was wrong." I stormed into the hall and tugged on my trainers.

Stan followed me, looking distressed. "I just want everything to go back to normal."

"Newsflash," I said, slinging my bag over my shoulder. "Nothing will be normal again, including us."

"Listen, Amy," said Stan and I stopped. I waited a moment for him to open up some more, but he just stood there looking at me with that tortured expression.

"You shouldn't walk home on your own," he said at last.

"Like you care," I said. And I opened the front door and left.

# CHAPTER 18

I was on our road when the car screeched to a halt beside me. Mum got out, her cheeks flushed with fury.

"I told you not to go anywhere alone. Get in the car *now*."

I did.

We drove in silence. When we got home, she hauled Harry down from his room and shouted at both of us in the hall, and when she marched into the kitchen and slammed the door, Harry said, "Nice one, Amy. If you'd been hit over the head, imagine how the rest of my life would have been. You're so selfish."

"*I'm* selfish?" I retorted. "All you're doing is thinking of yourself. I've just had a big row with Stan."

He stopped at that. "You and Stan never argue. What's he said?" He sat down on the last step of the stairs. He sounded sympathetic, but I had a feeling he was only settling in for the gossip which he would probably share with Cooper.

"I don't understand him any more, that's all." I eased past Harry and went upstairs to my room. There were no messages on my phone. Nothing from Stan, nothing from Dom. I put my phone face down on my bedside table.

The wall next to my bed was covered, top to bottom with photos.

There was one of Mum and Dad giggling in front of a boat on a disastrous family holiday, taken just after Dad had accidentally steered it into a riverbank, one of Harry proudly holding a cookery competition trophy age eleven – but most were of my friends. There was one of Jada near the bottom, pouting into the camera with orange eyeshadow next to the guess-how-many-shreds-in-the-marmalade stall at our orange-themed day. The rest were of the four of us: Stan, Hollie, Aden and me. We looked like the best friendship group ever. In the majority of the photos, one or other was cracking up at something someone had said or done. Sunbathing by the river, Hollie dripping cold suntan lotion on to Aden's back, all four of us in a tent at Reading Festival looking rough as, Aden being attacked by a sheep in Wales, Stan wearing a werewolf costume for Halloween that made him look like a drowned squirrel. Aden photo-bombing me and Stan while we gamed at his house, the four of us linking arms and posing in sunglasses at the Year Eleven prom.

I sank into my bed and buried my head in the softest pillow so I didn't have to see the photos. Tomorrow, when I had more energy, I'd take them down.

The next day was the one-week anniversary of Hollie's murder, the day that everything had fallen apart. I wanted to stay in bed. Mum had other ideas. Their shifts meant Dad was going to drive me and Harry to school and she was going to pick us up.

"This is non-negotiable," she said. "We'll give Stan a lift too. I've already messaged Karis to say we'll pick him up en route."

Luckily Dad and Harry were in the middle of a fierce discussion about cancel culture when Stan got in the car, because the awkwardness was off the scale. He was looking on his phone at anything related to the murders. I counted backwards from one hundred in threes. I stopped at eighty-two because it was giving me a headache.

Dad had to drop us in a neighbouring road to school because of the cordon and the amount of parents driving their kids to school. There were more press people today, leaning over the crash barriers and the do-not-cross tape with their long lenses and their microphones. A police officer marshalled us into the school grounds instead of staff. Some students asked her questions, mostly along the lines of why it was taking so long to arrest someone.

"Lots going on behind the scenes," she said. "You're safe in school. Please move along."

In form, Stan and I sat together at the back as usual but without communicating, Stan still flipping through news sites on his phone, me playing *Plants vs Zombies*. Everyone in the class was wearing muted clothing apart from Jada, who was wearing bright pink loose trousers with a tight red T-shirt, and a red bandana round her hair. Aden said hello, then wandered to the front of the room to speak to her.

"What reading are you doing?" I heard him ask her.

"A poem about being remembered," Jada said.

I understood then. They'd been asked to do readings at Hollie's funeral next Thursday. It pierced me with a sharp physical pain.

"All right, everyone?" said Ms Reid, sweeping in. "Good to see you." She propped her many bags against her desk. "Now, has anyone had any thoughts about Ms Arnold's suggestion? A commemoration for Hollie and Kristen?"

"An art project," Aden called out. "Hollie loved art."

"Remember when she campaigned for plastic bottles to be banned from the canteen?" said Hussein. "Maybe some kind of recycling thing?"

"Was that when she tried to organize a picket line?" said Jake. "That was chaos. So fun."

"I'm working on something," said Jada loudly.

"That sounds mysterious," said Ms Reid. "Care to share?"

"Not yet," said Jada.

At break, I went to the art room, mainly to avoid the café and the sofas. There were a few students there discussing the memorial art project with Mr Pitter, the art teacher. They were all from younger years and I doubted any of them had known Hollie or Kristen. I sat at the back, behind them.

"My dad says we shouldn't start any memorials yet in case there are more murders," said a boy who looked as if he was in Year Eight. "We'd have to start all over again."

His mate laughed. "Your dad's got a point."

Mr Pitter said, "I very much hope there won't be any more murders." He looked at the clock. "Go away and do some research and we'll put forward ideas to Ms Arnold for approval when we've worked on them tomorrow."

At lunch, I went to the library to research memorial projects on a computer. I stared at handprints with messages on them, tree leaf plaques, poems, scrapbooks, photos of sponsored events, and tattoos. I looked at tealights spelling out a person's name in the dark and read about how dangerous sky lanterns and helium balloons were for the environment.

I felt the loneliest I'd ever felt.

At the end of the day when Mum stopped the car outside Stan's house to drop him off, she said, "Amy, if you want to stay at Stan's for a bit, I'll come and collect you."

"I've got loads of work to do," I said.

Stan nodded. "Yeah, same."

When he'd got out of the car, Harry said, "You two still not made up?"

"Shut up," I muttered.

"Oh no!" said Mum. She turned to look at me. "Have you and Stan fallen out? You need each other now, more than ever. What's it about?"

"Nothing," I said. "Just the strain of everything, I think."

"Do you want me to speak to Karis?"

"No! God, no. Don't get involved," I said.

"Lol, Mum," said Harry. "We're not kids any more."

Mum sighed. "Everything feels odd at the moment," she said, almost to herself. "I wonder if I should ask to reduce my hours. Be at home more to keep an eye on you two."

Having less money coming in sounded as if it would be more stressful for everyone and Mum mostly loved her work and her colleagues. "You don't need to," I said.

Harry said, "Whatever works for you, Mum, but could we go home via Tesco because we've run out of cocktail sticks? I'm going to make mini cakes that look exactly like strawberries. Let me find you a photo." He got TikTok up and showed us a series of incredible cakes that didn't look like cakes at all. "A blog post on super-realistic cakes will get loads of shares and likes. People are really into them right now."

"So you decided that pushing your blog at the moment wasn't insensitive?" I snapped at Harry.

"It's better to be busy and get on with things than get massively depressed and be falling out with my friends," retorted Harry.

"Shhhush," soothed Mum.

The way back from Tesco took us past Mr Peaty's block of flats. I'd been paid for looking after Hector via bank transfer and Mr Peaty hadn't said anything about the bag of cat poo waiting for him when he got back from his trip, so I assumed we were good. There was someone going into the flats as we drove past, a girl with pink trousers, struggling with the main lock.

"Is that Jada?" I said.

Harry pressed his face to the glass. "Yep," he said. "I didn't know she lived there."

"She doesn't," I said. I'd only been to Jada's house once but it was definitely the other side of Markham.

"Ha!" said Harry. "Mr Peaty's sacked you and replaced you with Jada."

"Ha ha, very funny," I said. "How would he know Jada? She and her mum only moved here in the summer."

"If you've really lost your job with Hector, it's not a disaster, Ames," said Mum. "You'll find something else."

She didn't know that it wasn't the job I was bothered about. Whoever had texted me from Liam's account had known about the cat poo. If Jada knew someone in the block, could she have found out?

Dad got home shortly after us. He burst into the living room where I was watching *Gogglebox* and said, "I heard on the news that the police have got a visual of someone they want to question in connection with the murders."

I reached for my phone and saw the police were hailing this as a breakthrough. The image was pixelated and grainy, from private CCTV footage, but I could see it was a man, between thirty and forty, wearing a close-fitting jacket and jeans. "Thank god for that," I said.

Dad sat down beside me and put his arm round my shoulders, drawing me to him. "They'll catch this person now, Amy. You wait and see." He went off to the kitchen, where Harry was labouring over various versions of super-realistic strawberry cakes.

The news made me feel brave. I picked up my phone and messaged Jada. *I know you don't want to hear from me, but serious question: what were you doing going into Hillrise View House?*

I figured I had nothing to lose. She could ignore me, she could send back a hateful message or she could tell me the truth. At the very least she would know I was on to her if she was the one sending the messages.

I forced myself to watch the latest press conference that evening. It was too much to be in the same room as Mum, Dad and Harry, though. I sat in bed and watched on my laptop.

Kristen's mum couldn't get any words out at all because she was crying so much. It was another appeal for witnesses. DCI Mark Gorling, his forehead glistening, said, "Despite the breakthrough with the CCTV image, we want to hear from anybody who was on the riverside on Monday evening between eight and ten p.m. It was relatively mild that night – but did you see anyone wearing gloves? Acting suspiciously? Have you found discarded clothing, perhaps with blood on it? This could be someone close to you, someone you know. Please call our helpline." He looked down at his piece of paper to read off the helpline number.

As I lowered the lid of my laptop, I thought of Stan doing more around the house, including the washing... I squeezed my eyes shut. I was being paranoid. I knew Stan better than anyone, didn't I? Surely I'd know if he was behind this.

Besides, the police were after that thirty-something-year-old man.

I got out of bed and took down all the photos from my bedroom wall. I put them into two piles, one for photos Hollie was in and the other, much smaller one, for photos where she wasn't. My wall looked diseased afterwards, with the remaining tiny lumps of Blu-tack still attached and grease marks.

I picked up a photo from the Hollie pile. She was smiling her usual huge smile. We were on a train, going to Reading Festival. Hollie already had glitter on her face, Aden's bucket hat covered his eyes. Stan's face appeared at the side of the photo, a sideways photobomb. He'd had food poisoning twelve hours later but had refused to go home and bounced back. At the end of the festival the four of us had taken the coach home. Hollie and I had sat in front of the boys. I remembered looking back at the two of them, snoring because we'd had to get up so early to take down our tents, still hungover.

"What are those two like?" I'd said to Hollie at the time.

"So grim and yet they seem to belong to us," said Hollie.

I'd looked at Stan's face, his head leaning on Aden's shoulder, snoring with his mouth open

I'd thought we'd all be best friends for ever.

Someone took that away from us and I wanted to know who.

# CHAPTER 19

I woke the next day and sent a message to Dom saying: *Can we talk?*

No reply.

In form, Aden sat next to me and Stan, but Jada sat away from us. She hadn't replied to my message about Hillrise View House and was acting as if Stan and I didn't exist.

While Ms Reid stepped out of the classroom to use the photocopier, people started talking about the press briefing the previous evening.

"I wonder if the police have brought in a profiler," said Hussein. "It's a really interesting job. They can figure out what sort of person the killer is from the characteristics of the crime itself." He sounded as if he was giving a careers talk.

"The guy must be confident," said Jake. "Walking around with a hammer and gloves, killing people in public places. Anyone could have walked past."

"You're assuming it's a man," said Jada. Her voice carried across the classroom. "Assumptions are dangerous." I heard a faint sniffling beside me and turned to see that Aden was crying. He was looking down, hoping no one would notice. I searched in my bag for a tissue and handed it to him. He took it and blew his nose, but his tears kept falling.

"I'm taking you to student services," I said softly. "You shouldn't be in school." He didn't reply but when I said, "Stand up, Aid", he did. We walked out of our form room, meeting Ms Reid in the corridor on her way back to the classroom.

"What's happened?" she asked, looking swiftly at Aden. "Is everyone talking about the murders?"

I nodded. "They're going on about the press conference last night. I think he needs to go home."

"OK," she said. She tried to make eye contact with Aden who was still staring at the floor. "Take care, Aden. These feelings, they're normal. Everybody understands how hard it is." Her words seemed to make it worse. He began to sob.

I guided him downstairs to student services where Ms Hadley was in her office on the phone. She gave us a sympathetic smile and indicated through her sliding window that we should wait on the seats outside while she finished up. There were more tissues on the low table, and I grabbed a wodge for Aden.

"I should have saved Hollie," he said through sobs. "I can't stop thinking back."

"I keep thinking about the 'what ifs' too. Like, what if Stan and I hadn't catfished her? But you've done nothing wrong," I said quietly.

"I've done everything wrong," he said, gulping air between sobs.

I rubbed his back. "Like what?" I asked. "Tell me."

Ms Hadley came out of her office. "Now, then, you two. What's going on here? Hmm?" Without waiting for me to speak, she said, "You go back to lessons, Amy. Don't worry, I'll look after Aden."

I spent break and lunchtime in the art room, where I pulled the photos of Hollie from my bag and colour-photocopied them. As a sixth former I had generous photocopying privileges. Mr Pitter made a "huh" noise when I began to cut out Hollie from each picture but left me alone in the corner of the room. I placed them on a plain sheet of A3 card, moving them around to see where they fit best. People came and went and had discussions about memorials made out of glass and clay, and I kept on cutting and sticking, as if I were back in infant school. It was soothing, and looking at each photo of Hollie, I felt my sadness swell then settle. This was her life, or pieces of it.

I heard decisive footsteps come towards me, looked up

and saw Ms Arnold. "What a great project," she said. She stood next to me, looking at the photos I'd stuck down. Her grey wool jacket looked itchy compared to her white silk blouse, her perfume woody and strong.

"What a sweet, sweet girl Hollie was," said Ms Arnold, one hand against her cheek. "Such an angel."

I reeled back slightly. Sweet wasn't the right word for Hollie. Not at all. And she was no angel. I glanced at the photo of Hollie pulling a disgusted face on Aden's sofa, fresh from learning in Year Eleven that she'd got the most boring teacher in the school for history, Mr Worthing. As I looked up again, I caught sight of Jada, standing near the next table, listening in. Our eyes met and she mouthed, *Seriously?*

"*Sweet* isn't the word I'd use to describe Hollie," I said. "But that's why she was awesome. She was always one hundred per cent herself."

I saw Jada nod.

"Well. It's a lovely collage," murmured Ms Arnold and she moved on to examine someone's sketch of a memorial sculpture.

Jada came over and sat on the stool next to me. "I love those photos," she said.

"What are you doing in the art room?" I asked, eyeing her cautiously. This was the first time Jada had spoken normally to me since she'd found out what I'd done.

"Came to see if anyone was working on a decent way of remembering Hollie," she said.

"I'm honoured you're talking to me again," I said, with more than a tinge of sarcasm. "Why didn't you reply to my message last night?"

"Thought I'd talk to you about it instead," said Jada. "It was weird. Why did you want to know about Hillrise?"

"Because my cat-sitting job is in those flats and I" – I searched around for an excuse – "wanted to know if you'd taken over my job."

Jada laughed. "Paranoid, much? What's the name of the person you cat-sit for?"

"Mr Peaty."

"Never heard of him. Nah, my mum cleans for an old couple in those flats and she forgot the keys so I had to take them round." She watched me take this in. "I reckon your job is safe."

"Did anyone tell you I'd left a bag with cat poo in it inside his flat?"

"No! Ew, why did you do that?"

"It was a mistake," I said and went back to my sticking.

"Understandable," said Jada. "Everyone's all over the place with Hollie and Kristen. If my A-level grades are terrible I'm going to blame the murders. Maybe school will put in a special plea for us?" She gave a faint smile. "Hollie would be all over that like a rash, wouldn't she?"

"She probably would," I said.

Hollie loved finding loopholes, ways to work the system, and going off-piste in her pursuit of what she wanted. Her aunt, who'd made her own wedding dress, had done some of Hollie's GCSE textiles coursework, for example, and when I gave her a hard time over it she brushed it off and said that she'd come up with the idea and sourced all the materials and it was, "more about the vision than the actual workmanship".

Hollie was all about the vision. To be fair, her vision was always bold, colourful and amazing. She followed through as well. When she wanted to learn belly dancing in Year Eight, she set up a mixed club and the PE department found an instructor and the club was still going.

"Have you had any more messages from Liam's official BubbleSpeak account?" I asked.

"No. Have you?" Jada's eyes searched mine as I lied, shaking my head. "It gave me actual shivers," she carried on. "Thinking someone was targeting me. It had to have come from someone close to me. I haven't been in Markham that long."

"It could have been random?" I suggested. "Someone coming across your account?"

"Nah. Whoever it was seemed to know me. That Eng lit comment – it was too precise. Still, sounds like they might have caught the real killer."

I nodded. "Thank god."

Jada touched one of the images of Hollie. "She had such a beautiful smile," she said.

"I'm making it for Hollie's family," I said. "They won't have seen all these photos of her." I waited for a bitchy comment about how her family wouldn't want a collage from me. I thought Jada must know Stan and I had been asked not to attend the funeral.

"Nice. I think they might totally love it." Then she hopped off the seat. "See you," she said, and headed out.

I watched her go. We weren't friends again – maybe we never would be. But it was a start.

After school, Mum picked me and Harry up and when she said, "Takeaway tonight?" my heart sank a little. I loved Takeaway Fridays, but it just reminded me it was the weekend. I had a whole two days to get through without Stan or Dom for company. Aden and Jada weren't lining up to hang out with me either.

"Feel free to invite any friends round this weekend," said Mum brightly to me and Harry. "Probably safer at home."

"Sounds claustrophobic," said Harry. "I might get Coop over, though."

"God, not Cooper," I said. "The last time he came round, he was a real delight, showing me the stuff he watches on TikTok."

Harry groaned. "Yeah, that was awks. But he's fine. He's just got into some slightly weird stuff lately. You know Coop, always jumping on a trend – thinking he's found some new guru to guide him in life."

"People who advocate 'keeping your girlfriend in line'? Who talk about what 'women owe men'?"

Mum frowned. "I don't like the sound of that," she said.

"Coop likes to shock people," said Harry. "I know he

goes too far sometimes but he's harmless. He doesn't mean any of it."

"I don't want anyone promoting hateful stuff in our house," said Mum. "Why would you be friends with someone like that, Harry?"

Harry contemplated this for a second. "He can be funny and I ignore the rest. I feel sorry for him. You know his mum's got a horrible partner."

"You can't ignore what comes out of his mouth," I said. "You need to grow a backbone, Haz. Stop letting him latch on to you."

Harry rolled his eyes. "Don't lecture me about friendship, Ames."

Mum shushed him gently. "Teenage friendships aren't straightforward," she said. "I may be old but I remember that much."

As I went into the house my phone vibrated with a message from Dom.

*Want to meet tomorrow for brunch to talk?*

I left it a dignified few minutes before replying: *I'd really like that. Where and when?*

We agreed on Clemmy's, a café in Markham High Street, and I decided the strange churning in my stomach might just be hope.

# CHAPTER 20

Dad left the car engine running outside the café on a double yellow while he leaped out to check through the window that Dom was there.

"Thanks for the lift but this is over the top," I said.

"Have a nice time, Ames," he said, legging it back to the car as a traffic warden showed up on a scooter. "Let me know when you want picking up."

I checked myself in the mirror in the entrance of the café, suddenly nervous. I'd spent a long time perfecting my natural make-up, covering up the spots which had appeared as a stress reaction. Under my denim jacket, I wore my pink crochet-look cami top, the one I was wearing at the party where we had first met and Dom had come over to talk to me. My hair was artfully tousled. I looked … fine.

But inside my stomach was churning. The horrible truth was that Kristen might not be dead if I'd spoken up about how she was messaging Liam's BubbleSpeak account. Would Dom ever be able to forgive me for that?

I took a deep breath, then walked over.

"Hi," Dom said. "Full English, no black pudding, bacon well done? With freshly squeezed orange juice."

I smiled. We'd only been out for brunch once before and that had been exactly what I'd asked for. The waitress came over and we ordered quickly. I picked up my paper napkin and folded it into a hat, as shown to me by Granddad about ten years ago. It gave me something to focus on. It reminded me of Hollie – I'd shown her how to make paper-napkin hats once when her parents took us out for pizza, and we'd worn them all evening, in a competition to see who could keep theirs on the longest.

Everything always seemed to come back to Hollie.

"I'm sorry I got so angry about the message," said Dom, rearranging his fork so it sat precisely on the navy line of the navy-and-white striped table mat. "You weren't to know something so terrible would happen. And you called the police. You did the right thing."

My shoulders lowered a little, the tension ebbing slightly. "That's OK. But I wish I'd called them sooner." I let go of the paper napkin hat as the waitress placed two orange juices on the table.

"How are you doing?" I asked gently as she walked away.

"Not gunna lie," said Dom, "I can't stop thinking about Kristen. The way she died… It's messing with me. I was one of the last people to see her alive. I keep thinking I could have done something to prevent it. I feel guilty. I suppose that's why I was so angry with you. I was really angry with myself."

*Guilty.* We were all feeling guilty, in our ways – me, Stan, Aden, Dom.

He took my hand and traced round my nails gently. "I'm sorry I took out all my guilt on you. Threw that whisky." He cringed. "Did it take ages to clear up?"

"It wasn't too bad," I said, squeezing his hand. "OK, it was fairly bad but other people helped." We pulled away as the waitress approached again with our breakfasts. "Sauces?" she said.

"Ketchup, please," Dom said.

"What do you have to feel guilty about?" I asked, picking up my knife and fork.

"Kristen told me something at the funeral. She said she thought somebody was stalking her."

A prickle went up my spine. "Stalking her?"

Dom rubbed his forehead. "Aghh. I should have taken more notice at the time, but I thought she was being over-dramatic. Or…" He screwed his face up with embarrassment. "Trying to make me jealous."

I nodded, encouraging him to keep going.

"I remember a few things. She said she'd been sent flowers a few days before her grandma's funeral and there was no note attached. Think she found a box of chocolates in her dance bag another time. A couple of random accounts had left messages on her socials, telling her how pretty she was, until she blocked them."

"But if she thought she had a stalker, why did she agree to meet someone from a BubbleSpeak account she had every reason to suspect was dodgy? She knew Stan and I had pranked from that account."

"I keep asking myself that," said Dom. "She was sharp, but she did have a thing for Liam. He's basically a celebrity in Markham, isn't he? The person messaging her must have convinced her that he really was Liam. God knows how." He shook his head. "I wish she'd told me. I'd have told her not to go. I wish I'd listened more."

"It's not your fault," I said, and he nodded. I'm not sure he believed me.

We ate for the next few minutes in silence and then we talked about Dom's biology coursework on insects and it started to put me off my food. I moved the chat on to travelling and told Dom about Harry's plans to go on a trip to France with Cooper in the Christmas holidays to get some good photos for his blog. That led me on to a long diatribe about Cooper which I realized I was making too humorous because Dom was laughing and saying, "He sounds like a right charmer," but it lifted my heart to see his face lit up.

"I'd better call my dad," I said, when we'd asked for the bill. "I'm not allowed to go anywhere on my own because of everything going on."

"I'll wait until he gets here," said Dom. We split the bill, then stood awkwardly outside the café in the small patch of November sunshine.

Dom pulled out his phone. "I meant to ask you. Have you been followed by a new account called the Catfish Catcher?"

I looked. "Oh. Yes, I have." The profile photo for the account was of a big brown fish with what looked like giant whiskers, which I presumed was a real catfish. The account was following most people in both Markham High and Ivy Green sixth forms.

The bio said: *On the hunt #MarkhamMurders*

"Who started this?" asked Dom.

"No idea," I said. The first photo was a statement saying the account had been set up to keep track of what was going on in the investigation, a place to collate information. The second photo was of the flowers at Pennington Park, the third the police tape by the river. "My money's on Stan or Jada. Stan's kind of obsessed with the news at the moment, always on his phone, and Jada loves being at the centre of everything."

I sent a DM to the Catfish Catcher. *Stan?*

Dad messaged: *With you in two minutes.*

"Dom," I said, dredging up the courage to say what I needed to before Dad turned up. "Can we talk about *us*?"

He must have been expecting it but he still didn't look ready. "Um, yes. Sure."

"Could we … keep seeing each other? Because … I'd really like that. I really like you."

Dom paused. "I really like you too, Amy," he said. "But my head's all over the place right now."

I was more interested in where his heart was at. "Sure," I said. "Of course." It didn't sound wildly promising.

Dad pulled up in the car.

"Take care, then," said Dom. We hugged but didn't kiss.

It was because Dad was right there in the car, waiting for me. That's what I told myself, as I said, "You take care too."

# CHAPTER 21

In between downloading and decorating a house on Sims, I kept an eye on the Catfish Catcher account that afternoon and tried not to think about the heavy feeling in my stomach whenever my thoughts turned to Dom. People had added comments under the post, variations on: *Who are you bro?* But the Catfish Catcher didn't reply.

I also noticed that Jada had posted a photo of Hollie on Instagram, with a caption about how she was planning a non-official memorial in the next few days and to "watch this space".

There was a knock on my door and Mum put her head round. "Odd request coming up. Just had Aden's mum,

Sally message me to ask if she could come round for a chat with you about Aden. She says she's worried about him."

I climbed off my bed. "I have no idea what's up with Aden – apart from he's lost his best friend," I said, feeling nervous, though I didn't know why.

"Don't panic," said Mum. "I haven't got back to her yet. What do you think?"

I bit my lip. "I want to help," I said cautiously. "I'm just not sure I can."

Mum nodded sympathetically. "Why don't I tell her to come for a cup of tea and I can hover in case it gets tricky?"

"All right, thanks," I said, although I'd rather have been adding little touches to my Sims house.

Sally turned up in a pale blue jumper and beautifully fitted dark jeans with a selection of mini cakes in a cardboard box from the Old Markham Bakery near Liam's house. "Thank you for agreeing to speak to me, Amy," she said, as she sat down at the kitchen table. "I didn't tell Aden I was coming over. I don't like keeping secrets but there it is. Up to you if you want to tell him." She accepted a mug of black tea and refused a cake. I selected a red velvet cupcake from the box and sat next to Mum.

"I gather you were very kind yesterday at school. He said you took him to student services. Thank you." She gave me a small smile. "That's the first time it's happened at school but he's been crying a lot at home. I know it's understandable for him to be extremely upset about Hollie's murder – and Kristen's too, of course – but I worry. He won't talk to me at all. He keeps saying I won't understand – but I want to. I can't help thinking there's something he's not telling us." She let out a breath. "I'm not asking you to betray a confidence, Amy. I just want to know if there's anything serious I should be worried about."

"I think he's just trying to blot it all out," I said uncomfortably. "You know, with drinking quite a bit." She knew that already – she must have seen him after I'd left their house on Tuesday night.

"Hmm," said Sally. "Yes, I've spoken to him about that. His drinking has to *stop*." She made a slicing action through the air on the word *stop*. "He's lost enthusiasm for everything, even rowing. Is there something I'm missing, Amy?"

I hesitated. I thought of Aden crying. Those terrible sobs. I thought of his note in Pennington Park. *I wish I could take it all back.*

"Have you spoken to the school, Sally?" Mum chimed in. "Ms Reid always seems to be on the ball."

"I've had calls with Ms Reid and Ms Mackie – they've both tried talking to him but he says he's fine. Won't see a counsellor. They can't force him to speak, can they?" She shrugged sadly.

I took a deep breath. "He told me yesterday he feels … guilty about Hollie's death."

Sally looked up immediately. "He had nothing to do with it," she said. "He was rowing that evening and stayed on for food at the clubhouse."

213

"I didn't mean that," I said hurriedly. "I think he felt he should have saved her." I looked at Mum for help. "A lot of us feel like that."

"That's understandable," said Mum.

Sally said, "I see." She forced a bright smile. "I suppose it's just a question of being patient, and hoping he opens up. Thanks for talking to me, Amy, I appreciate it."

The conversation was closed. Sally sipped her tea and Mum asked how her kitchen design business was going and they talked about the cost of builders for a bit, while I ate my cake in tiny chunks. As she left, she said, "I'll see you both at Hollie's funeral. That'll be tough, right enough."

I held it together until the front door closed and then I burst into tears.

"Oh, Amy!" Mum grabbed me and wrapped her arms round me. "Was it the mention of the funeral?"

"Yes," I sobbed. "I understand why I can't go but I wish I could. And I don't know what's got into Aden either. Everything is just a mess."

"I know, it's horrible and hard. Things will get easier." She pushed the hair back from my face with both hands so she could see me properly. "Why don't I run you a bath? You can get into your pyjamas and relax."

I let her run me a bath even though it was four-thirty in the afternoon, and I lay still in the bubbles for a long time, listening to the sounds of our next-door neighbours playing football in their garden with their small kids.

My phone on the side of the bath pinged with a Bubble

notification from Liam's account. I dried my hands on the bath mat, the closest thing to hand, and opened it quickly, like ripping off a plaster.

*What will it take for you to notice me, Amy?*

I climbed out of the bath immediately, grabbing a towel and tucking it round me, shivering.

I quickly put on my ugliest pyjamas, which also happened to be my most comfy, emailed the screenshot to the police email address, then sat at my desk. I'd force myself to work on an economics presentation I had to give on Monday which would help me forget about that Bubble. Mum peered round my bedroom door to tell me she was going to the supermarket. "I'll bring you back some chocolate," she said. "Looks as if you could do with some. Dairy Milk Oreo?"

I managed a feeble smile. "Thanks, Mum."

Minutes later I heard her scream so loudly I lost the breath in my lungs.

I was down the stairs as fast as I could, taking them two, sometimes three at a time, stumbling at the bottom on unreliable legs.

Dad and Harry had got there before me. They were staring at something on the doorstep. I nudged Dad to one side so I could see.

There was short brown fur, a long tail, claws, dark red blood and blobs of unidentifiable organic matter. A raw meat smell.

It was a crushed, headless rat.

# CHAPTER 22

"What the hell is that doing in front of our door?" asked Mum. She was shaking.

Harry held his stomach and retched. "I knew I should have gone to the cinema with the lads. This is worse than the horror film they wanted to see." Then he lifted his phone and took a photo. "Deeply gross," he said.

"I'll get rid of it," said Dad, but I saw his face as he went to the understairs cupboard to find gardening gloves and a bin bag. He looked as if he was about to throw up too.

I sat on the second from bottom stair, leaning forward to stop the dizziness, worried I might faint. I couldn't shake the idea that this was some kind of message in rat form.

Someone putting it there to make me afraid. To make me take notice. *What will it take for you to notice me, Amy?*

"How d'you think it got there?" I asked, as Dad lifted it up by its tail and put it in a bin bag.

"A cat?" suggested Dad.

"A big aggressive cat," said Harry, standing well back. "Look at the size of it."

"A fox," said Mum. "They don't usually come out until dark but they're getting too tame round here."

"You don't think it was…" I knew it would be better to voice my fear than to keep it hidden. "Maybe someone putting it there to scare me?"

"I think that's rather far-fetched," said Dad matter-of-factly, tying a knot in the bag. "That's a lot of trouble for someone to go to."

"Why would someone want to scare you?" asked Harry. "Ew, it stinks."

We watched Dad go outside to the dustbin and heard him shove the lid down hard.

"I opened another couple of Bubble messages from Liam's account," I said when he came back in, and I caught the glance between him and Mum. "I got one just now when I was having a bath. It asked what it would take for me to notice them – and the other one mentioned the cat poo I accidentally left in Mr Peaty's hall."

Dad flinched. "Oh, Amy."

"Yep. So I think that rat might be part of it."

Dad discarded the gloves on the door mat and held out

his arms for a hug, and I stepped into it, despite his recent close proximity to the rat. "Listen, Amy. The police have a lead on Hollie's killer. And they're making progress on whoever is hacking into Liam's account and it will be some lowlife who's eavesdropping on your life because it's so much better than theirs. I doubt they have anything to do with the murders but they're enjoying the notoriety."

I didn't know what to think but I was glad I'd told them about the messages. It was good not to have everything jammed up in my head.

"Who knows you hate rats?" asked Harry.

"Everyone who knows me," I said, my face against Dad's thick-knit jumper.

"Most people hate rats," said Mum. "Including me."

"Whoa," said Harry, holding up his phone. "The police have found the guy from the CCTV!"

We crowded round Harry's phone and read that a thirty-eight-year-old man had been taken to Markham Police Station for questioning in connection with the release of the CCTV image.

I puffed out my cheeks and released the air noisily. Thank god. I went up to my room and messaged Dom and Stan separately, saying: *Seen the news?*

Dom messaged back: *They finally got him.*

Stan replied: *I hope they've got the right person.*

Could that thirty-eight-year-old man be the one messaging me? I didn't think so. He wouldn't have had time to send that message when I was in the bath – or to leave the headless rat. He wouldn't have known about the cat poo.

I told Dom and Stan about the headless rat on the doorstep and they sent appropriate crying, horror and vomit emojis. Meanwhile my socials were out of control. Did anyone know who the thirty-eight-year-old man could be? How had he been caught? Did anyone have a name we could google?

The Catfish Catcher account posted a photo of Markham Police Station with the caption: *Gotcha #MarkhamMurders*. It currently had four hundred and twenty-one likes. I added mine. Soon there was another post – the name of the man had been leaked. Robert Courtney, a lorry driver who lived out of the area.

The name meant nothing to me – or anyone following the Catfish Catcher account.

Then another: the police were now requesting anyone who had been within a half-mile radius of the bridge across the River Mark on Monday evening between 8.30 p.m. and 10.30 p.m. to contact them. *We cannot stress enough that even if you don't think you have any relevant information, we still want to hear from you.*

Jada messaged me: *Can I call you?*

She immediately video-called me and I picked up before I remembered I was in my ugly pyjamas and my hair hadn't quite dried.

She was in her room, cross-legged on a cushion on the floor, next to a towering pile of books. They'd been graded in rainbow order. She scrutinized me, and said, "You look different."

"Just had a bath," I said. *Been sent another creepy Bubble. And a headless rat.* Jada was wearing a big yellow-and-pink patterned shirt over black leggings and long glittery gold earrings.

"Great they found that man," she said. "What. A. Relief."

"It took a while," I said. "But, yeah. Just hope they have the evidence."

"I really hope so." Then with typical directness, she said, "So here's the thing: a true crime podcast has contacted me on Instagram and asked if I wanted to go on it. It's about being the friend of someone who's been murdered. I thought you might be interested. You could go in on the guilt angle."

I sank into the silence of that request. The pain hit me in the chest like a netball at close range, knocking the breath out of me.

"Hear me out," said Jada, readjusting her legs. "It's an interesting angle. Like, you've had the extra weight of people thinking badly of you when Hollie's death wasn't your fault. And you would get a chance to talk about how much Hollie meant to you. It's a great podcast – and could be something for your personal statement?" She raised an eyebrow.

"The answer's no," I said. It was time to stop feeling cowed and guilty.

"Fair enough," she said. "I'll do it, then, and hope Ms Arnold doesn't dismember me. I'm sorry I was a cow about the catfishing. I shouldn't have overreacted like I did."

"Thanks," I said. I could have done with the apology a while ago but it still felt good to hear.

"Are you behind the Catfish Catcher account on Instagram?" she carried on.

"No. Are you?" I shot back.

"Sadly not," she said, with genuine regret in her voice. "Is it Stan? He's always on his phone."

"Maybe. I don't know."

"Have you two fallen out?"

"No," I said coldly. Apology or no apology, this was still none of Jada's business. "We're just coping with Hollie and Kristen's deaths differently."

"Oh," said Jada, straightening a glittery earring. "Because I'm picking up on some strain there. Shame. I always thought you two were solid."

"We are," I said. "Me and Stan are good."

I wasn't sure who I was trying to convince – Jada, or myself.

I had a lie-in on Sunday. When I woke up, I heard Cooper's voice downstairs and immediately decided to stay in bed a bit longer. I messaged Mum, requesting breakfast in bed so I didn't have to be anywhere near him. The last thing I needed right now was his "banter".

Mum brought me up honey-nut cornflakes and a mug

of tea, and sat on my bed, telling me she'd seen a tattoo on Cooper's upper arm which read: *Your worst nightmare.*

We exchanged a look. "He's awful," I said. "Like, completely awful."

Mum pulled a face. "I hope none of this rubs off on Harry."

"I doubt it," I told her. "Harry might be easily led but he draws the line at anything really weird."

Luckily, Cooper had to leave before lunch. That left me, Mum and Harry making Sunday lunch while Dad sorted the week's washing.

"Shame Cooper left," I said, pinching a roast potato from the tray as Harry finished off the lunch. "Not."

"Amy," said Harry, stirring the gravy, "I could say things about your friends, but I wouldn't because I'm not mean like that."

"What could you say about my friends?"

Harry clamped his lips together.

"No, come on," I said. I knew I was overreacting but suddenly I was spoiling for a fight. "Let's hear it."

"Calm down, you two," said Mum. "Amy, can you get the horseradish, please."

"I want to hear what's so problematic about my friends," I said.

Harry poured the gravy from the roasting tray into a jug. "Nothing, Ames, I was out of line. Just – Jada's taken centre-stage as mourning friend. Aden is a walking ghost. And Stan – well, are you telling me you haven't noticed anything weird about him at all lately?"

"Our best friend just died," I said. "In case you missed that."

"I know," Harry said. "Like I said, I was out of line."

"Enough," said Mum. "Time to eat. And we're not going to talk about anything horrible. Especially now that man has been taken in for questioning." She wiped her hands on her apron. "This is going to draw a line under the investigation, and you can all start to move on."

We sat down for lunch and I thought about how nice that would be. To move on. For the messages to stop. Mum thought it was possible. So why didn't I quite believe it?

Mum and Dad went for a walk that afternoon and Harry went to the gym. They were still out when I took a break from my essay writing and went to make a tea. As the kettle boiled, my phone almost levitated off the work surface it was buzzing with so many notifications.

*Suspect in Markham Murders released without charge.*

*Police back to square one.*

*The investigation continues.*

*Markham murderer still at large.*

I was trembling with shock and disbelief. The murderer was still out there. I suddenly felt very alone. I wished Mum, Dad and Harry weren't out.

I ran to lock the front and back doors. Then I sat on the sofa to message Mum, asking her to come back. My phone was hot from all the activity. Notification after notification, piling up like an online game. Speculation about the man they'd arrested, who else the killer might be. And then—

No.

I blinked. Was I reading them properly?

*Another teen falls victim to the Markham Murderer.*

As I stared at the headline, my fingers icy, a message came through. From Liam's account:

*Amy, I had to do it.*

# CHAPTER 23

I sank to the floor.

I was screenshotting the message when another one came through. From Jada. And it brought my heart to my throat.

*You might have heard, but if you haven't … they're saying online it's Rory who was killed. Aden's brother. Stabbed while he was running along the towpath.*

I lowered my phone.

A third murder in ten days, all the victims under eighteen. All from the same school, all of them known to me. The dead rat. The messages from Liam's account. Was I connected? Was I a potential victim too?

Everyone thought the murderer had been killing

girls – confident, pretty girls. But now Rory? It didn't make sense.

I sent the screenshots of the last three messages to the email address DS Haig had given me to let him know I was still receiving things. I hoped the specialist police officers in the lab had been monitoring the account and seen where they had been sent from – but I expected they'd simply be led to an account set up on a burner app or phone.

I heard the key in the front door and I called out, "Hello?"

Finally Mum shot into the living room, then Dad and Harry, who dropped his bag and sat down on the armchair, his face in his shaking hands. He'd changed out of his gym kit but he looked dishevelled. Under his sweatshirt I could see the bottom of his T-shirt and it was inside out.

Mum scooped me up in her arms and pressed her soft cheek against my forehead. "Oh, Amy. Such horrendous news. Poor Rory, poor Sally, poor Aden."

"I'll make everyone some tea," said Dad.

"I ran back as soon as I saw on my phone. It's hard to imagine Rory dead," said Harry quietly. "Like, he was a strong bloke. He played rugby and everything."

Harry was right. Rory had always been so sporty, and a real extrovert, it was impossible to imagine him dead. And why had the killer broken his pattern? It was hard to imagine a motive for his murder – unless…

"I remember him saying he'd been near the riverside on Monday," I said. "He put it on Instagram too. Maybe that's why he was killed? He saw something and the killer knew it."

Mum looked at her phone, sniffing. "The poor lad was going on a run. Says here that the passer-by who found him must have missed the murderer by minutes. It's unbearable. I'm going to text Sally, see if there's anything at all we can do."

I knew I should message Aden too. After typing, deleting and retyping, I put: *Am so sorry Aden. Let me know if you'd like me to come over x*

I could see him typing. *Thank you. Yeah. I could do with some company.*

I showed it to Mum and within ten minutes she was driving me round there. A girl of about fourteen I didn't recognize opened the door.

"I'm Maria, one of the cousins," she said. Sounds of chatter and the TV news came from the living room.

Sally appeared, as if she was sleep-walking, unable to speak. Mum stepped forward to hug her and Sally let out a wail and fell into her arms. It was a frightening, animal sound.

Aden came down the stairs, red-eyed and puffy faced. We hugged too, soundlessly, and he put his hand on my back to steer me up the stairs, away from our mums.

"Whole extended family's over," he said behind me. "I keep thinking Rory's going to burst through the front door in his running gear and say, 'False alarm, everyone.'"

"It's unreal," I agreed.

His room didn't look any different from how it had five days ago. The same clothes were on the floor, the photo of him and Hollie in their school uniforms in Year Seven was still on his bedside table.

Aden sagged on to his bed and I sat cross-legged on the chair at his desk.

"I don't want to talk about Rory. I don't want to think about anything," he said. "But I don't want to be on my own either."

"I get that," I said because I wouldn't have liked to have been on my own if it had been Harry who'd died and my house was full of relatives, not that I had a tenth of Aden's.

Aden cracked his knuckles and said, "There's something going round in my head over and over and it won't leave."

"What is it?" I asked. He was silent for a moment and I waited, sensing that he needed the time to talk.

"The wrong brother died," he said at last.

"What?" I snapped my head up. "Why would you say something like that?"

"Because it's true. I'm going to be a massive disappointment to my parents."

"Oh, yeah, right. As if." I meant it. "They adore you, Aid."

"Fact is," said Aden, "I'm already a disappointment. They just don't know it yet."

"Why?" I pushed.

He started to cry.

"Tell me what's going on, Aid," I whispered. "Please." He was making me nervous.

There was silence in the room. I heard a door bang downstairs and the whine of his closed laptop which hadn't been shut down properly.

At last he spoke. "I did something stupid," he whispered. "I liked Hollie. I mean, really liked her, not just as friends. I have done for ages. We were all a bit in love with her, weren't we?"

I nodded. It was true.

"But I actually, properly loved her. I didn't say anything. Kept hoping it would go away, that I'd get over it. But then she set up the date with Liam – or I thought she had – and I decided I had to say something. On the night she died…" His voice cracked. "On the night she died, she asked if she could come round here, and of course I said yes. As soon as she arrived, she said she needed me to walk with her somewhere, but she wouldn't tell me where. I took her hands and seized the moment. I told her that I was in love with her. She – she was *angry* with me. Said I'd ruined our friendship and…" He pressed the base of his neck as if the words were sandpaper against his throat. "We had a row and she went off." His hand had moved from his throat to his head, pressing against his skull. "I let her go, Amy. I let her go off and I didn't follow her. She must have gone straight to Pennington Park and I wasn't there to protect her." He turned away from me, unable to make eye contact. "I was on my own when she came round so

229

nobody knew. I guess I should have told the police but … I just … couldn't." His voice had tapered to a whisper.

"It's not your fault," I said, understanding everything about the regret, embarrassment and self-loathing.

I said it again louder but he shook his head. "I should have gone with her, Ames." He made an unbearable howl-like sound. "Then she wouldn't be dead, Amy. She'd be alive and the attacker would have been caught because I'd have been there looking out for her, and Kristen would still be annoying and making us roll our eyes and my big brother would be coming back from his run." He cried properly now, loudly with his shoulders shaking, lying down, curling himself up. I thought about running downstairs and finding Sally, but she had enough to cope with on this terrible day.

His phone pinged repeatedly and he fumbled for it on the bed. "It's Jada," he said, lifting his head to read the messages. "She's outside. You'll have to let her in."

"You asked Jada to come over too?"

He thumped back down on to his duvet, his phone tumbling out of his hand. "Yep, right after you messaged. Not sure if Stan's coming or not."

"How many people did you invite, Aden?"

"Squad," said Aden in a sad voice. "Except there's no group chat any more, right?"

His phone pinged again. I saw another message light up from Jada: *Aden, where are you at?*

I went down the two flights of stairs to let her in. From

the living room, I could hear the sounds of a wedding video and someone said, "Look, there he is. Behind Auntie Lisa."

Jada didn't look surprised to see me, and enveloped me in a hug that nearly knocked me backwards. I could smell coconut on her hair and feel the chill of outside on her skin. "How is he?" she asked as she took off her fluffy coat. She was wearing a jumpsuit made from thick stripy red, white and green material. She looked like an Italian flag or a Christmas elf – but in the most awesome way. Hollie would have given it a ten out of ten.

"In a bad way. He thinks the wrong brother died," I said. I wasn't going to tell her about the rest just yet. "Come and help me."

"Okaaaay." We went upstairs together. "By the way, Stan can't make it. He's in Birmingham apparently. I called him."

"Birmingham? What's he doing there?" It was miles from Markham.

"Dunno. He didn't say."

Before Jada walked into Aden's room, she took a deep breath and said, "Hello, Aden. It's Jada," in her breeziest voice. He was still on his bed.

"Hi, thanks for coming," he said in a robotic voice. He lifted his head. "Want a drink?"

We shook our heads. Aden lay back down. I looked helplessly at Jada.

"What's his favourite film? His comfort watch?" she

231

asked me as she picked up his laptop from his desk, and I was stumped for a moment, then I remembered. "*Shrek*."

"Laptop password?"

Aden waved her over and put in a password that started with Hollie's name. Jada took the laptop from him and found *Shrek*. She rearranged the pillows on his bed and climbed in. "You get one of us either side of you, Aden," she said. "You can watch or you can fall asleep but we're not going anywhere until the film ends, are we, Ames?"

She leaned over and squeezed my shoulder and I gave her a ghost of a smile. Jada certainly knew how to take charge of a situation.

"No," I said. "We're not going anywhere."

"You two are mini dictators," said Aden.

I realized as he shuffled under the duvet into a position where he could see the laptop screen, complaining about us having taken up too much space, that one of the kindest things you could do for a person was to make them feel less alone.

# CHAPTER 24

Unsurprisingly less than half my form group were in the next day, despite Ms Arnold sending an email that said: *Now is the time for the community to pull together, and to focus on safety and learning.* Being at school felt like a good distraction to me.

Aden wasn't there, of course, but Stan was. He was on his phone – *The New York Times* website. I could see a photo of Rory in his rugby kit. The third murder was now international news.

"Hey, Stanley Maloney," I said, taking my seat. "Thought you might still be in … Birmingham, was it?"

He coloured and said, "I was there yesterday, seeing someone … from the computer science lot. Came back late." He turned the screen off.

I looked at Stan thoughtfully. Had he really been seeing a new friend in Birmingham? I'd have bet money that he was lying. Pre Hollie's death I'd have known he was going to Birmingham and why. I nodded towards his phone. "Why are you so obsessed?" I asked. "I never see you off the news sites."

"Why *aren't* you obsessed?" he shot back.

"We missed you yesterday evening at Aden's," I said.

Stan swallowed. "I feel really bad about that. How is he?"

"Not good. Obviously." By the time *Shrek* had finished, Aden had been asleep, twitching and crying out now and again. Jada had stroked his hair and said, "It's OK. We're here." But we'd had to leave him to go home. I hoped he hadn't woken in the night and been scared, alone.

Now Ms Reid came in, followed by a few people who'd got to school late. Normally they'd be issued with automatic fifteen-minute detentions, but today Ms Reid smiled at them and said, "Glad you're here." She sat on top of her desk, grey roots showing in her red hair, and said, "The police have asked me to share that they will be on the premises today at lunchtime. They are asking any students with information to come by – and they can also answer questions you might have."

"I want to ask why they're so effing useless," said Jake. "They should have been quicker to shut down that BubbleSpeak account. And they should be doing DNA tests. It's a small town, there's no excuse for this."

"As a police cadet, I can tell you there are procedures in

place," said Hussein, rising to the bait. "You can't just run a DNA test on anyone you want – the police need grounds for that."

Jake rolled his eyes. "Oh my *god*. Don't give me excuses, mate."

"I'm giving you an explanation," said Hussein, raising his voice. "You can't force the whole of Markham to do a DNA test."

"I'd do a test," said Jake. "I bet everyone would – if you're innocent you have nothing to hide. And the person who refuses – well, there you go."

"D'you want to live in a totalitarian state?" asked Sabine in her high voice.

"I don't know what you're talking about," said Jake. "Not one clue."

"This murder was more reckless," said Hussein. "So many people use the towpath at that time of day. We've got to ask why they risked getting caught."

"Let's shut this conversation down," said Ms Reid. "Take any questions to the police. The drop-ins are taking place in the café and the library. Now, it's time to move on to other things. Ms Arnold is keen this doesn't disrupt your studies…"

I looked out of the window as Ms Reid talked about preparation for the Year Twelve mock exams. Ms Arnold could pretend the biggest thing facing us was exams. But we all knew that wasn't the case.

At break time, there was a buzz of activity. The police had released more details about Rory's murder, and everyone was talking about it.

He had been stabbed in the neck with a small knife, similar to a penknife. The murder weapon hadn't yet been found, despite a thorough combing of the area. The attacker was likely to have returned home with blood over them and their clothing.

"Why d'you think Rory was stabbed, not hit over the head like the others?" I heard a boy behind me in the library ask.

"Maybe this murder was more premeditated. Like, who walks round with a penknife on them?" his friend said.

Another person said, "Some kids do. For protection." That last person was right. When Harry had been in Year Seven and I wasn't at Markham High yet, one of his friends had been mugged at knifepoint for their phone and most of his year had started carrying penknives. A couple of boys had been caught admiring each other's penknives in school, the knives were confiscated, and the boys were suspended for a couple of days and made to attend a police talk on the escalation of knife crime. Granddad had thought it was outrageous. In his day, a penknife was fine for a person to have in school.

Stan and I had been fascinated and we'd looked up penknives online, wondering if we needed to get one for secondary school. In the end it had fizzled out. I wondered how many students still walked around with one.

At lunchtime, I bought a pasta pot in the café and sat in our usual spot which seemed to have been taken over by Hussein and a few of his mates. "Sorry," he said, as I sat next to him. "Thought you guys had vacated the sofas."

It seemed that we had. I had no idea where Stan was, and Jada was the other side of the café with the English lit crowd and their maxi skirts.

"It's cool," I said. "It's not like they're reserved or anything." Though we all knew perfectly well there was an unwritten code they belonged to our group. Only now there was no group.

Ms Arnold arrived with a police officer and I recognized him immediately. DS Stuart Haig. A crowd gathered but he spotted me as Ms Arnold introduced him, and he acknowledged me with a nod of his head.

"DS Haig has kindly offered to come in and answer some questions, which I'll be fielding," said Ms Arnold. "May I remind everyone that you are representing Markham High and I don't want any inappropriate questions. Please also bear in mind that DS Haig is not allowed to give out certain information that may affect a court case further down the line."

Hussein put his hand up, and DS Haig smiled and said to Ms Arnold, "That's one of our police cadets. What is it, Hussein?"

"Is there really no decent CCTV evidence?" asked Hussein.

DS Haig said, "The locations of the murders have been

in places where there isn't CCTV and we've been unlucky with the cameras nearby. One by the towpath was tampered with. If any of you have heard about someone destroying a CCTV camera, please get in touch on the helpline."

We nodded.

I saw Stan arrive and stand next to the water fountain. He looked anxious, his hand clasped round his phone.

"What about criminal profiling?" asked Hussein crisply. "What have you got?"

"We believe the killer of Hollie and Kristen is potentially the same person who stabbed Rory. They understand social media well, so perhaps a younger person," said DS Haig. "Someone who knows the local area and where the CCTV drops out. The killer took an overgrown footpath leaving the riverside the evening of Kristen's murder, again indicating familiarity with the area. We know the person is around five foot ten inches and was wearing shoes with a certain tread that suggests a Nike sports shoe. This is information that is being released at a briefing at the same time as I'm talking to you."

There was a buzz at this — it felt as if we were important, getting information at the same time as the press.

"What about the online angle?" called Sabine.

"We heard both girls got messages from Liam Henderson's account. Is that true?" called someone at the back of the crowd.

"Hollie's messages came from two known individuals," said DS Haig, and I felt sick, then grateful he didn't mention me and Stan by name. "Kristen Sorrenson was corresponding online with a different individual whom she believed to be Liam Henderson," he continued. "Liam Henderson himself has been cleared of any involvement. He has alibis for the murders and also confirmed he never accessed the account. Someone else was using it."

"Can't you trace them?" interrupted Jake and Ms Arnold glared at him for not putting his hand up.

Hussein muttered that it sounded like a "burner phone situation".

"I'm afraid I can't comment," said DS Haig.

Jake shot his hand up. "Are you going to pay Robert Courtney compensation? The man you wrongfully arrested?"

"Inappropriate," barked Ms Arnold. "No more questions from you, thank you."

"How are you going to stop this person?" asked Lou from my history class. Her voice was thin and shaky.

"We're waiting for new forensic evidence from Rory's murder," DS Haig said. "This killing differed from the previous two – this was the first young man killed, indicating a different motive. The murderer would have got blood on their clothes and needed to dispose of them. Secondly, it was a riskier crime because it took place at a time when there were more people around." Hussein nodded along as DS Haig spoke. "We suspect that the perpetrator may have killed out of panic. Perhaps they thought the net was closing in."

He looked around at us all. "I know it's unrealistic for me to say stay off social media, but please be hyper-vigilant and never assume anything. The team have seen lots of Liam Henderson accounts spring up over the last few days, either joke accounts or people trying to instil fear. It's not helping and it's wasting police time when we need to be focusing our resources." He rubbed his forehead wearily. "Please don't go out on your own, and report anything that doesn't feel right. We'd rather it came to nothing than miss an opportunity."

As DS Haig talked more about online safety, I looked at my trainers – Adidas – and thought about the opportunity I'd missed when I saw Kristen interacting with Liam's BubbleSpeak account. I could have saved her life and Rory's if only I had acted.

"Time for one last question," said Ms Arnold.

Jada put up her hand. "Yes?" said the head.

"I'm organizing a memorial event in the cricket pavilion next to Pennington Park for the entire sixth form," she said. "To honour those who have died. Food, music, chat and an open mic. Details are being announced later today. Any chance we can have a police presence?"

This was the first I'd heard about plans for a memorial event. How did Jada have so much energy? But I felt warm too. The idea of coming together for food and drink and music, to honour Hollie, Kristen and Rory – it felt right. And Stan and I would be welcome. Jada had said "the entire sixth form".

"Let's discuss this later, Jada," said Ms Arnold quickly. "I'm not sure that this is advisable under the circumstances frankly."

DS Haig smiled at Jada. "Done in the right way, I think that's a cracking idea. Young people need to come together to make sense of what's happened in their own way—"

"Do you even have permission to use the cricket pavilion?" broke in Ms Arnold.

"Yes," said Jada with a note of triumph in her voice. "I've spoken to the chair of the Markham Cricket Club. He says it's fine as a one-off. Kristen used to play in the Under-Fourteen girls cricket team and my mum is the cleaner there, so there's a personal connection. It's free this Wednesday. The night before Hollie's funeral, which feels fitting."

"This Wednesday? But it's Monday now. That's impossible," said Ms Arnold. "These things take a lot of planning and in all good conscience there'd need to be a risk assessment and—"

"I want to be spontaneous. Seize the moment and bring people together," said Jada calmly. "If enough adults are available to supervise, and the venue is free, there's no reason not to go ahead." She swivelled round, speaking to her audience. "It wouldn't be anything to do with school. This would be about our friends."

Ms Arnold sucked in her breath, clearly about to say something, but DS Haig got in there first.

"I do need to stress that we are very stretched at the

moment, but I think we could agree to police support for a few hours in the evening," he said. "This seems like a good way to remember Hollie, Kristen and Rory. You'll need adequate adult supervision and a strict policy of no alcohol for under eighteens." His expression was kind as he looked at Jada. "Come and see me afterwards and we'll work out the details."

Jada nodded. "Sure."

I couldn't help smiling as Ms Arnold bristled. Jada had certainly won that battle.

# CHAPTER 25

As soon as Harry and I got home that afternoon, I went round checking the doors and the downstairs windows were locked.

Harry was already at the kitchen table, chopping one of his little strawberry cakes into pieces to film in slow motion. "The murderer's not going to come storming in here, Ames. That's not their modus whatever. You're being paranoid."

"Modus operandi," I said. I shoved the screenshot of the last Bubble in front of him. "Look. *What will it take for you to notice me, Amy?* And, yes, I've emailed it to the police. So forgive me for being *paranoid*, Harry. And, no, I haven't shown Mum and Dad because they're scared enough and

243

probably won't let me leave the house till I'm fifty. But I would say this pretty much confirms that the person sending the messages is the killer, right?"

Harry read the screenshot. "Man. Have the police got back to you about it?" he asked.

I shook my head.

"You don't think…" Harry trailed off and shook his head. "Nothing."

"What?" His usually cheerful expression was unhappy and worried. "What is it, Harry?"

"Hear me out," said Harry. He pushed the plate of cake away from him and took a deep breath. "I know you won't want to hear this but – could it be *Stan* sending the messages?"

I laughed. "You have to be joking?"

Harry shrugged miserably. "It's just – well, I've always thought he was very into Hollie. The way he looked at her. And you too, Ames. He's always followed you around like a little puppy. He's never had much luck with girls, has he? It might have made him angry. You read about people like that."

"Stan was at home for both murders," I said firmly. "You're being ridiculous."

Harry said slowly, "But was anyone with him? He looks absolutely terrible – as if he hasn't slept for weeks."

I thought about it. I'd left Stan's house to sort out the parcel for Mr Peaty the night Hollie died, leaving him on his own with enough time to get to Pennington Park and back. He'd been home alone when Kristen died. But he'd been in Birmingham when Rory was stabbed. At least that's what he'd said.

As for a motive, Harry was right. Stan had never had much luck with girls. Had he enjoyed pretending to be Liam, flirting with Hollie and Kristen? Then when he'd shown up, the girls had laughed at him. Had Rory seen him in Markham the night Kristen died? He'd boasted about it on social media enough. Perhaps Stan had panicked and followed Rory and—

No, it was outlandish. Ridiculous. I felt sick even thinking such a terrible thought.

But it had given me an idea. Another boy who hadn't had much luck with girls – and, unlike Stan, had pretty bad views on women.

"I wonder if it could be Cooper," I said.

Harry's eyes widened. "No," he said. "Cooper talks a lot of rubbish but he's not violent." We were silent, thinking about it. Then Harry put his elbows on the table and ran his hands through his hair, depositing a couple of cake crumbs in it. He gave a weak laugh. "Listen to us, discussing whether our friends could be murderers."

I laughed too, but I still felt uneasy. "I know. This is making us *all* paranoid."

Mum came in from work, holding her phone. "What's this about a memorial event at the cricket pavilion on Wednesday? Because you two are not going, let me tell you that now."

"I want to go, Mum," I said. "I'm not going to be at the funeral and I wasn't at the vigil in the park. The police are going to be there, and other adults. You could be there to supervise too." I swallowed. "Hollie would love that it's taking place."

Mum chewed her bottom lip. "I think it's a bad idea," she said, but she sounded quieter, as if she was thinking about it. "Besides, Dad and I have both got shifts tomorrow evening."

"Harry would come," I said, turning to Harry.

He shook his head. "It sounds like The Jada Show to me," he said.

"Please, please, *please*," I said, giving him big eyes.

"I'll think about it," he said reluctantly.

"Nothing is decided," said Mum. "I'll talk to Dad. Now, someone start peeling some potatoes."

In the car on the way to school the following morning, I looked at the Catfish Catcher account, which managed to upload news stories as soon as they hit the sites. Today they had screenshotted an article about the murders from the *Markham Gazette*.

I enlarged it.

*Markham students continue to live their lives in fear,* the article began. *One student, who wished to remain anonymous, has a fresh theory on the killings.*

*"There was a group at school that liked to play pranks on each other and they were getting more and more out of hand. Everyone*

*knows that's how the murders began — it was a prank that went*
*wrong. I think everything that's gone down is to do with what went*
*on within that group. I've even heard one girl was into ritualistic*
*animal killings."*

My head was hot and pounding. I passed my phone to Harry who was sitting in the back seat. "Read this."

Harry read it out loud and snorted. "Ritualistic animal killings at Markham High? Really?" Then his eyes widened. "Oh, wait. The rat on our doorstep. Are they talking about *you* here, Ames?"

"Maybe," I muttered quietly.

"Ignore it," Dad said, glancing at me as I took the phone back. He looked old and tired.

When we got out of the car I said, "Did you tell people about the rat, Harry?"

"Yes," said Harry. "Loads of people. Nobody told me not to."

As I walked into our form room, everyone looked at me. Stan was already there, in his usual seat, AirPods in, scrolling. Ms Reid arrived at the same time as me, struggling with all her bags.

"Morning, guys," she said. "Phones away. Now, some of you might have read an article in the paper that puts forward some ridiculous theories about the murders. I hope you all know better than to pay attention to such nonsense."

She was trying to shut down any rumours sparked by the article, but I could tell it was hopeless. The damage had been done.

"Some of you will be attending the memorial event tomorrow," continued Ms Reid, catching Jada's eye. "It will be taking place at the Markham Cricket Pavilion from four-thirty until six-thirty. The school want to make it clear that you will be attending at your own risk. But I for one will be there to support – along with my son, Michael."

If Ms Reid and one of her sons were going to be there, the event had been officially endorsed. It meant most of the sixth form would turn up.

It was much later when I caught up with Jada in the art room. She was photocopying fliers for the event and I was putting the finishing touches to the collage I'd made of Hollie.

"How do you have so much energy, Jada?" I asked, as I pasted a final photo of Hollie, wearing bunny ears, on to the bottom right corner of the card. "Why are you doing all this?"

"Because…" She stopped. "I don't know. Having a memorial event is something different. Something that the adults aren't taking over. Something that Hollie would have actually loved. The real Hollie, not the perfect, saintly Hollie they want us to remember."

We smiled at each other, then she turned businesslike. "And if Harry could bring some of his famous sausage rolls, that would be great," she said.

"He'll be happy to make some, I'm sure," I said.

248

Jada pulled my collage round and looked at it in more detail. "Can I make some photocopies later for the cricket pavilion?"

"Of course." I loved that idea.

Jada pointed to a photo. Hollie had her hand up to shield her eyes from the sun. We were in my garden. It was this summer because she was wearing the bracelet I'd given her for her birthday. She was making the face that meant: *I have the funniest story to tell you*. "Hollie was amazing, wasn't she?" she said.

"Yes," I said simply. Then I added, "And you took her away from me."

My hand flew to my mouth. I couldn't believe I'd said that out loud.

But Jada nodded. "I'm sorry," she said. "I couldn't help getting close to her. We got on so well." She twisted a piece of her hair round her finger. "I've never told anyone this, but – well, I hoped it would be more than a friendship. Obviously it never was." She looked at me. "We both loved her in our own way, didn't we?"

I nodded. It was true. We had all loved Hollie.

"What's that phrase that people use?" I said. "'Burned brightly' – that's it. Hollie burned brightly."

"Yep." Jada stood up. "And we keep her light shining, right? We give her a stonking memorial. The funeral's for her family. The memorial in the cricket pavilion is for us."

I nodded. "For us," I repeated softly. The bell was about to go so I stood up.

As I turned to go, Jada laid a hand on my arm. "Amy, wait. I forgot – there was something I wanted to ask you. Something about Hollie. Something strange that happened before she died…"

# CHAPTER 26

Jada looked around the art room. We didn't have long before the bell went. Satisfying herself that there was nobody within listening distance, she sat on a stool opposite me and leaned forward. "It was such a weird thing," said Jada. "Hollie had her hair in plaits with a band near the bottom. At the end of the day, she came to tell me that one of the ends had been chopped off. A big chunk of hair, gone. It could have happened at any point in the day. Her mum had to neaten it up."

Hollie's hair had been long, blonde and shiny. She'd told me many times that she considered it one of her best features, along with her attractive knees. "Not many people have attractive knees, Ames," she'd said. "I'm proud to say mine are top tier."

"That *is* weird," I said slowly to Jada.

"It's not all," she continued. "Hollie had little things go missing in the run-up to her death, didn't she? But we just told her she was careless."

I remembered the hedgehog pen, the hairbrush and her crochet rabbit key ring, none of which were found.

I sucked a breath in. I recalled something that Dom had told me – about Kristen thinking she had a stalker.

"Do you know if Hollie was ever sent flowers anonymously?" I asked.

Jada's mouth was open. "Yes! She thought they'd been sent to her by mistake. Why?"

"Because Dom told me Kristen was sent flowers the week before she died," I said. "She told Dom she was worried someone was stalking her. He thought she was being dramatic. She *was* dramatic. But now, I don't know…"

Jada's eyes widened. "Do you think someone *was* stalking Kristen and Hollie?"

"It's possible." I tapped my fist lightly against my mouth as I thought of the messages I'd received. *Hey Amy, will you notice me now? I want to be closer to you. You look stunning in that green scarf. Haven't you worked out I'm doing all this for you? What will it take for you to notice me?*

I brushed away the tiny thought in my head which said: *Stan.*

"I don't know," I said, "but I should speak to Aden. See if anything weird happened to Rory before he died."

"Let's go and talk to him together," said Jada, and without checking that I was free, she messaged him, her thumbs moving at lightning speed. She kept her eyes on her phone screen.

"Yeah, he says that's cool," she said, moving towards the door with her photocopies. "We'll go round after school."

"Actually my mum is picking me up today so…"

"Great. She can give us a lift to Aden's," said Jada. "Let's get Stan to come too. We need to figure this thing out, once and for all. It's not like the police are solving it."

"But—"

"I know things are frosty between you two, but it'll be fine. I'll be there to referee it. See you by the gates at the end of the day." She strode out of the room. She reminded me of Hollie – the way she assumed things would work out.

Sometimes, though, they didn't.

Mum took it in her stride when I messaged to tell her the plan to go round to Aden's after school. *As long as everyone's safe, I'm happy to help*, she replied. Stan met us after school at the gates, as directed by Jada. When we reached Mum's car, Harry made a grab for the front seat and I was uncomfortably wedged in the back between Stan and Jada. Jada kept the conversation going, joking with Harry about him failing his driving test twice.

"Are you the one organizing the memorial event tomorrow?" Mum asked Jada, when there was a lull. "Because I'm a bit worried about it, to be honest. The killer is still out there."

"Yes, I am," said Jada easily. "But there's no need to worry about safety. There'll be wall-to-wall security – police, parents – and CCTV at the entrances. It's going to be a safe way to remember our friends. I know that Amy really wants to be there."

I nodded vigorously.

"You'll help, won't you, Harry?" said Jada. "You can be security, and get some other hefty Year Thirteens to help?"

Harry turned round from the front seat. I could tell he was flattered to be called hefty. "Sure."

Mum smiled. "You seem very determined," she said to Jada in the rear-view mirror. "I guess Amy and Harry can go. It's important to remember your friends."

"Thanks, Mum," I said. "It means a lot."

We pulled up at Aden's and spilled out on to the pavement. Aden opened his front door. He looked genuinely pleased to see us and, for a moment as we hugged, time fell away. Hollie was just late, like always, and would be along any minute.

"Mum and Dad are out for a walk, along with everyone else," Aden said. "Come on in while it's quiet."

We went into his living room, where the thick carpet had been so recently hoovered it looked like a mowed lawn with neat rows. On the mantelpiece and every other available surface there were cards. So many cards. Some had the word *sympathy* on them, others were of nature scenes or flowers. There was an open tin of biscuits on the coffee table. "Help yourselves," Aden said, nodding towards it. "Everyone's been bringing food. We have So. Much. Food."

The four of us sat self-consciously on the sofas. In previous times we'd have sprawled over them, and Stan would have been setting up a game on the huge TV screen, and maybe Hollie would have thrown a cushion at Aden for saying something silly – but today we were straight-backed and quiet. Stan kept a firm grip on his phone; he hadn't said a single word since he'd said hi to Aden.

Only Jada seemed oblivious to the tension. "The police suggest we have a guest list for the memorial," she said. "Let's keep it to Markham High sixth formers – but, Amy, you could ask Dom, if you want? He might want to be there because of Kristen."

"I'll ask him," I said, taking out my phone from my hoodie pocket. It was good to have an excuse to contact him.

"Have the police said anything to you about the investigation?" Stan suddenly asked Aden. I glared at him for being so insensitive. "Anything that's not in the press, I mean?"

Aden breathed out slowly. "Not really. Rory kept telling people he was near the river the night Kristen died – one line of inquiry is that maybe the killer overheard or found out

255

somehow and panicked that Rory had seen something. That might have been why he was killed. His phone was taken, unlike with Hollie and Kristen. The police say that might be because the killer had made contact with Rory under their real name. Maybe he was getting rid of the evidence."

We nodded.

"So here's a thing," said Jada, leaning forward. "Amy and I have realized that Hollie and Kristen both received flowers in the days before they died. No note or anything. Some of Hollie's things went missing too, remember? And Kristen told Dom she was worried she was being stalked."

Stan and Aden stared at us.

"What are you saying?" said Stan. He looked pale and gaunt. "That the killer was sending them things? Why?"

"Who knows," said Jada. She turned to Aden. "Did Rory get sent anything?"

Aden shook his head slowly. "Don't think so." He screwed up his face as he thought. "Someone sent him a picture of your headless rat, Ames."

"Harry sent it to half the school," I said. "I'll throttle him. It was traumatic enough seeing it once. It's going to be bouncing around for ever."

I could see it again – the glistening red, the raw meatiness, and the claws.

"So that's another way the crimes differed," said Jada, clearly bored with the rat conversation. "Hollie and Kristen were sent things in advance of the murders. Rory wasn't. The killer had a different motive for the third murder."

I stood up, needing space and air. "Aden, can I make a tea?"

"'Course," he said. "I'll come with you. Who else wants one?"

Jada put her hand up.

"I'll have a water, thanks," said Stan. He still looked pale and shaken. I didn't blame him. I knew that Jada just wanted to get to the bottom of this, but it was stressing me out as well.

In the kitchen, I filled up the kettle and took deep breaths.

I placed three mugs on the counter and I dropped teabags into them, and Aden filled a glass with water for Stan. As Aden poured boiling water into the mugs, he said, "Listen, Ames. What I said to you…"

"About feeling guilty about Hollie?"

"Yeah…"

"It's OK. I haven't told anyone." I went to the fridge to get out the milk. "But you shouldn't feel guilty, Aden. You weren't to blame, any more than Stan or I were."

"Thanks." He mashed the teabags against the side of the mugs. "It was stupid, declaring myself like that. It would never have worked between me and Hollie. We were too similar. Hollie was fixated on Liam – but she'd have been happier with someone like Stan."

I stared at him, the milk in my hand. "Stan?"

Aden laughed. "Yeah, they always got on well. He was quiet and she was loud. And Stan liked her too, you know."

I swallowed. We'd joked about us all being in love with Hollie – but had Stan felt more seriously about her? Had he thought there'd been hope for him and Hollie? Could he have been the one sending her flowers? He'd known about the fake date with Liam. What if he'd gone there that night? What if she'd rejected him and—

"Stan liked Hollie?" I repeated and Aden nodded.

"Besotted with her, I'd say." The doorbell rang and he looked panicked. "Can you see who it is? Journalists keep trying their luck."

Jada got to the front door half a second before me from the living room, and opened it.

It wasn't a journalist. It was Cooper.

# CHAPTER 27

"What are you doing here?" asked Jada coldly.

"What does it look like, you clown?" said Cooper. He held out a large serving dish, covered in foil. "I'm delivering food from my mum." He nodded his head at me and grinned. "All right, Amy?"

"All right, Cooper," I said. I reached out to take the dish from him, but he resisted, stepping into the house. He made his way to the kitchen. "Got something here for your family, mate," I heard him say to Aden.

Jada raised her eyebrows at me. "That guy gives me the creeps," she muttered, and I nodded. We followed Cooper into the kitchen.

"Oh. Cooper, hi," said Aden, sounding confused. "Thanks."

"My mum threads your mum's eyebrows," Cooper said, by way of explanation. "It's shepherd's pie. And she wants this dish back, so could you put it into something else so I don't have to come back and get it?"

Aden looked nonplussed, so Jada opened cupboards at random until she found a serving dish and began to decant it quickly.

"You going to wash that up now?" said Cooper.

"No," said Jada, giving him an obviously false smile. "But feel free to do it yourself." She shoved the dish back into his hands.

"All right, no need to be so aggy," he said with a smirk, taking it to the sink, and making a show of pushing back the sleeves of his dark green bomber jacket. The hot tap gushed out water too fast and he leaped back. Karma for the smirk. "FYI," he said in Jada's direction, "I'm going to be a bouncer at the event tomorrow. Harry asked if I was interested and I said I was happy to do it. Bet you ladies will be glad to have me there."

"Really?" Jada said, surprised. "Well, thanks. Appreciate that."

"No worries," said Cooper. "As I said, happy to help. My way of paying my respects to Hollie, Kristen and your brother too." He tipped his head at Aden. "It's going to be a great event, I reckon," Cooper carried on with misplaced joviality, using a tea towel to soak up the residual orange grease.

I realized that Stan had come into the kitchen. He'd

picked up his glass of water, and was hovering like a shadow next to the tall radiator. "It's a memorial, not a party," he said quietly. He was rubbing his neck as if it was stiff. Cooper ignored him.

"See you all tomorrow, then," he said. "Have a good one." He sauntered towards the front door with the dish under his arm.

"Ugh," said Jada as we heard the door shut behind him. "He thinks he's all that. And he so fancies you, Amy."

I clamped my hands to my ears to show her what I thought about that.

Aden sighed. "Nice of his mum to make that, though… I guess." He looked at the heap of unappetizing slop in the dish Jada had plonked it in and widened his eyes comically, a goofy expression of horror that was pure Aden – the old Aden, before so many terrible things had happened. "Anyone want to stay for dinner?"

We burst out laughing and I knew if I closed my eyes I would almost be able to convince myself that life hadn't changed at all.

I woke to the comforting smell of sausage rolls. Harry must have been up for ages. Grabbing my dressing gown, I went downstairs to hoover up as many as he'd let me.

He had them on three cooling racks which I guessed were for meat, vegetarian and vegan, all golden brown and unfurling every tastebud in my mouth. "I've counted them, Amy," Harry said when he saw me, his face sweaty from the steam of the oven as he placed another baking tray on top of the hob. "They're for the memorial event. You can have one from each rack. Got it? *One from each rack only.*"

Dad appeared. "The veggie ones are my favourite. The herb combination is incredible."

"Got to go," said Mum, grabbing one. "Busy day. Taking Granddad to an appointment then racing back for a late shift. Now" – she eyeballed me and Harry in turn – "promise me that you two will be sensible tonight. Anything feels off to you, call Karis – she's going to pick up and drop off and she'll have her phone on. The police will be there too. But I don't want you taking any chances."

"It's OK, Mum. We'll be fine," I said. "I really appreciate you letting me go."

Mum ignored me. "Your dad's giving everyone a lift in to school this morning. I've told Karis he'll pick up Stan. Tell Jada too. I don't like to think of her on public transport alone."

Mum hugged each of us in turn. "See you all later."

Harry went to shower, and Dad went to finish getting ready. I messaged Jada about the lift. She replied with: *Cool, thanks*, and as I was looking at my screen an Instagram notification popped up. Someone had started following me on Instagram.

It was a new account – @NewLiamHenderson. No followers yet. I could hear Dad searching for the car keys in the hallway when I got another notification: *The account wants to send you a message.*

My heart was racing but I had to see what it was. I clicked accept.

Then I read four chilling words: *See you tonight, Amy.*

# CHAPTER 28

All morning as I sat in lessons, I was thinking about that message. *See you tonight, Amy.*

What could I do? I could tell DS Haig about it, but he'd said lots of people were being targeted by these new accounts. We'd been told not to interact with them. People were setting them up for a sick laugh, not realizing how much they would be hampering the investigation by wasting police time. If I told Mum and Dad, they wouldn't let me go to the memorial event.

I didn't need to take it seriously, I told myself. But I couldn't help it. I was scared.

At lunch, I looked into the café on my way to the art room. Stan was there on his own, eating prawn cocktail crisps, looking closely at his phone, his long hair falling forward. He was never not looking at his phone these days.

Jada was at a table with Sabine and others, talking intently, clearly going over plans for later.

I wanted to tell them both about the creepy message, but something stopped me. I stepped out of the way of Hussein coming in and walked away.

In the art room, I kept my head down, doodling on a piece of A4 paper with a set of coloured pencils, most of which needed sharpening, hoping I was giving off strong "leave-me-alone" energy.

"You all right, Amy?" said someone. Cooper.

"Oh, piss off," I said. I was already on-edge, anxious, and he was the last thing I needed.

Cooper came closer. He stuck his thumbs in his front jeans pockets, and stood with his shoulders back, casually aggressive. "Show me a bit of respect, Amy," he said. He was smiling but there was a mocking look in his eyes.

I gave a hollow laugh. "Respect you? Why, exactly?"

His expression darkened. "I'm your brother's friend."

"Oh, OK, in that case," I said sarcastically. I balled up my piece of paper. "Excuse me, Cooper, I've got somewhere better to be."

"All right. See you tonight, Amy," he called as I left at speed, making sure the door banged shut behind me.

After school, Harry and I got ready for the memorial at our house. He set out three large Tupperware containers

265

of sausage rolls. I swapped my jeans and dark green sweatshirt for my brightest multicoloured top with a red mini skirt and turquoise tights, borrowed from Mum, and black ankle boots, and Harry wore all black as requested by Jada for his bouncer role. Then it was time for Karis to pick us up.

When we got in the car, she gave us a thin smile. I saw Stan was wearing the green Hawaiian shirt he wore for special occasions with his regular black jeans. I'd been with him when he bought the shirt in May half-term, in between revising. I remembered everything about that shopping day – the way he'd taken ages to choose between the green shirt and the pinky-red one. The browsing in the Apple Store, the strawberry milkshakes and how we'd shared a chocolate chip cookie. Simple stuff that had made us happy.

"Let me know when you want picking up," said Karis, as we climbed out of the car, each of us carrying a Tupperware. Harry looked warm in his lined black leather jacket, but Stan and I shivered in our thin clothing, hoping the venue would be warm. "Have fun." She sounded absent-minded and I wondered if she'd forgotten what this event was for.

The cricket pavilion was swathed in fairy lights and seemed almost magical in the misty air. Two women sat in puffa coats at a table on the wooden veranda, with a list that was a few pages long. We gave her our names and she ticked them off the list. "I'm Loretta Simmonds, Jada's mum, and this is my sister, Jada's Auntie Joy," said the woman. "You let us know if you're worried about anything tonight."

"I'm one of the bouncers," said Harry.

Loretta said, "I'd give you a hug, young man, if you weren't carrying whatever it is you've got there."

"Sausage rolls," said Harry. Loretta beamed.

"Save me one, will you? Communal food goes on the table upstairs. Oh, and, kids?"

We stopped and she raised a stern finger. "No drinking, understand?"

We nodded meekly.

"And just to let you know we're aware of the rumours and they're rubbish," said Loretta.

"What rumours?" asked Stan, speaking for the first time. He sounded hoarse.

"Accounts on social media have been saying the killer would show up tonight," said Loretta.

"Geez," said Harry, with a nervous laugh. "Am I going to need a stab-proof jacket?"

Loretta shook her head. "The police are happy for us to go ahead," she said. "It's all safe." But I could see that her eyes were worried.

I elbowed Harry to tell him to shut up, and pushed him through the door.

Inside there were more fairy lights, making up for the fact that the club had the feel of an old man's pub with dark furniture and a bar which had its grill pulled down shut.

On the walls there were multiple photocopied photos of Hollie, Kristen and Rory, including my collage. Three people whose lives had been cruelly and prematurely taken. I held back a sob. The room was slowly filling. Stan melted away after handing me the Tupperware he was holding, mumbling about the toilet, and Harry and I went up the narrow wooden staircase at the back of the room, and came out into a room with a second bar, also closed. It was colder up here because two sets of rickety glass doors leading to a balcony were open. A group from my year, including Jake, were out there singing what sounded like two different tunes. He waved at us drunkenly, and I wondered how he'd got past Jada's mum. There was no sign of Jada herself.

This room was thinly carpeted apart from an area of wooden flooring, where I imagined people like my parents danced with their arms flailing about when it was rented out for parties and charity dos. There was a long table with a paper tablecloth on it and a few plastic bowls of crisps and olives and a plate of nuggets of unlabelled origin. Three two-litre bottles of soft drinks stood at one end with plastic glasses. Harry put his Tupperware boxes down, opened the lids and retrieved three folded over pieces of cardboard from the pocket of his jacket. With a calligraphy pen he'd written *organic meat, organic veg, vegan*. He arranged them neatly in front of the boxes, stood back and took a photo. "You don't think it would be disrespectful to post this on the blog, do you?" he asked.

I shook my head and reached for a crisp. I wasn't hungry but I didn't know what else there was to do.

Jada emerged from a door of what looked like a cupboard. Her hair was in a half-up, half-down style and she wore a thigh-length tight pink dress with glittery high heels. She smiled at me. "Amy, I'm glad you're here." Then she turned all business again. "Help. Can't get the music working."

We followed her into the tiny room which was essentially a junk room that housed, among lots of random things, a sound system. Between us, Harry and I managed to sync it to Jada's phone and Taylor Swift's "Champagne Problems" blared out, one of Hollie's favourites. Jada and I looked at each other with glistening eyes. We'd sung this loudly with Hollie at her house only a few weeks ago.

"I hate this song now," I said, and the two of us fell into a hug, clinging to each other, crying.

"I've got to go and check Mum and Auntie Joy are OK," said Jada, pulling away. "Harry, could you take over on the door so they can come inside and warm up?"

"Sure," said Harry and headed off towards the stairs. Jada pulled the cupboard-room door shut as we walked out. "I'll get the microphone sorted. I thought it would be nice for people to have the chance to speak about their memories of Hollie, Kristen and Rory."

"Jake will hog it complaining about the police investigation and how everyone should get down to Markham Police Station for a DNA test," I said, looking out to the balcony where he was yelling to someone on the grass below.

Jada said, "Good point — we don't want people like him going off-piste. I'll time people. What d'you reckon? Three minutes each?"

"Nah, two. Max," I said. My phone vibrated and I tentatively took it out of my jeans pocket, worried it was another message from "Liam". Instead, it was Dom. He was waiting for me outside. "I'll come down with you," I said.

Jada took my hands. "Thanks again for coming. I didn't realize how much I needed you here. You, Aden and Stan. Sorry I've been a cow recently. I just miss Hollie so much. You let me into your group and I should have been nicer."

I gave her a half-smile. "To be fair, *Hollie* brought you into our group and we always did what she wanted."

Jada laughed. "I know I didn't know her as well as you, and I bet you think I've been presumptuous doing this." She waved her hands round. "But I'm someone who needs to *do* things. Doing things helps with the pain." I nodded; I understood. "Promise you'll stand up and say something during the open mic? Speak about Hollie. Say what she meant to you."

"Hmm…"

"I'll give you whichever slot you want. First?"

"Second," I said. "After you."

She smiled and we went downstairs. There was a group of five parents who had volunteered to help out, standing together in a clump, nervously watching the room, which was rapidly filling with people. It was like being watched over at the Year Six disco all over again – except now they weren't looking out for kids who'd eaten too much sugar. They were here to protect them from a person who had already killed three times.

Sixth formers were arriving, sitting at tables, spreading out food between them, pouring drinks and chatting in low voices. People looked over their shoulders, darted worried glances. Everyone was on edge. I saw Stan with a group from our psychology class, not making an effort to talk. He was watching the room like a hawk in between glances at his phone.

Hussein was walking around with a large camera round his neck, taking photos of anyone who would let him. A girl from my economics class carrying a tray on which there was a large flat cake covered with chocolate icing and Haribo rings stopped to pose for a photo. "I was on the hockey team with Kristen," she said to Hussein. "She'd eat Haribo rings, like, all the time. It's my way to remember her."

I headed outside to find Dom. Dom was shivering without a jacket near the cricket pitch. He looked nervous too, I thought. I wanted to kiss him full on, while cupping his head lightly, feeling the softness of his hair, before tracing his sharp jawline.

Instead, I gave an awkward wave. "Good to see you," I said.

"How are you doing?" he asked. He adjusted his backpack, and I heard bottles clinking. The memory of whisky splashed across Aden's kitchen wall flashed into my head.

"Not too bad," I said. I took his hand and led him to the pavilion. "Tick Dom's name off, will you?" I called to Harry, noting that Cooper was here too now. He'd slicked his hair back, which wasn't a look that did him any favours and he gave me a wink which I'd never be able to unsee.

"Hold it just a minute," said Cooper officiously, blocking the entrance. He stared at Dom. "You're Ivy Green. You're all nobs. You can't come in."

"He's on the list," I said, rolling my eyes at Dom.

Cooper scowled. "Well, you can wait in line like everyone else," he snapped at Dom.

I tried to catch Harry's eye, but he was busy searching the guest list for a name and hadn't heard. We walked to the end of the line and I was aware of people staring at me. I was still the girl who had tricked her friend into going to the park that night, to her death.

Maybe I always would be.

# CHAPTER 29

Dom and I had almost reached the front of the queue when a ripple went through everyone waiting. Ms Reid was walking up to the porch. She looked quite different in jeans, a burgundy misshapen jumper and Doc Martens – but it was the boy next to her who was attracting the attention.

He was tall and muscular, with dark eyes and hair and strong features; he was wearing perfect fit jeans and a navy Nike sweatshirt. He also looked as if the cricket pavilion was the last place he wanted to be.

"That's my teacher," I said. "And that must be her son Michael." Who was approximately a hundred per cent more handsome than I'd expected.

"Hello, Harry. Hi, Cooper," Ms Reid said. "Hope it's OK for us to push in. We're looking for Jada – Amy, you'll show me where she is, won't you? Michael is going to help out a bit tonight." Cooper glared but he had no choice but to nod and let us past.

"Of course," I said, tugging Dom inside and smirking at Cooper. "Happy to."

Dom stopped abruptly as soon as we were inside the pavilion. I followed his gaze and saw he was looking at a big photo of Kristen smiling as if she'd just heard the news she'd been cast as the lead in a play. "Oh, god," he said. "I didn't think it would be this hard."

I pointed Jada out to Ms Reid and then turned to Dom. "Let's go up to the balcony," I said encouragingly. "The views are nice. You can see into the allotments."

"Sounds wild," said Dom, but he followed me through the open doors and we squashed up against the railing, next to some of Rory's friends who were talking about the time they'd been standing on this exact spot with Rory, watching a cricket tournament.

Dom reached into his backpack and pulled out a bottle of beer and offered it to me. I shook my head – I didn't feel like it tonight. I could see uniformed police officers talking to people outside the pavilion, and the shadows in the allotments beyond. Above us, the darkening sky was streaked with clouds, stringy like stretched chewing gum. I huddled closer to Dom, breathing in his smell of fresh clothing and beer. He told me about a football match he'd played in at lunchtime. I listened to the sound of his voice rather than the individual words, but I understood that he'd scored one of the two goals and his team had won.

"I got a message from one of the fake Liam Henderson accounts this evening," I said suddenly, knowing I was bringing the mood down but unable to stop. "It said: *See you tonight*."

Dom squeezed my shoulder. "I'm sorry. I've heard there are loads of those accounts springing up at the moment. It's impossible to get them shut down. But I won't let anything happen to you, Ames. Nobody would be stupid enough to do anything at this event with the police here."

I nodded. I wished I could feel safe, but I didn't. In spite of the police, the parents and Dom, standing right beside me, I felt on edge. Watched. Not that I would ever have admitted that to anyone. I looked around at the crowd and felt an unpleasant tingle up my spine. Was the killer out there in the darkness, waiting to strike? Or were they here in the club itself? Was it someone I knew, someone I walked past every day?

"Amy. You're shivering," said Dom.

"Let's go downstairs and warm up. Wish I'd brought a coat."

It was crowded downstairs but I saw two free chairs on the edge of a table of Year Thirteens. Too late, I saw they were friends of Kristen's, which meant Dom knew them. This might be awkward for both of us.

"How ya doing, Dom?" called one of them. Her name was Saskia.

"All right, yeah. You?" he said quietly.

"It's been pretty rough," said Saskia. She lowered her voice. "You were one of the last people to see Kristen alive, weren't you?"

"I was, yeah," said Dom. "I went with her to her grandma's funeral."

"She was made up about that," said Saskia. "She was proper gutted when you two finished."

They talked quietly, Saskia ignoring me.

I looked round. One of the police officers was speaking into their radio by the door. *Everything is OK,* I told myself. It was safe. I could say that over and over but it wouldn't change the anxiety in my chest.

I noticed that Aden had arrived. He was in a corner talking to Stan, pain etched on his face, holding a can of Coke. I was glad he wasn't drinking beer. People were glancing at him – he hadn't been at school since Rory died and now they didn't know how to be with him, whether to hug, talk or give him space. I watched Ms Reid go up to him and give him a warm hug. Stan saw me looking and his eyes darted away. He looked nervous. No, more than nervous. Keyed up. Almost excited.

*Why?* I wondered. Was it the same anxiety and grief we all felt – or something else? Guilt? I remembered Harry's words in the kitchen. *"I know you won't want to hear this but – could it be Stan sending the messages?"*

I shook off the thought as the music cut off mid-song and everyone stopped speaking to see what was going on. Jada walked to our end of the room with a microphone, kicked off her high heels and climbed up on to a chair with the help of her mum and Auntie Joy.

"Hey, everyone!" she called.

A few people called back, "Hey."

"I hope tonight is letting you guys remember our friends in the way they would have wanted," said Jada. "Because that's what it's all about. On that note, there's a mic here and I hope some of you will come up and spend a few minutes talking about Hollie, Kristen or Rory. What you remember about them, what you miss, what made you laugh. I'll start, then it's" – she looked round the room and saw me – "Amy, and then anybody else who wants to speak can line up here." She looked out at the crowd. "Let's remember our friends," she said softly, "*our* way."

Slowly, hesitantly, people began to gather around.

I saw Harry and Cooper by the door which was shut now. At the back of the room, the parents stood in a line next to one of the police officers, the one who'd been on his radio. I guessed the other one was stationed outside. Harry gave me a small wave and a thumbs up.

I went over and stood beside Jada. I hadn't thought about what I was going to say. There were over a hundred people here, maybe more. Ms Reid beamed at me and Hussein was standing in a prominent position with his camera. My legs wouldn't stop shaking and I wished I'd gone to the toilet. This was my GCSE French oral all over again.

Jada spoke about how kind Hollie had been when she'd started at Markham High, and what a fun person she was, and how they'd had such a laugh in their Eng lit lessons, and how she'd never do anything half-measures. One of her enduring memories of Hollie would be her dressed as a pumpkin on orange-themed day, not caring that she was the only one in full fancy dress while everyone else was just wearing a token splash of orange in a scarf, nail varnish or socks.

"Hollie welcomed me into her friendship group – they all did," she said, taking my hand and squeezing it. "I realized they liked to play pranks on each other. Isn't that right, Ames?" I nodded, a lump forming in my throat. "It was mostly Hollie coming up with the pranks, to be fair, but it was never malicious. She wouldn't have wanted her friends to be punished for what happened." There was a faint murmuring from the crowd, which sounded supportive. "It made things fun." Jada paused. "Hollie showed us that life didn't have to be bleak and boring, and all about CVs and personal statements. She showed us how to live in a light-hearted way and I'll always be grateful to her for that."

Someone near the front started clapping and faint applause rang out. Jada grinned through tears. "I didn't know Kristen and Rory well, but I can tell from how many of you are here how loved they were. I'll let you all share your memories. But first, Amy – you're up." She handed me the mic.

Jada's mum took my hand and somehow got me up on the chair. I felt dizzy and my hands clutching the mic were sweaty. Fairy lights seemed to sway and blur. I could see Harry through the crowd, looking worried. Dom, frowning. Aden gave me a quick, encouraging nod.

"Hollie and I became friends in Year Seven," I said. My voice sounded small and shaky. "Remember when we had to work on dances in groups of four and perform them to half the year group?" I pulled a traumatized face. "There was a ripple through the crowd, of people remembering and laughing. "But I lucked out because I was in a group with Hollie, Aden and Stan. We just clicked and spent the whole time laughing. Didn't practise at all, we were having too much fun. But because we had Hollie, who was a serious dancer, we managed to pull off a few stellar moves and win." Somebody in the crowd whooped. A few people were holding up phones, recording me and it was making me flustered. "I know people have a lot to say about the prank we played on Hollie the night she…" I swallowed. "… the night she died. What they don't understand is that it's what we did. We played jokes on each other. It was never meant to be mean. I'd do anything to take it back, but…" The room went out of focus. "But I can't. I made a terrible mistake and—" I gulped in more air to keep going, my heart was pumping too fast, and I felt myself sway.

Someone grabbed my hand and squeezed it. I looked

down gratefully into Auntie Joy's face. She helped me off the chair and hugged me against her huge floaty floral top.

"There's only one person responsible for your friend's death," she murmured. "And it's not you."

# CHAPTER 30

In the uneasy silence, Jada said, "Thank you, Amy. We know how much you loved Hollie and how hard it was for you to speak about her in front of everyone, so we appreciate it."

Auntie Joy sat me down next to her and rubbed my back until my racing heart became steadier. Jada called Dom up to speak about Kristen. He spoke smoothly, his words flowing, explaining how much she'd meant to him, how her family had been everything to her, especially her grandma. His voice was full of pain and regret.

Then one of Rory's friends went up to speak. Dom came and sat next to me. He was trembling.

"That was so hard, wasn't it?" I whispered to him.

"Yeah," he said. His jaw was set. As Kyra climbed on to the chair, he said, "I have to go."

"I'll come with you," I said. I was meant to wait for Karis but I'd had enough too.

Dom shook his head. "Amy, I'm sorry. I need to be on my own."

"But you can't," I said. "No one's supposed to be out on their own at the moment."

What I meant was that I wanted him to stay with me.

"I'll call my dad when I'm outside," he whispered. "I'll see you soon." He gave me a brief hug as I analysed his words, *see you soon*, vague and unsatisfactory.

I could see Harry by the door and went over, realizing too late that Cooper was there too.

"What's up with your boyf?" asked Cooper. "Come outside and have a drink with Uncle Coop."

I wanted fresh air but the last thing I wanted was to be alone with Cooper. "Harry, you'll come outside for a bit too, won't you?" I said pointedly.

"Sure," said Harry. "We shouldn't be drinking, though."

"Don't be a wuss," said Cooper.

The three of us slipped out. The police officer who'd been outside was in the car park talking to another officer through the window of a patrol car. I could hear them laughing. Cooper produced a small bottle of whisky from his jacket pocket and once we'd sat down on the porch steps, me making sure Harry was in the middle between us, I wasn't too proud to take a sip.

It numbed my tongue and burned my throat. A large fluffy scarf had been left on the decking and I wrapped it round myself.

"It's good stuff," said Cooper. "It's what my nan drinks. She pays a fortune for it." He leaned round Harry who took a swallow and coughed. "By the way, my nan knows you."

"How?" I asked, bemused.

"She lives in the flats where you feed some old guy's cat. I only know because he was complaining about you."

"Mr Peaty? She knows Mr Peaty?" I said.

"Yup. Mr Peaty, that's the one." Cooper snorted. "Apparently you left him a nice little welcome-home present on his mat the other day!"

The cat poo. So, all this time, Cooper had known about it. My head buzzed with alarm.

"Nan is devoted to her cat," said Cooper. "You know those all grey, very furry cats with pissed-off expressions? She's got one of them. She doesn't like Mr Peaty's cat at all. Says he's ugly." He laughed.

"Don't diss that cat," said Harry sternly. "Ames is very fond of Hector."

I shivered. I didn't really think Cooper had been sending me those messages, did I? I glanced at my phone. No. Thirty minutes of this event to get through, then I'd be back in Karis's warm car, then home.

"Harry and I have been watching Suspicious Stan," said Cooper, nudging me.

"Suspicious Stan?" I said absently. "What do you mean?"

"Have you noticed he's been on his phone all night? Messaging. Looking dodgy. Well stressed. Guilty, you might say." He leaned closer to me past Harry and I could smell his sour breath. "It's always the quiet ones, Ames."

Jada came outside. "You all right, Amy? We're winding down now. Guys, fancy helping me clear up?" She handed Cooper a black bin bag, leaving him no option. "One of you could hand round the rest of the food too."

"She's so bossy," muttered Cooper. "Needs taking down a peg."

I went inside, leaving the scarf on a chair to be claimed by its owner, and went upstairs to where most of the sausage rolls had been eaten, which would please Harry. There were still full bowls of crisps, some ragged pieces of cake and a tub with some broken cookies inside.

Downstairs Loretta and Joy were talking to Ms Reid, and her son Michael was speaking quietly into his phone, one finger in his ear to block out the noise. The other parents were sitting at a table, looking more relaxed now the event was ending and no killer had made an appearance. The police officer who'd been on his radio had disappeared somewhere.

I could see Stan and Aden still sitting together, but both were on their phones. I tidied the food away, dumping it into bin bags and stacking the Tupperwares. I looked again at Stan and Aden, both locked in their own worlds. At Ms Reid now sweeping up some broken glass. Then I stopped.

Something wasn't right. Someone was here who wasn't meant to be.

There. There, sitting at a table in the corner with an older guy, was Liam Henderson.

Liam looked up and our eyes locked. His gaze was cool and defiant despite having snuck in without being on the list. He said something to the guy next to him, who looked at me with interest. Then he waved me over.

If he was going to make a scene, I was ready.

"Hey," I said as I reached them. I stayed standing. I tried to keep the anger out of my voice and sound calm, like Jada. "You shouldn't be here, Liam."

"I'm Will," said the guy next to Liam. He put his hand out for me to shake. "Nice to meet you, Amy."

So Liam had already told him who I was. Perhaps he didn't need to be told. "Why are you here?" I asked, ignoring Will moving closer.

"Wanted to pay our respects," said Liam. "Will's a … mate. I was telling him about the Markham Murders."

"Hadn't you heard about them before Liam told you?" I asked with an edge of sarcasm. I hated the phrase "Markham Murders".

"Of course," said Will easily. "Liam was telling me about how it started with the prank you played on Hollie Linton, using his official BubbleSpeak account. Must have been distressing, Amy. Tell me about it?"

Realization hit me. "You're a journalist." I turned to Liam. "You brought a *journalist* to a private memorial event?"

# CHAPTER 31

Liam looked away, fidgeting uncomfortably, but Will nodded.

"That's right," he said smoothly. "I'm doing a piece about Liam's year in tennis and I thought it would be of interest to include how he found himself caught up in the Markham Murders." He gestured to a seat. "Sit down, Amy. I'd hate to get the facts wrong. It would be good if you could clear up a few things for me. Set the record straight, as it were. I know you've had a rough ride."

I sat down heavily. There was no reason I had to talk to him, but after the last article about me, I did want to set the record straight – as briefly as possible.

I placed my phone pointedly on the table and pressed record. Will gave a faint smile.

"Whose idea was the prank?" he asked. "Yours or Stan's?"

"I don't remember," I said. I couldn't see another phone on the table but I had no doubt he was recording our conversation too.

Will nodded slowly. "You sure?"

My stomach heaved. This reminded me of my initial conversation with DS Haig. The truth was, I did remember – it had been Stan's idea to do the prank, and his idea to keep it going when I had wanted to stop. *But that meant nothing*, I told myself.

"We feel terrible about what happened. Really terrible, and would turn back time if we could. That's all I'm going to say." I sounded prim but better that than saying something I'd regret.

Will nodded. "I heard you're in regular contact with DS Haig."

I recoiled. "Who did you hear that from?"

"Come on, Amy. Everyone knows you're the one who put the police on to the social media angle when they were still running around, arresting the wrong guy. Perhaps you've got some theories of your own about the killer?"

"I know the same as anyone else," I said carefully. "But what about you? Any journalistic insight into the case? You must know more than me." Flattery could work both ways.

"Will's got a contact in the police who's familiar with the case," said Liam and I almost laughed because he sounded so superior and pumped up about his new mate who wasn't a mate at all.

"I do know the police have been looking for a bracelet Hollie was wearing when she left home," said Will, watching me closely. "It was a gold chain one. Wasn't found at the scene. Kristen was also missing a pin badge from her jacket collar—" He broke off, frowning. "What's wrong?"

"I gave Hollie that bracelet," I said. I pressed my hand against my eye to stop a tear from falling.

"You did?" said Will. His eyes were shiny with something that might have been excitement. "That's tragic."

"The whole thing is a nightmare for everyone," said Liam, trying to shift the attention back to him. "But it's been really hard for *me*. You can quote me on that."

I got to my feet. I hoped Will *would* quote him; it would show him up for the utter self-absorbed jerk he was.

"Don't go, Amy," Will said persuasively. "Give me your number. We can pick this up—"

"What are you doing?" Ms Reid's son Michael was standing beside me but he was talking to Will. "Are you a journalist? Because this isn't the place."

"Mate," said Liam, standing up. "Who even are you?"

Michael raised an eyebrow and considered him. He was taller than Liam and broader. "My mum works at Markham High," he said.

Liam sniggered.

"You two should leave," said Michael calmly, but stepping closer.

The two of them squared up to each other as Will backed away fast. I heard someone, possibly Jake, yell, "Fight! Fight!"

Ms Reid strode up behind Michael, watched by the group of parents. She had on her you-have-crossed-a-line face. "Get them out of here, Michael," she said. "Quietly, though." She heaped a look full of scorn on Will, then Liam. "You should be ashamed. This is a memorial event."

Jada came up to me. "What was all that about? Thought it was safe to take a toilet break and I miss a fight?"

"Liam and a journalist got in," I said. I suddenly felt exhausted. "Listen, Jada, I'm going to go soon. You've done an amazing job tonight. Hollie would have been really proud of you."

"It means a lot that you said that. Thank you. Come here." We hugged and she said, almost shyly, "I hope we can be friends? Real friends."

"Yeah, I hope so too," I said. I looked over at Stan and Aden. "Need to check that Stan's ready to go. His mum is giving me and Harry a lift home. I haven't spoken to Aden yet either." I walked across the room. "Hi, Aden. How are you doing?"

He put down his phone and gave me a tired smile. "Holding up, just about. Rory's mate Tom is driving me home."

"Sounds good," I said. I turned to Stan. His knee was bouncing up and down – he seemed keyed up still.

"You OK, Amy?" he said.

"Yeah, you?" I asked.

"You still getting messages?" he asked, his eyes locking on to mine.

I held my hand up to stop the conversation. This wasn't the place. "Let's not talk about them now."

"You ready to go home?" he asked, almost urgently. "I'll give Mum a shout."

"Sure," I said. "I'll round up Harry." I stood to go but, over Stan's shoulder, I saw the message he was writing – and it wasn't to his mum.

*Yeah. Bench by the lake. 20 mins?*

I moved away, my mind in overdrive, my heart thudding.

There was only one lake in Markham and that was in Kingsley Park. Stan was meeting someone there, at night.

It sounded frighteningly familiar.

Was he meeting a girl? A girl he had messaged, pretending to be someone else? Liam Henderson, the good-looking celebrity he could never be?

I stumbled away, mind still racing. Had I been in denial about Stan all this time? Was he the one behind these messages, these murders – quiet, unassuming Stanley Maloney, who had barely even had a girlfriend? I went to the toilet to splash water on my face, blotting it away with a green paper towel, taking big breaths in and out.

I'd speak to him. If I did it with lots of people present, there was nothing to be frightened of.

As I emerged, Aden passed me, swept along with Rory's friends, who were squeezing his shoulders, ruffling his hair, bantering to distract him from the winding down of his brother's memorial event. In a daze, I watched him leave with Rory's friend Tom. I could see Cooper high-fiving someone, Harry chatting to Sabine, Stan—

I froze. I realized then – I couldn't see Stan at the table.

Loretta and Joy and the other parents were bustling round with rubbish bags and a broom. One of the police officers was laughing with Ms Reid. Jada and Sabine were perfunctorily wiping tables with faded blue J-cloths. I went upstairs, then back downstairs. Stan was definitely missing.

"Where did Stan go?" I asked Jada.

"Outside?" she said. "Some people were talking about letting off fireworks. I'm keeping out of it."

I raced outside, along with a crowd of others. It was hard to see who was out there in the dim lighting from the veranda. The temperature had dropped even further and people were huddled together in little groups. Suddenly there was a loud bang and everyone screamed. Bright clusters of lights lit up the cricket pitch and people laughed, knowing that it was just a firework.

"No more fireworks!" a police officer called. The patrol car had gone and he seemed to be on his own, aside from some panicked-looking parents. He ran across the grass to a group who were squatting down, pushing fireworks into the ground. "This isn't safe," he said loudly. "Stand well back, everyone."

I spotted Harry and Cooper on the edge of the pitch. "The cricket club is not going to be happy," Harry was saying as I came up behind him.

"They'll be so pissed off," agreed Cooper with a laugh. "This'll be the last time they rent it out to a load of teenagers."

"Have you seen Stan?" I asked, out of breath.

"No. Why?" asked Cooper, turning to face me. He squared his shoulders. "What's he done?"

"Nothing. Nothing," I said, backing away.

"Are you OK, Ames?" Harry said.

"I'm not sure," I said. A bad feeling was growing in my chest, pressing down on me. I'd ignored so many red flags. I pulled away and ran back into the pavilion. It was pretty much empty apart from Loretta and Joy who were stacking chairs and a couple from Year Thirteen who were slow dancing to Tom Odell. I went upstairs, scoured the balcony, came down and burst into the men's toilets. They were completely empty.

Stan had vanished.

I'd seen that message with my own eyes: *Yeah. Bench by the lake. 20 mins?* Was that where he'd gone – Kingsley Park?

I tried his phone. It went straight to voicemail.

I called Karis who said, "Hi, Amy! Are you ready for me to come and pick you all up?"

I didn't know what to say because she'd already told me what I wanted to know. That Stan hadn't called her.

"Um. I just wanted to say we're going to stay a bit later. Is that OK?"

"Of course," said Karis. "Just call me when you're ready."

I went back outside to find the police officer, who was looking increasingly harassed.

"What's up?" he asked, holding out his arm as if he was directing traffic, trying to move people away from the cricket pitch.

"I saw someone write a weird message," I said weakly.

He frowned. "What did it say?"

"*Yeah. Bench by the lake. 20 mins?*" I said. It sounded silly said out loud. The bench by the lake was known as a romantic place to sit. Lots of old people liked to sit there, hand in hand.

"Ohh," he said, elongating the word. "One of those messages. We've had so many reports tonight. We'd just advise everyone to go straight home and stay safe. Is an adult picking you up?"

"Yeah – but my friend's gone missing," I said. "It's Stan Maloney. He hasn't gone home. We were meant to be picked up together."

*Bang.* A firework went off, whistling and flying low over our heads. The officer's head jerked around.

"I'm sorry. This situation is getting out of hand. Call the helpline if you're worried," he said. He turned and yelled. "Everyone is to clear the cricket pitch. NOW."

I was on my own.

# CHAPTER 32

There was only one person left who could help.

I ran to Harry, who was making his way back to the pavilion with Cooper.

"What's up, Ames?" he said. He squinted at me. "Are you OK?"

"I need to talk to you," I said. "Now. Alone."

Cooper shrugged and hung back.

"What is it?" said Harry. "You look like you've seen a ghost."

"I saw Stan sending a message, arranging to meet someone at Kingsley Park. By the bench by the lake in twenty minutes. That was about ten, maybe fifteen, minutes ago." I gulped air. "Why is he meeting someone at the park when we're supposed to be going home?"

Harry frowned. "What are you saying, Ames?"

"I'm scared that you were right. That Stan's the one who's been messaging girls, who showed up to meet Hollie, who messaged Kristen…"

"You serious?" Harry looked shocked. I expected him to tell me he'd been right all along, but he stood there with his mouth partially open, staring at me.

"I – I think so," I said. "What if there's about to be another murder?"

Harry gathered himself. "When did Stan leave?"

"It can only have been a few minutes ago. There's still time if we go there now…"

"We should call the police," Harry said.

"Let's call them on the way," I said frantically. "Not that they'll be interested. Come on – we don't have time to waste. It's only ten minutes if we run…"

"All right." Harry looked at his shiny black shoes which had last seen action at our uncle's wedding. "Not sure I can run very fast in these."

"Well, try."

Harry and I ran down the gravel track and left on to the main road, his shiny shoes slipping on the pavement. "You really think this is a good idea?" he gasped.

"I might be overreacting, but I've got a bad feeling," I said. "Everyone thought something was going to happen tonight at the memorial – but what if Stan was just using it as a distraction to plan another meet up?"

Harry clutched his stomach. "Urgh, running after

drinking whisky is not fun." He straightened up, and said, "All right, let's go."

We didn't speak again until we saw the gates of the park up ahead; we slowed down and caught our breath. Although I'd been running, my bare arms were chilled. I rubbed them as I walked, wishing I still had that scarf. The gates were padlocked together, cold to the touch. The elaborate ironwork had plenty of potential footholds and looked easy to climb. If you weren't wearing a mini skirt.

"D'you really think Stan is in there?" said Harry, peering into the darkness.

"I don't know," I said. I was starting to think maybe I *had* overreacted. Maybe I'd misunderstood the message. Maybe Stan was waiting for me back at the pavilion, getting annoyed. I checked my phone: there was nothing.

Harry hesitated. "I can climb over and take a quick look?"

"I'll come too," I said.

Harry shook his head. "No. Stay here. Call DS Haig on that number he gave you. Tell him about the message you saw, and that Stan's been acting strangely." He tapped his back pocket where his phone was. "Message me if you need me. It's on silent."

I shivered in my thin clothes. "OK. Can I borrow your jacket? It'll be easier for you to climb the gate without it."

He shrugged his leather jacket off and handed it to me. It felt warm, heavy and oversized on me, comforting. I watched him haul himself up and over the gate. He gave me a thumbs up on the other side, then put his finger to his lips and slipped into the darkness.

With terrifying speed, Harry was swallowed up by the dark and all I could see were the silhouettes of the trees and a round area of tarmac which turned into a stony path. It was silent apart from the occasional car driving on the road past me and the swish of the leaves in the light wind. No bird song, no human voices. Peak creepiness.

I fumbled for my phone and called DS Haig's number, pacing up and down in front of the gates. It went straight to voicemail, to his deep, calm voice. I pictured him at the pub with his police mates. Was he looking at his phone, thinking, *Not her again*. He'd assured me he listened to his messages regularly. How regular was regular?

Mouth dry, I spoke softly and urgently into my phone. "It's Amy Mathews. I know this sounds stupid, but I'm at Kingsley Park with my brother. We're worried that it was Stan Maloney messaging the girls. I saw a message tonight on his phone agreeing to meet someone at the bench by the lake in twenty minutes. That was over twenty minutes ago. He's been acting a bit weirdly recently and…" I hesitated. What else could I say? "Er, can you come? Thanks."

I hung up. Then I waited by the gate, checking my phone constantly. I thought I heard the flapping of ducks on the lake and the creak of a tall tree as the wind picked up.

I stuck my cold hands into the pockets of Harry's jacket, trying to warm them. The lining was smooth but there was something in the pocket. I pulled it out. A necklace.

No; it wasn't a necklace.

It was a gold-link bracelet that I recognized. The bracelet I had given Hollie for her sixteenth birthday.

My heart slammed against my ribcage. I put my hand in again cautiously and felt something else, something small and hard. An enamel pin badge – a pair of red sparkly shoes.

Hollie's bracelet. Kristen's badge.

I sank to the ground.

If these things were in Harry's pocket, that meant—

"Stan!" I shouted, stumbling to my feet. "Stan!"

I shoved the bracelet, the badge and my phone back into the jacket pocket and hitched my mini skirt higher so I could move. I climbed the gate, ripping Mum's tights against a rough bit of iron, holding on with sweaty hands. I landed awkwardly on the tarmac and ran to the path.

There were several turn-offs for the lake. I took the first, running past thorny bushes and thick-trunked trees, faster and faster, the sound of my own panting echoing inside my head. There was the lake. Shiny black water, rippled with reflections.

The bench was round the next curve in the path.

I stopped. I couldn't see anyone, but there were plenty of dark bushes to hide in, plenty of shadows to conceal.

"Stan?" I screamed. "Harry? Where are you?"

My eyes had adjusted to the dark and now they snapped back to a shape on the ground, between the bench and the lake. A human shape. I recognized the bagginess of the shirt, the shoulder-length hair. "Stan!" I shouted as I ran towards him. "Stan!" He lay face down on the damp grass, motionless.

I crouched and tried to roll him over. His body was surprisingly heavy. I'd done first aid instead of PE last year. I needed to get him into the recovery position or he might choke.

As I turned him over, I saw that his eyes were closed. His neck was sticky with something – with blood. A knife dropped from his limp fingers on to the grass.

"Stan, it's Amy," I said, through gasps, vaguely remembering I had to speak to the patient because they might be able to hear you even when they were unconscious. "I'm going to apply some pressure and try and stop the bleeding. Remember I did that first-aid course? Then I'll call an ambulance. It'll be OK, Stan."

With clumsy, bloody fingers, I wriggled out of the jacket, folding it so the cotton lining was outwards, and I held it against Stan's neck, scared to push too hard in case I blocked his airway. Then, with stiff fingers, I took out my phone and dialled 999—

I felt a sharp pain on the back of my head and then nothing.

When I came round, I was lying on the sandy gravel path. Harry's face swum into my vision.

I stared up at my brother. The face of a killer. He looked nothing like himself – he was hard and angry and wild. There was blood all over his T-shirt and hands.

"I told you to wait," he shouted, spit gathering at the corner of his mouth. "Why didn't you wait, Amy?"

"You wanted me to think it was Stan," I sobbed. I thought of the knife that had been in Stan's hand. Harry must have placed it there after...

"You never listen," hissed Harry. "That's your problem."

I thought of the branch coming down on Hollie's head, the hammer-like object, which had never been found, making contact with Kristen's head, and I flinched. I'd never finished calling 999.

"Help!" I cried hysterically into the night. "Someone, help me!"

"Stop it! Stop it!" screamed Harry. "You're making this worse." He spoke more quietly. "I didn't want to hurt you, Amy, you know that, right?" I blinked hard to get rid of my tears; I needed to be able to see. I needed to keep myself together.

"You weren't meant to be in the park," said Harry. He wiped his face, leaving a trail of blood and dirt. "I did all I could to protect you. I was going to keep you safe. The others had to die, but you didn't."

I quietly scooped up two handfuls of earth and gravel. I counted down in my head.

*Three.*

"I never meant for any of this to happen."

*Two.*

"But this was your fault, Amy—"

*One.*

I threw both handfuls of earth and stones into his eyes, rolled sideways and pushed myself up. My legs were wobbly but they took my weight.

I ran, jumping over Stan's body, round a clump of roots. I ran fast, my throat hurting as I sucked in breath, my thighs burning. I could hear Harry running after me, swearing and shouting. I had hold of the gate when he caught me, rugby-tackling me to the ground.

I fought back but it was futile. Harry was furious and it made him strong. I was too terrified to speak or cry. I closed my eyes, went limp and he dragged me along the bumpy ground. The slightly rotten smell of lake water grew stronger.

"The catfish is taking you for a swim," Harry said. I could hear the smirk in his voice. He didn't sound like himself. He sounded like Cooper. Cooper had never been the bad influence, though; I saw that now. He had been influenced by Harry, not the other way around.

He dragged me to the water's edge, forced my head into the water. Icy cold, stinky water filled my mouth, my ears. I scratched and kicked, heard him swear, got my head above water for a gasp of air, but then the shove came and I was submerged into liquid darkness. Something plant-like and stringy draped across my face. My lungs strained, I arched and rolled. There was pain in my head and my chest. Panic distilled my thoughts down to one pressing one: *I don't want to die.*

I heard muffled shouting. Louder. More urgent. Sirens wailed somewhere close.

The pressure on my head was suddenly released and with the last of my strength I flicked my head up and back. I gasped for air. Strong arms hauled me out of the lake. DS Stuart Haig's face was above mine.

"She's still alive," he yelled. More quietly he said, "I got your message, Amy. I came as soon as I heard it. The paramedics will be here in four minutes." He put me in the recovery position, pulled vegetation from my mouth, and wiped my face with a blanket. "It's going to be all right, Amy. Just hold on tight."

# CHAPTER 33

**Five months later**

Nothing made any sense for a long time and that wasn't just due to being hit on the head with a rock next to the lake. Gradually the police and a counsellor called Vicki helped me piece things together, even if I couldn't fully understand why Harry did what he did.

Harry had realized Stan and I were planning something when he saw us faking a photo from Liam in the garden. He'd explained that he liked to go through my phone regularly, so he saw Liam's passwords which Stan had sent me. Our plan to catfish Hollie had given him an idea.

Harry had always had a thing for Hollie – he'd taken

her things, as a warped way to get close to her. Although the messages between "Liam" and her had been deleted by the app, he knew from messages between me and Stan where and when the date was going to be. He decided to go along and declare himself, hoping she'd be feeling low about Liam standing her up. He sent her flowers in advance. But she'd laughed at him. She'd been walking away when he'd picked up the branch that killed her. It was spur of the moment, he told the psychiatrist. He had an alibi because Cooper – who'd always done what Harry had told him – had signed him into the after-school art trip. It had been a casual trip, the students old enough to come and go to the exhibition by themselves. He'd told Cooper to keep quiet and Cooper had agreed. He'd thought Harry had met someone on Tinder. It hadn't occurred to him for one moment his friend might be a killer.

That could have been the end of it. But pretending to be Liam – confident, handsome Liam – had given Harry a way to speak to girls he wouldn't have normally. He chatted with Kristen easily. He had always liked her, taken small things of hers. Sent her flowers too. But when they met up, she'd been confused, then angry. He'd brought a hammer with him to the park, just in case.

It had been easier the second time, he said.

They were ungrateful girls, he said – ungrateful and spiteful. They deserved it.

Harry had been the one sending me creepy, stalkery messages. He was hoping I'd think it was the killer – someone unrelated to the family, just in case I had suspicions. He'd thought he was safe because of the inadequate CCTV, which he'd researched last year during a geography project. He'd invested in a few burner phones. And then the police had a suspect. But the guy was released without charge – as he suspected would happen – and he needed a real-live scapegoat.

Which was when Harry started to push the narrative that Stan was the killer. He left the rat, hoping to build a picture of Stan as a desperate stalker. And, most importantly, to throw suspicion as far away from him as possible.

He never wanted to kill a third time, he said. But Rory had seen Harry walking near the riverside the night of Kristen's death, as if he was on his way to the gym. Harry knew that eventually he would tell the police – and that everything would start to collapse. He arranged to meet Rory, saying he was worried about Aden. It had been a frenzied stabbing and Rory had fought back. Harry had thrown his clothes in the river, bunched up together so they'd sink, and decided it was time to kill Stan and make it look like self-defence or suicide.

Mum and Dad sat in on one of the interviews. Harry had sounded almost proud, they said.

"I messaged Stan the night of the memorial," Harry had said in the interview. "Said I was worried about Amy, that I'd seen a message she'd been sent about meeting at the bench by the lake at Kingsley Park and suspected the killer had her in his sights next. That I was scared she would go there to video him or something as evidence – that she was the Catfish Catcher. I let him think that if Amy went missing she'd have gone to the park, and we had to go after her.

"I said if she went, she'd probably let DS Haig know so there'd be back-up on the way but we couldn't be sure the police would get there in time. Stan was never very bright. And he'd do anything for Amy, I knew that. As soon as he lost sight of her in the cricket pavilion, he went charging off like an absolute fool, messaging me to meet him there. I was about to tell Amy that I was going back to Cooper's around the time she saw that phone message over Stan's shoulder. Then I was going to go to the park."

Harry's plan was that the police would arrive and find Stan dead by the lake, the knife in his hand. The same knife that had killed Rory. A suicide, because of his guilt.

"I hadn't counted on Amy seeing the message," he'd said. "To be honest, that was annoying and I had to think on my feet."

Mum and Dad blame themselves for not noticing changes in Harry's behaviour but when the three of us look back we don't think there were many. As Harry had told the doctors who assessed him, he'd enjoyed what he'd done. He'd found it exhilarating. He'd been cleverer than the detectives for almost two weeks.

I haven't seen him in prison yet. Mum and Dad go regularly and so, to my surprise, does Granddad.

My parents were interviewed over and over, and DS

Haig says they didn't do anything wrong. I don't know if they can believe that yet, though.

As well as me seeing Vicki, Mum, Dad and I have counselling together with a man called Jonathan. It's a bit embarrassing, like you'd expect. Lots of crying. But the relationship between me and my parents has changed. We have more time for each other now, and we listen better. We talk about holding each other up. I've realized how much I love them.

I feel a wave of horror every time I remember finding Hollie's bracelet and Kristen's badge in my brother's jacket pocket. The gold chain lying in the palm of my hand. It was Harry's downfall in the end – he couldn't bring himself to get rid of his trophies.

Stan was alive when the police got to the park – just. He was still in hospital when I was discharged and I wrote him a card saying how sad and sorry I was about everything, and asking if I could visit. I showed it to Vicki before I sent it. She said I had to be prepared for him not wanting to see me, but he did.

Mum came with me but waited in the canteen. I was shaking as I stepped through the door to his ward. Stan had been sitting in a chair by the window, playing a game on his phone. He'd looked up and seen me and smiled. We'd hugged then, and I knew that no matter how bleak everything was, I still had Stan.

His odd behaviour in the weeks after Hollie's death hadn't been only in my mind. Stan had been keeping a secret from us all. His dad had been having an affair and had left a few weeks before Hollie's murder. Karis hadn't wanted anyone to know because she was hoping he'd come back. But he hadn't. That's why Stan had been in Birmingham – he'd been visiting his dad.

"I was hit hard by Dad leaving," said Stan, as we sat next to each other in the high-backed chairs. "I was desperate to tell you, but I wanted to be loyal to Mum too and I'd promised not to tell a soul until she was ready. Dad leaving out of the blue like that – it did something to me. I stopped trusting people."

I bit my lip. "I was preoccupied with Dom," I said sadly, thinking of all those nights that Stan had wanted to talk and I'd been busy. "I should have been there for you."

"I was pleased you were with Dom," said Stan. "Seriously. But I was lonely too and then Hollie was killed. I became obsessed with figuring out who had done it. It was a way of coping with everything. I didn't have to think about Dad or my sadness about Hollie."

"I'm sorry I thought you were involved." I put my head in my hands. "I let you down."

"But you saved me too," said Stan quietly. "You came to the park, you called the police."

"I could have got to you sooner," I said.

Stan put his hand on my arm and said, "Let's stop. We can come back from this. I've got some prawn cocktail crisps in the locker by my bed, and I think we should build a new fortress in *Colony Survival*."

Dom and I officially split up. Unsurprising, really, given that my brother had murdered his ex-girlfriend. He was nice about it, though. He said he didn't blame me and I heard he always stuck up for me at Ivy Green if people talked about the case. He made a point of stopping to say hey whenever we met in Markham.

Aden couldn't talk to me for ages. He couldn't even look at me. Sally still refuses to speak to Mum. But Aden found me crying under the stairs by the sports hall recently, and he sat next to me in silence, back against the wall, knees up to his chest, sharing my pain. It reminded me of the time Jada and I sat with him in bed after Rory died.

I'm starting to realize all the ways that people can be kind.

I miss Hollie badly, but I have friends: Stan, Jada – and Hussein. They sit with me at lunch, distract me when the black moods take over. They shut down whispers behind my back. Hussein turned out to be the Catfish Catcher. He said it was time he put his police cadet training into practice. "Didn't catch anyone, though, did I?" he said glumly the other day.

My friends helped me laugh when I read the article which came out about Liam, written by a journalist called Will Hemworth. The title of it was:

*Markham Murders: This Has Been Really Hard For Me*

We discovered the student who'd talked to the press about ritualistic animal killings had been Kyra, the girl who'd pushed my jigsaw pieces to the floor in the library – she couldn't resist boasting about it to a boy who reported her. Ms Arnold made her go to counselling. I hope it helps her, but I'm not angry any more. It all feels a really long time ago.

Hussein and Jada run a podcast together now called *Social Media and Me*, and one day I might go on it and tell my side of the story. Stan and I help them with the editing and production.

Ms Reid says I'm not going to slide into self-pity on her watch. She calls it tough love. Somehow she wangled me on to the same volunteering programme as her son Michael, with an opportunity to go abroad if we stick at it. She's on my case about getting good grades and going to university, and she says I can get away from Markham and be myself then. Treat it as a fresh start.

So I work hard and I plan my future, and I hold on tight.

# Acknowledgements

The basic outline for this book was thought up in a coffee shop in Wimbledon with my super-talented editor Linas Alsenas. Thank you, Linas, for letting me talk it through with you every time I stumbled. I also had incredible editorial help from Genevieve Herr. Gen, your comments were perceptive, supportive, sometimes hilarious, and always useful.

Thank you to Sarah Baldwin who designed the impactful cover, Jenny Glencross for copyedits, Sarah Dutton for fantastic proofreading, Harriet Dunlea and Stephanie Lee for PR, Eleanor Thomas in marketing, Lucy Page for championing my books to supermarkets and bookshops, Antonia Pelari, head of sales, Yvonne Murphy and Su Inglis from the schools' channels, Alice Pagin in production, and managing director Catherine Bell, for her ongoing support of my books. I am proud to be published by Scholastic.

Thank you to my agent Becky Bagnell for continuing to make my publication dreams come true.

Big thanks to P.R. who helped me understand police procedure concerning social media. Any errors are my own.

Thank you to my creative writing group at Teddington School who helped with some of the gaming content in this book, and who write clever things on Friday afternoons:

Gregory, Belle, Alex, Bea, Polly, Arabella, Evie, Alicia, Sarah, Lilia and Charlotte.

To everyone who's chosen my books, put them in readers' hands, tagged me in nice posts, sent lovely messages, invited me into their schools, given me opportunities, listened during the lows, celebrated the highs, given me wine and crisps and encouraged me, I am truly grateful.

I'm lucky that each time I have a book out, I can publicly tell my family how much I love them. Shout out to the gang (that includes you, Eddie, the best-looking Border Terrier in South London). Dad, you left us with so many good memories. I'll always remember our Saturday morning trips to the library, and how before every holiday we'd go to Bookends in Christchurch and you'd buy me a stack of books because it was impossible for me to only select one or two.

Sophie, thank you for reading an early version of the book and giving really helpful feedback. Thanks to you, Maia and Phoebe, for keeping me on the straight and narrow, and being your wonderful selves.

# Other books by Sue Wallman: